THE NUDEST DE

G000164458

DEDICATION

To my kind, creative, hilarious, adventurous sister
– rest in peace

I wish I could have shared these works with you before you left. You would have helped me make them better, and I know we would have had a great laugh

FORWARD

Now we've lived through 2020, my storylines don't appear as fantastical as they did before a pandemic. The amazingly swift production of vaccines, the bizarre politics, and the raft of conspiracy theories being promoted by those who should know better has changed many people's view of the world. As people seem ready to believe anything these days, I should state the Le Perjure and the abilities of the Nimbus in this novel are figments of my imagination.

Books one and two are set in 2018 and 2019 and this book's story followed on in 2020. I admit to losing my writing focus as the world took a radical turn but when I put my author hat back on, I faced a big decision. Should I reset the complete story timeline to pre-pandemic, or weave in the pandemic (border closures et al), or just adopt the alternate reality of a 'normal' 2020. I chose the latter.

I've dedicated this book to my late sister, but I do want to thank all of those countless people who saved us, helped us keep going, focussed on keeping society on track, or just brought some joy and happiness into a world that needed it badly.

1: MEET THE GANG

Vancouver, May 2020

[Marcy] – You are probably wondering why the girlfriend of one of the world's richest men is standing behind a tripod on the roof of an SUV, pointing her camera at a group of 30 naked cyclists who are racing up Vancouver's charming Beach Avenue. I'm really just focused on one sexy cyclist in particular; the rest are there purely for framing and effect. Ethan is easy to pick out for two reasons: his currently green-coloured, super-buff-bod sets him apart from the all-shapes-and-sizes posse behind him; and the fact that said posse is at least 20 feet to his rear, and he will not allow them to catch up. As instructed, by me.

Let me share Ethan Booker's day so far:
- Sleepy, cuddly sex (with me) in the Booker Building penthouse suite. This 26-story building is our home and base of operations here in Vancouver, Canada.
- An hour-long butt-kicking-cum-workout in our dojo, supervised by Gia. Gia was Ethan's personal trainer and martial arts instructor until she left to lead a charity helping people escape the sex-traffic trade. She and my brother, Max, returned last week with the happy news that they were "getting hitched." Gia thought that Ethan's replacement trainer was not torturing him sufficiently, and she took back the role. She took me in hand, too, and I have as many bruises as Ethan, now. It's a relief fighting someone so accomplished, as I can put everything into each session without fear of hurting anyone (but myself).
- A steak and egg breakfast, over which his girlfriend (me again) informed him he had a challenge to complete today.

- A trip to a private makeup specialist. Vancouver is a film-industry mecca and has a ready supply of special-effects gurus. The professional fantasy-figure makeover included prosthetic facial enhancements and all-over (and I do mean *all-over*) body paint. Ethan makes a very tasty-looking Bike-Boy; think a green Superman, with Bike-Boy stencilled across his broad, sexy chest and back. The colour of the body paint making his eyes pop deliciously. His eyes being the only recognisable part of his face, thanks to the fantastic disguise created by the makeup woman.
- A car ride to Vancouver's annual naked bike ride event – of which he had no prior knowledge – where he was dumped on the street with only body paint to keep him warm, and the clear instruction (me again) that his cute ass better be leading the pack by at least three bike lengths when he passes me on the route. I omitted to mention to him where I would be standing, of course, which meant he would have to be way out front the whole way or face the consequences.

In our youth, immaturity and bad timing foiled several attempts at being a long-term couple but we've loved each other since we were teens. When Ethan and I picked up our on-again, off-again relationship last year we both knew it would be for life. We haven't delved into the marriage and baby discussion yet; we have been too busy fighting off criminals and exploring our more adult selves. I was shocked to discover that Ethan has had been hiding this long-standing 'kink' about being forced into positions where he might be caught naked by others.

At first anything resembling forcing and domination was very difficult for me, as my brother Max and I came from an abusive home. My battle to vanquish the demons spawned in my childhood led me to apply to the Vancouver Police Department, specifically to fight for the abused. Finding out that the love of my life had a kinky side initially worried me greatly as I had often associated domination with abuse, and assumed any consent was a form of Stockholm Syndrome. But thanks to some tactful education by our neighbour, Gwen, who is a professional sex therapist – and not forgetting many tearful nights re-evaluating my experiences and searching my soul – I've become quite comfortable with the difference between non-consensual abuse and enjoyable, fun, kinkiness.

Ethan and I are on a slow journey of exploration of our newly found, kinky selves. I must admit, though, that coming up with creative ways to playfully torment, tantalise and tease Ethan while indulging his almost-caught-naked kink remains one of my favourite roles in our sex life.

Today's kinky mission was very much on the extreme side of our naked-in-public game. Typically, I put him in predicaments in which he thinks he *could* be exposed, but then let him off the hook by the skin of his teeth. It's the tease I enjoy the most. But as he pointed out himself, knowing there is a limit I probably won't push him past tempers that feeling of dread he so enjoys. An occasional leap past that point, like today, proves I'm prepared to take him way out of that uncomfortable comfort-zone. On these rare occasions I stress out worrying if I've gone too far, but afterward he says he is genuinely pleased I pushed him.

Pedalling hard, Ethan shot by me. I am so glad that my high-end camera has sophisticated autofocus and continuous-shot modes, so I just concentrate on framing the shot to best capture an ass a girl (me again) can bounce coins off. I click away. Perfect. Perky ass against the Vancouver skyline. Another of it receding into the distance. I mentally patted myself on the back for thinking of choosing this raised-camera platform, so the posse didn't block that great ass-shot. I may have snapped pictures worthy of adding to the collection I started when I made Ethan go to a boudoir photographer, but if not, there is always next year. Perhaps with less makeup.

*

I picked Ethan up at the finish line, not making him endure the beach party the other cyclists would have to wrap up their day. While I was waiting for him, I went through some of the photos I had shot and noticed a missing triangle of paint on a strategic spot. I would have to photoshop that!

I put a blanket on the car seat to prevent the body paint smearing on the seat, as it had on the saddle of his bike. Ethan playfully tried to give me an enthusiastic green hug – I was wearing a white blouse over my jeans – but I put on my stern Phoenix voice and made him behave.

I named my Mistress persona Phoenix, and I have a beautiful Phoenix tattoo on my shoulder, which signifies my rebirth in several ways: As a private detective, no longer a cop; as a member of the wealthy set (we certainly use the money, but we don't flaunt it); and, most of all, to provide balance to the tattoo on my hip of a stop sign which I've had for seven years. The stop sign was to ensure I never forgot my promise to relentlessly challenge abusers; the Phoenix reminds me to check each time that what I do is fully consensual. But the best part is that in public – when I can't be overt about giving Ethan kinky commands – if I casually touch the tattoo, Ethan knows that what I am saying is more than a suggestion.

It took Ethan an hour in the shower to remove all the paint and makeup. Well, perhaps the last ten minutes was more about me popping into the shower to 'inspect closely' that all was clean. Afterward, over lunch, Ethan downloaded his version of events; he was nicely terrified, thought it was incredibly thrilling, and confirmed his renewed respect of how far things *might* go if Phoenix had a mind to torment him to extremes.

Our phones buzzed in unison; it was time for our regular meeting with the gang. We headed down to the boardroom which was located in the offices below our suite. Our select group communes every two weeks to review our most confidential projects.

THE NUDEST DETECTIVE

The Booker Building had many well-designed spaces, but this boardroom was one of my favourites: space for up to 20 comfortably, an upright grand piano, a whisky bar, and a modern, open fireplace. The Oscar Peterson Boardroom looked out across the city towards Stanley Park and the North Shore mountains. It was subtly chic, bedecked in gunmetal greys and glass, joined by tasteful inlays of recycled Pine Beetle wood that linked it to the forests and times gone by. Each place at the diamond-shaped table – which was finished like the glossy, upright grand – had a small workstation inset so as not to block eye contact with even the shortest person.

Kelsie and Naomi had every geeky feature of their workstations lit up; the rest of us had ours turned off, and a single finger of Tamdhu 50 whisky in a Nolan Rauk heavy tumbler sat before each of us.

When you enter the Oscar Peterson room to start a meeting, there is always piano jazz playing softly, and a replica of our Canadian jazz hero's eight Grammy Awards tastefully placed on their own wall shelves. As the meeting organiser presses the 'start the meeting' button in their console, the music fades gracefully, the windows turn opaque, and the lights reorganise themselves to put the focus on the participants, not the walls.

As we settled in, I looked around the table and it struck me that although some of the attendees were unknown to me just last year, they all felt like family now.

Let me introduce you.

Ethan you've met. He's a 32-year-old, five feet, ten inches tall man with a rangy physique and a serious, narrow face topped with side-parted brown hair he wears short. He projects competence, intelligence, humility, and don't-fuck-with-me strength. Even when I have him tied up and bent over a chair. His family money from land purchases in the early 1800s and canny investing since are the least of what defines him.

Max Bremmer is my younger brother who fled our abusive home and enlisted in the Canadian Special Forces. Soon afterwards, he was killed by a roadside bomb in Afghanistan, or so we thought. But then the quiet, lost boy who fled abuse and apparently died, suddenly re-emerged last year to save Ethan and me from assassination.

He had become a successful undercover operative who used the explosion we thought took his life to slip into the murky intelligence community. Here he uncovered a criminal ring stealing arms from his unit and selling them to rebels in the region, who in turn passed the weapons on to their terrorist brethren in Europe. Max slowly won the confidence of the terrorist organization across Europe, and was in the process of rolling it up with Interpol, when he heard about an assassin targeting me, his then-cop sister, for defying an infamous sex-trafficking gang. He secretly flew back to Vancouver, acquired some military-grade weapons, and took out a helicopter that had just killed two RCMP officers and was poised to gun down Ethan and me.

Max met Gia as she was giving me a thumping in our dojo, and despite the instant chemistry between them, Max foolishly got all brotherly and stepped in to teach Gia a lesson. His combat training is phenomenal, but Gia put him on the mat hard without him getting in a single shot. Perhaps I should have mentioned to him she was a mixed martial arts instructor, Tae Kwon Do medallist in the 2012 Olympics and, more than that, she had escaped the sex trade at an early age by learning how to see things at superhuman speeds. I might have mentioned that, but that was the day he returned from the dead and I was a little miffed about the deception; I enjoyed seeing him suffer.

Max is a little shorter than Ethan, at five-foot-seven, but much stockier. Where Ethan is rangy, Max is bulky muscle. Where Ethan has a cute but serious face, Max's is rounder and cheeky. The quiet, lost soul I used to know as my brother has been replaced by a confident man's man. Always a joke in his eyes. He could charm the pants off anyone.

I had a short marriage to a great man, Terry Stone, who tragically died in a road accident soon after we wed. The emotional fallout from that loss sucked me down an emotional drain, and it was Ethan who pulled me back up. The Phoenix concept was initially inspired from that rebirth; from my suffering from chronic depression to emerging as the woman with her mojo back It also fit well with all of the other reinventions-of-Marcy I was undertaking.

Gia was orphaned in Alicante, Spain, and fell into the foster care system. Following a subsequent tragedy, she and her younger foster-sister Jenjing were sold to a pimp and forced into the sex trade. Gia had learned martial arts for self-defence and developed her fast-speed sight, as she has always referred to it which have her an edge over other fighters. One life changing day she came across a customer assaulting her sister and stepped in to protect her. The customer hit his head on the way down and died. The fallout eventually resulted in Jing being forced to move to a different pimp to pay off a local kingpin.

When it became known that Gia was a gifted fighter on a rage-driven search for her sister, Jing was killed by her captor. This melting pot of emotions made Gia an ardent protector of sex-trade victims and fuelled her drive to become one of the best fighters on the planet – male or female. Gia is a 36-year-old Asian beauty with long, silky, black hair that hangs to her mid back, an athlete's build without an inch of fat, but stocky, not slim or skinny. Where Max is funny and charming, a wise-ass comment on his tongue at all times, Gia is quiet. She says the minimum and is serious more than funny. But quite often as you walk away from a conversation with her, it dawns on you that she had several subtle pokes at you that took time to register. Ninja-funny. She and I had friction until I realized her interest in Ethan was to protect him as a devoted bodyguard, not to pursue him romantically. Since then, we have been firm friends and, in a short time, she has come to be close person in my small circle: The intense, ass-kicking sister I never had.

Sitting to Gia's left is Dr Naomi Eldridge. Naomi's doctorate is in neuroscience, and last year Ethan and I had desperate need of an expert in that field. Years ago, Gwen had covert-crush on the then married doctor, who has since become a widow. We approached Naomi to join our team and used our resources to furnish her with a top-class laboratory in which she made some startling discoveries about two others at the table today, Moy Lei and Jim. During this process, the renewed proximity between Naomi and Gwen allowed their relationship to flourish; they've been a couple for the past several months and are rarely apart. They live in the other penthouse suite on our floor.

Naomi has a boyish five-foot-tall figure, smooth mulatto skin, and smartly braided hair that starts off tightly pulling back from her intelligent brow and ends in the small of her back. She has quick, curious eyes and a sharp nose. Following the death of her wife Jane, she sought solitude and cultivated an unfriendly, stern demeanour. When I met her last year, *resting-bitch-face* was an expression that crossed my mind, but there is none of that look now. Jane is not forgotten; in fact, Naomi and Gwen visited Jane at the crematorium's Garden of Rest just recently, and while Naomi still mourns Jane's passing, Gwen's boundless and infectious personality and non-stop pranks are hard to be sad around.

It was Gwen who told me about Ethan's nudity kink. She had accidently caught him in the act – so to speak – blundering around trying to scare himself with self-inflicted predicaments. Partly because Gwen sees teasing as a sport she could represent Canada in; partly as she is a bit of a sadist (in a fun way); and partly to protect Ethan from his own experiments, she forced him to agree to her choosing the predicaments and controlling them. He was at her mercy for a few months before I came back onto the scene as his romantic partner.

I should point out that no one could ever force Ethan to do anything he didn't want to; he may play at being my bitch sometimes for fun, but he is an alpha to the core. My alpha.

Anyway, back to Gwen. I tripped over a Polaroid of the two of them and all but broke her door down – she was nearest, otherwise I would have tackled Ethan – to find out what the hell was going on. To be fair, this was literally day one of Ethan and I dating again, and Gwen explained how the agreement came to be, and promptly stepped out of her role of Ethan-torturer and handed the reins over to me.

Gwen's first career was as a psychologist and professor of all things sexual at a local university. This led her to open a kink-aware counselling business, which she runs from our office's downstairs. But she is also the flamboyant owner of Vancouver's best coffee shop, conveniently located now at ground level of the Booker Building, having been relocated from a block down the road to accommodate its growing following.

Gwen is so sex positive that it can be too much on occasion, but she was certainly a great resource in helping Ethan and me understand BDSM's history, psychology, laws, stigma – and our very confused feelings on the topic. We've become self-sufficient at researching since then, and our trips across the hallway to see Gwen and Naomi are now purely social or to retrieve Elvis, our inherited pooch, who has a Houdini-like ability to sneak out of our secure apartment to theirs. I'm convinced he follows the bacon lures they deliberately leave out to tempt him over. In their minds, Elvis is at least half theirs.

If you combined Hollywood's Jane Lynch with a bit of Ellen and Charlize, and add a wicked facial expression or two, you have Gwen. A fifty-something, tall, gregarious, blonde troublemaker, and sex-Yoda. I should mention that Gwen is the only person in our gang who is aware of Ethan's and my unusual sexual games.

Next is Kelsie Kobe, our Head of Operations and logistical wizard. She operates two floors below our suite out of a control room that is staffed by brilliant, hand-picked experts in everything we need in our private detective business, as well as our lives as 'billionaires-about-town.' As we are potential kidnap targets, Kelsie orchestrates four teams of bodyguards, as well as our fleet of private aircraft, yachts, cars, and so on.

Kelsie's older sister Darcy, not present at today's meeting, is our 'mad-inventor' who, along with her husband Jimmy Fullerton – himself a military scientist – creates the technically amazing gadgets we always seem to need in our James Bond-like lifestyle. Ethan sells some of this ultramodern technology to the military and police forces for a tidy sum. And what Darcy dreams up and brings to life, Kelsie finds ways to exploit to the full.

Kelsie and Darcy are both of Japanese descent, born in Vancouver but schooled in Europe and the USA, where both scored in the top 2% at MIT in science subjects. Both are on the shorter side, a shade under five feet, and both have very short, very fashionably spiked hair. Darcy's is brown, almost verging on ginger, and Kelsie keeps hers black.

Which brings me to the final pair at the table. Two very special people from quite different backgrounds: Moy Lei and Jim. Special because, technically, we don't think they are human at all.

2: I DIDN'T SEE THAT COMING

[Ethan] – I reluctantly shifted my morning 'funishments' to the back of my mind and called the meeting to order. I was particularly eager to hear Naomi and Darcy's report because it sounded like they were on the edge of a breakthrough. I was about to speak when my cell phone buzzed with its 'urgent' vibration pattern. I glanced down and saw it was from Maurice Bernier, so I parked the message for later.

Maurice, my Group CEO and Fatima Sousa, his CFO, essentially run all of my mainstream business interests. I delegate to him almost completely, trying to stay as far away from the corporate world as possible. He does sit me down at least once per month to update me, but I would even skip some of those if he would let me. It was unlike him to message me on an urgent basis, as he knows I pay *him* to deal with pressing issues so I don't have to. Just because it is urgent in his world, doesn't mean it is in mine. I decided I would pop down and see him after we were done here, so I got the meeting started quickly.

"Why don't we start with Silent Souls. Gia? Max?" Earlier this year, the Toussaint family, who specialized in drug and human trafficking, hired a group of international assassins – led by Moy Lei's mother (a story for another day) – to kill Marcy. In her role as taskforce leader with the Vancouver Police Department, Marcy had thwarted the Toussaints' Vancouver operation. The family had a mean reputation for swiftly making examples of anyone who stood in their path. We fought for our lives and eventually took them down – permanently. Using millions of dollars drained from the traffickers' accounts, we established Silent Souls as a charity with the mission of rescuing the Toussaints' many victims around the world. Gia and Max eagerly stepped up to lead that mission and have been leading it since.

"We are happy to report we now have over 400 sex-workers using one or more of the Silent Souls' programs," declared Max.

14

There was a heartfelt round of applause celebrating the milestone. Gia's passion for saving those forced into prostitution made her the charity's natural leader, but she is not much of a talker and leaves most public speaking to Max. He continued to lay out some seriously impressive statistics.

"We have repatriated well over half of the victims with their families or to their home countries. We have 255 engaged in anti-addiction programs and approximately 170 have signed on for educational programs with scholarships, aimed at reintegration into society. There are just over 80 who believe they want to remain selling sexual services and have accepted our offer to establish them in better circumstances to do so; almost half in this group have already relocated to New Zealand, where their trade is completely legal and typically operates in well protected, safer environments."

"That's excellent, Max, Gia. Well done, you guys," interjected Gwen.

"Hang on. There's more," said Max. "Some 28 are in various stages of pregnancy and we are helping them plan for whatever future they choose. And there are roughly 40 we are monitoring who are accepting food and health programs but are unsure of their next steps." He paused, proudly looking at his fiancée, to whom – despite his own efforts in support – he gives all of the credit.

"There is one statistic Max saved for me," smiled Gia, making a rare contribution to the meeting. "We have recruited 14 of the victims to join Silent Souls as city-wide leaders or case workers, or both. They are helping their peers and are *so proud* to be able to put your resources to work, Ethan."

"Thank you, Gia, but we don't think of that money as ours at all. I like to think of it as the Toussaints', may they not rest in peace, giving back to the community," I laughed. "What are you busy with in the next month?"

"A few weeks ago, we switched our personal attention to two specific priorities. The first is hiring a senior team to manage operations; we have some great résumés and need to replace ourselves so that we can step up and focus on longer-term programs. The other priority is raising more money. Eventually, even the Toussaints' generous seed money will run out, and we want the program to be self-sustaining. Since the beginning of the month, we have held auctions and fundraisers to get our name out. We have already hired two full-time staff to manage that aspect."

Marcy jumped in. "Sounds like you two will be able to put your feet up soon and start planning your wedding," she half-joked.

My phone buzzed once more. Maurice, again. I silenced it, again. There was no more on Silent Souls, so I invited Naomi to take the floor.

"I have two items of interest today. The first is a bit of a temporary disappointment, if I'm honest, and the second an unlooked-for bonus, with significant potential. The bad news first." She paused, shuffled some papers, and took a nervous sip from her glass of water. If you didn't know Naomi and her incredibly high standards, you might think she was about to announce the end of the world. But as I suspected, what she called bad news, most others would be proud to proclaim loudly.

Since joining our team, Naomi has focused on researching an amazing discovery we made about Moy Lei and Jim – and perhaps as many as one hundred others like them. They call themselves Nimbus, a name derived from a faintly glowing aura that they can see surrounding their species, but which is invisible to most humans. Over centuries, if not millennia, Nimbus have existed among us and are probably the source of many myths and legends, such as sirens, vampires, and perhaps even gods.

Naomi has been using modern methods to research their physiology to understand the supernatural powers that set them apart from humans. They have a radar-like ability to track a small number of people, and a more powerful ability to project real or manufactured emotions, such as fear, onto others. This second ability gives them the power to overwhelm or control humans, and even incapacitate us entirely. We are still not sure what else is possible and are keeping this discovery a closely held secret; in the wrong hands, the potential for abuse is huge.

"As you know," she began, "we have been working on defences against Nimbus mental intrusions. I had hoped to be able to confirm positive test results to you today. There were some 'glitches,' so we are running a little late; but I am still quite confident we will soon have a solution signed off.

We are calling it the delta-blocker. Gwen came up with the term. It is technically inaccurate as the drug is not taken by Nimbus, or as I still call them, Adepts, such as Jim and Moy Lei, who actually possess a fourth super neuron – a delta; it is taken by their human targets, who only have three super neurons. But it is kind of catchy and the lay person would get the analogy. Besides, we won't be sharing any of this with the scientific community, so we have artistic licence to choose a fun name." She paused, forgetting that we still didn't know what the drug did.

"What does the drug do, Naomi?" prompted Kelsie, tactfully.

"Oh, pardon me. As we have discovered, a Nimbus essentially projects emotion through their delta neuron. Using Moy Lei, Jim, and some human volunteers as test subjects, we were eventually able to narrow down that part of the brain in a human that receives and translates the Nimbus' transmission. It's in the lower part of the amygdala, about here." She pointed to the side of her head. "The amygdala are two almond shaped clusters of nuclei responsible for memory, decision making and emotional response. The drug, the delta-blocker, interferes with the transmission from an Adept. I'll spare you the chemical formula; finding that and the delivery method was the easy part anyway, it turned out. The hard part was getting the exact dose to block the attack yet not overly disrupt the brain's normal functions. That is the part that has taken most of the time."

"How reliable is it, Naomi?" asked Max. Max's years in the military resulted in him normally being the first to employ attack and defence tactics.

"In perfect conditions of our laboratory, we can adjust the dose so it is 100% reliable, at least in the limited human subjects we've tested. That's not the issue. The issue is maintaining the precision of the dose required for 100% protection, outside of our lab. We are all slightly different to each other and require minutely different doses. Worse though, our chemistry changes constantly as we metabolise food, generally go about our day, and are affected by the world around us."

"If the dose is not spot on, what is the effect?' I asked.

"The dosage-effectiveness range is very narrow so if the dose is just a little bit low – even two to three percent – the blocking effectiveness falls away rapidly. If it is more than five percent over, we hit a tipping point and the drug skews how the subject processes emotion. The recipient essentially becomes quite ambivalent about, well, almost any transient emotion, such as fear."

"That could be quite helpful in, say, a soldier," suggested Jim.

"I prefer my soldiers to be scared easily but have the courage to manage through dangerous situations. I find we stay alive longer that way," said Max.

"Point taken," Jim acknowledged.

"We could still use this if we were under attack," I said. "Being emotionally flat, or only partially protected, is much better than fully debilitated. 'Twice I've been under the influence of a Nimbus and was so emotionally paralyzed, he could have cut my throat and I wouldn't have been able to defend myself."

"Well, if you let Naomi finish," interjected Gwen, inserting her usual sense of faux-drama into the proceedings, "my clever girlfriend has a solution."

My phone buzzed once more. Now I was a little worried. Perhaps someone is sick or something. I texted Maurice back, asking for some context, while Naomi picked up the thread.

"Actually, it is Darcy we have to thank. Leveraging some science that she and her husband pioneered for the air force, where sensors in a pilot's helmet detect, in real time, brain-oxygen depletion, she created an effective prototype device that can predict the required dose in any patient, in close to real time. That left the problem of delivering the adjusted dose on the fly. That part could be slower of course, but that is not how Darcy works, apparently."

"What do you mean?" questioned Moy Lei.

"Why do something slowly, when you can do it faster?" chuckled Naomi, obviously in awe of Darcy's achievement. "We needed a delivery system for the drug, and we spliced some enzymes and proteins together with an iron-based nanite structure. Darcy realized the iron would react to magnetism. You know how you can charge your phone without a cable these days, by placing it near a device that is emitting a vibrating electro-magnetic current? Darcy created something similar. She can make the iron in the delivery structure increase or decrease its atomic vibration, and the result slightly increases or decreases the effect of the drug. By marrying her detector to the vibrator-device, she solved our problem. It works."

"Fantastic! Well done, team. At the start of the meeting, you said it wasn't signed off yet. Is there still a problem?" asked Marcy.

"Err, yes. Her prototype is the size of a large suitcase. But she is confident she can boil it down to something wearable in a few weeks."

"You two, well, the whole team actually, are amazing. Well done. You said there was some other news?" I prompted, thinking I should get down to see why Maurice is so perturbed.

"Yes, thanks for the reminder. As you know, we have been doing scans on as many brains as we can get access to and applying what we have learned over the past months. Two surprises arose. Gia kindly gave us permission to share the first item, which relates to her fast-speed vision. We've solved the mystery of how she does it so well, and Darcy is looking at ways she could help others acquire some of that ability." Max, who evidently knew this in advance, jumped in with what felt like a premeditated comment.

"I've put my name down first, as I owe her a butt-kicking or two."

"Dream on, soldier boy!" laughed Gia, pinning him with a pretend tough-girl glare, undermined with the loving twinkle she couldn't mask fully.

"The last news is a little difficult, as this concerns the medical status of someone else, and I haven't had time to ask their permission to share something we discovered just before I walked into the meeting. So, without mentioning any names, Jim and Moy Lei are not the only people with a fourth super-neuron at this table." A heavy silence descended and stretched out for what felt longer than it probably was. It was interrupted by Kelsie's urgent security tone on her cell phone. She checked it and looked up aghast. There was some imminent threat. We all went on alert.

Suddenly the doors flew open, and Maurice Bernier's unusually small head poked in, looking distinctly panicked.

"Sorry to barge in, Mr Booker. You know I would only do so in an extreme set of circumstances," he apologised, in his overly cultured English accent.

"No, come in. Sorry I ignored you, Maurice. What's the flap?" I always seem to fall into using British Public-School terminology when we talk. I hadn't even noticed until Marcy chastised me for a spurious "tally-ho", thinking I was deliberately being irreverent and rude.

"Sir, I have no way to explain this at all but, unbelievably, the banks have frozen all of your Canadian accounts and have approached the courts for legal access to do the same for your overseas assets." Deciding he must be mad, I glanced at Kelsie to see if Maurice was, in fact, the security issue her team was in urgent contact with her about.

"Can you run that past me again, Maurice, please? I don't think I understand," I requested, not knowing quite what else to say.

"I know, sir. It seems quite implausible. Not on at all, in fact. We have the whole team engaged, of course, and have called in everyone we can think of to better understand the situation. Fatima flew back immediately from her family visit to Portugal and has reached out to the financial institutions. The banks themselves are being tight lipped, but it appears they are responding to a valid, legal instruction from the authorities. Poor Hamilton from West Bank is beside himself. Mortified, in fact."

Kelsie broke in. "Ethan. As bad as that sounds, I think you have a bigger problem!" I waited for her to continue.

Of all the surprises today, the fact that the unusually unflappable and highly articulate Kelsie paused without sharing the nature of a problem larger than my being destitute was the most astonishing. Typically, the bigger the crisis the more ultra-focussed she becomes, which is one reason why she is so invaluable in her role. I said as much, urging her to spill the beans so we could all start picking through them and getting them back into the pot, so to speak.

"Well...sorry, Ethan. Do you want to move to a private room? I'm not sure this is for everyone's consumption."

"Out with it, Kelsie," my frustration – and near panic – evident in my tone.

"Um... there is a large group of policemen downstairs with a search warrant. And... an arrest warrant, too."

"Kelsie, *who* are they here to arrest?" I could tell by the way she kept staring at me that it was me. The fact we had a surprise Nimbus among us, and I had cycled naked through the heart of Vancouver just hours before, was somehow forgotten.

With a final gulp, Kelsie announced, "Ethan, it's for you; for murder!"

THE NUD<u>EST</u> DETECTIVE

3: THE WRONG HANDCUFFS

Vancouver, May 2020

[Marcy] – The pregnant pause – following Kelsie's use of the word 'murder'– had barely formed a bump when the door burst open again to admit a string of people, led by Ethan's Head of Legal, Aiden Doyle. Having won the race to our meeting room, the soft-spoken, witty man from Cork, Ireland, stopped, turned, and held his hands aloft to the rapidly advancing crowd.

"Good people, there is absolutely no need to rush. I promise you it is only Scotch Whisky on the table, not Irish!"

Right on Aiden's heels came Jake Clerke, who one might assume is Gaelic based on his surname, but he is a six-foot-six-inch Jamaican. He leads Team Charlie, one of our four-person security details we always have on-call for our protection. Behind Jake, trying in vain to push past his rather wide frame, were four policemen; two in uniform I didn't recognise, and two detectives I most certainly did. Bell and Webb; homicide's finest, they were not. Straight-shooters – honest – but in my experience from my time in the force, they are lazy, surly, and small minded. They are the sort who resent anyone successful because they themselves didn't work hard enough to be so, and I knew that didn't bode well for Ethan.

"Sorry, Mr Booker," said Jake. "We held them at the entrance until these gentlemen started to get ugly and pulled out their weapons. I wanted to give Mr Doyle a head start." Max and Gia were both out of their seats as fast as I was, and I found myself side by side with them between Ethan and the police. Bell and Webb are cockier when they know their badge will protect them, but I could see them having second thoughts, with Jake towering over them. Max had stepped right up in Webb's face he was blocking his view of Ethan. Of course, it was Gia and me they actually needed to worry about.

In my peripheral vision, I saw Ethan and Jim make eye contact, the latter raising an eyebrow in an unspoken question.

Jim could stop these two clowns in their tracks with his thoughts, allowing Ethan to escape; but Ethan just gave Jim the slightest of head shakes 'no.'

"Simmer down, everyone," ordered Webb, in a voice that sounded more confident than he must have felt. "We have a warrant for Ethan Booker's arrest, and another that gives us the right to search this building."

"Excuse me detectives, if you don't mind. I need to read them before you do anything. I'm Mr Booker's lawyer, Aiden Doyle." Aiden's easy manner is quite disarming, and Detective Bell handed him a pack of documents. The room was strangely silent as Aiden read through the pack; I almost expected gameshow-countdown music to pipe up.

"Ethan, the arrest warrant is valid. Sorry." He passed the papers on to Maurice for safekeeping. "The search warrant is valid for your personal space, but not for the remainder of the Booker Building."

"Cut the crap, Doyle. Judge Meredith signed off on the whole building," complained Bell, loudly.

"Actually, no. He signed off on all property at this address owned by Ethan Booker. His suite is in his name, but the remainder is owned by Booker Holdings," corrected Aiden, with the face of an angel, not a smirk in sight.

"That's bullshit. Stone, tell them. We'll take Booker downtown and be back with the right warrant and a bad attitude." Webb made the thinly veiled threat a challenge. There was no love lost between us, even before I left the force. Some saw my resignation as a betrayal, and these two would jump on that bandwagon, especially as they would see me as joining the privileged set. The irony didn't escape me, having fought for years in a force that is trying hard to untangle its' systemic racism and sexism which these two clowns benefitted from for years. I opened my mouth to share the ugly thoughts that were welling up, but Doyle interjected.

"Ms Stone. If you please. Mr Booker has paid me too much money over the years, given how little he's asked of me, so please let me do my job today. I'm quite good at it."

"Aiden's right, and I appreciate everyone's loyalty. But let's find out what these two gentlemen believe I've done. Detectives?" Ethan stepped back and offered Webb and Bell a seat at the table but, as I expected, they had other ideas.

"Actually, we'll do this down at the station. The team downstairs can start the search on your suite while we wait for the judge to update the paperwork – he won't be happy about that!" I knew he wouldn't, but it would be the detectives he would blame.

Bell held out his handcuffs and made a sign prompting Ethan to turn around and put his hands behind him.

"You've got to be fuckin' kidding," growled Max, angrily.

"Easy, brother," I said, putting my hand on his arm. "Detectives Bell and Webb will want to take Ethan to their Cambie Street Station. Aiden, would you follow them there and sort things out? Let us know when you have some information, please."

"Of course, Ms Stone," replied Aiden, then addressed the room in general. "For the information of the others here, they will have to book and process Ethan first, so it will be a while before I see him. Oh, and Ethan: I doubt I need to remind you, but the only reason you should open your mouth without me at your side is to drink the coffee they may offer you. But even then, only if you are desperate."

"Why?" asked Ethan, puzzled. "Do you suspect it's drugged?"

"God, no. It's pure shite!" replied Doyle.

*

[Ethan] – My publicly acknowledged assets were being frozen – I would still have about 300 million hidden for 'stormy' days – and I'd been arrested, suspected of a murder or murders I had no knowledge of. I was surprised, of course, but that didn't stop Marcy and me from exchanging a secret glance that patently said *These aren't the fun kind of handcuffs.* She stepped in and kissed me on the cheek and whispered that she would leave no stone unturned to get to the bottom of whatever was going on.

I wasn't concerned about the search of the suite. All computer data resides in a cloud that is protected by everything Darcy and SkyLoX, our friendly 'white-hat' hacker – a hacker who works for good, not evil – could think to throw at it. I keep weapons, confidential papers, and a growing collection of sex toys in the suite, but in safes hidden so well that, unless searchers dismantle the walls, the contents would remain secure. There was even a 'throw-down' safe – well hidden, but one an expert thief could likely find – with some less valuable items inside, which hopefully would be enough to satisfy the police that they had found everything they wanted. My real fear is a search of the laboratory where my team was researching the Nimbus. Again, data would be safe in the cloud, but the equipment in the lab alone would raise many questions we wouldn't want to answer.

Bell and Webb were a little harsher than they needed to be and were enjoying themselves, exchanging snarky comments back and forth. I mentally tuned them out and racked my brain as to what, or who, could be behind whatever this was all about.

At the station, I was photographed, fingerprinted, relieved of any personal property, and led into an interview room, where the cuffs were finally removed. I was offered a coffee, which I declined, but took some bottled water.

The detectives removed their jackets, hung them over their chairs, sat down, then started a tape recorder. It was a surprise to see tape recorders still in use. It had two tapes that record in parallel: one copy for them and another for me. Bell stayed quiet – which I soon determined made him 'good-cop' in the unfolding drama – as Webb started in hard, obviously claiming the 'bad-cop' role.

"You know, I always suspected Stone was scum when she was on the force but hanging out with murderers and money launderers surprised me." Webb paused to see if his cheap shot would get a reaction, and when I stayed quiet, he continued.

"Is that how you top up your millions, Booker? Laundering? I respect your Dad, you know. Great man who has worked hard all his life. I know he is rich because of longstanding family money – heck he's as close to 'old money' as Vancouver could boast – but at least he works to grow his wealth. He must be pretty disappointed in his son, the playboy princess of Vancouver, eh?"

It's true the basis of the Booker-wealth is old money. We traced our family back four centuries and have French ancestors who came to Canada to join the Hudson Bay company, made a fortune in the fur trade, invested in the gold rush, and as they worked their way west, bought tracts of land around which many major Canadian cities grew. It's true too that Da, and Ma for that matter, continued to grow the family wealth. Da still loves the land and enjoys building and farming, while Ma is 'boardroom queen' on many commercial ventures. They would have done well without the head start from the family wealth. It's true, too, that I own – and Maurice mostly runs, to be fair – many companies that make millions from the military tech-sector, but most of that is classified, and Webb wouldn't know about them. So, I could understand why he tried to bait me by implying I am a loser.

The phrase he used that had made me nervous, which I hoped my face didn't betray, was the reference to money laundering. We had, in fact, taken the ill-gotten gains from the Toussaints and reinvested it – technically illegally – to create Silent Souls charity. Arguably, that could be classified as money laundering. Perhaps the murder allegation might turn out to the Toussaints somehow reaching out from the grave. I didn't pull the trigger, but perhaps their blood splattered in ways I didn't know and is now implicating me. Either way, Aiden's wise words stayed with me: As much as I was dying to know what I faced, opening my mouth was not the smart way to find out. I kept schtum.

"Ethan. Let me tell you how this works, son," soothed Bell, stepping into his 'good-cop' role right on cue. "You have this one small window to share what you know. We realise you are a good guy at heart; you must be dying to unburden yourself. It probably wasn't all your fault, anyway. But, once Doyle gets in here and you lawyer up, that window closes. Cooperation gives Webb and me something to take back to the judge. Silence, well..."

It felt like an episode of a cheap TV show, but Marcy had shared in the past that the police try these techniques at first because they have a bizarrely good success rate. I stayed quiet and took a sip of water.

Just then, the door opened, and Aiden stepped in. "Good afternoon again, detectives. I see you started without me. I'll need a moment with my client, of course, but first why don't you explain what it is you believe Mr Booker is guilty of?" There was no seat for Aiden, probably by design, but he knew how the game was played. He deliberately dumped his coat on the table in the space where Webb was making notes, and his briefcase in front of Bell. Then he stood near them, on their side of the table, invading their space. The detectives were not phased at all – they had played this game before, too – and Bell sighed and stepped out briefly, returning with a fourth chair.

"We have proof that your client," said Webb, in a sarcastic tone, "has been guilty of shady accounting and money laundering for casinos for three years, and probably for far longer, with clever people like you to cover for him." He threw a scowl at Aiden, for effect.

"We had a whistle-blower come to our fraud team, but before we could develop him into a confidential informer, he was found murdered; dumped in Deep Cove, presumably from the back of one of Booker's fancy yachts. The trail leads clearly to Booker, and here we all are." His face lit up as he said the last sentence. None of this made any sense, and my expression made sure Aiden knew I didn't know what they were talking about.

"Taking what you say purely on face value, Detective Webb, I wonder why you think someone with Mr Booker's obvious means would choose to dump a body in a cove, miles from the sea, where the lack of tidal flushing action would make it very likely to come to attention. Why not put it on one of his aircraft and leave it thousands of miles from civilization, buried under a frozen waste? I'm assuming you have more to go on, that you are holding back?"

"Of course we do, Doyle. We're not idiots, either. We know he is cunning *and* rich. But who knows what motivates criminals, eh? We have seen some dumb shit from smart people over the years. If Booker is so smart, though, why leave his DNA under our victim's finger nails?"

This crazy day just got even crazier.

"Understood. Now, if you could just provide the victim's name and a timeframe you believe these events occurred in, I will confer with my client," said Aiden, undisturbed by the revelation. I'd never want to play poker with him.

But then we descended another step down the crazy-event-ladder. The two men in front of us stopped, and looked a little... stumped? Yes, that's what it looked like: Stumped. They turned to each other, putting up a good poker face themselves, but they certainly looked puzzled. Eventually, Bell took the initiative, told us we would have to wait until they were ready to reveal information, turned off the recorders, and led his partner out of the room.

"What was that about, Aiden?" I asked, clearly puzzled.

"Not here, Ethan. Let's wait. There are no two-way mirrors anymore, but I never trust that the recording devices and cameras are all the way off. How are you doing?"

"Fine, oddly. Knowing this is all baseless, and that I have the resources to fight whatever's causing it, just leaves me worried about what Marcy and the team are up to back at base."

"That reminds me," said Aiden, pulling his phone from his pocket. He fired off a quick note to Marcy, advising her of the nature of the charges. I wondered what she was up to. Tearing down walls, I was sure.

"Well. Looks like we have some time to kill, Ethan. Let me tell you how my day started. Not quite as odd as this but, at the time, I couldn't imagine anything trumping it, to be sure." I knew he was just trying to take my mind off the events, so I let him continue.

"I was in Nanaimo overnight, visiting my cousin. The office called early this morning to tell me to get back, as we had started to hear that your assets were being frozen. To be honest, I assumed it was a mistake; I hopped on the first floatplane back, anyway." The airspace over Vancouver is some of the busiest in North America. In addition to Vancouver International Airport, we have three small, general aviation fields, and several floatplane operations ferrying people between Vancouver and the surrounding islands. Aiden was referring to the 1950s-era Beaver floatplanes, which carry up to eight passengers back and forth from dawn until dusk, after which it gets too dark for water landings.

"Anyway," he continued with a laugh, his face crinkling up, "I was just getting settled, when this woman... well, it's funnier if I repeat the story she told afterwards. Bear with me." He chuckled again, obviously genuinely amused by the whole affair. "She had travelled over the day before. Her first trip on a floatplane. Before the pilot cranks up the noisy engine, he briefs the passengers on the route and safety matters, and then points them to the sets of free earplugs, which they leave for anyone who wants them, in the pocket hanging on the back of the seat in front of each passenger. She had dug down, past the safety briefing card, and found a pair in a little plastic packet. She really felt they cut back on the fatigue the engine-noise caused and made the spectacular trip over even better. This morning, as we taxied across the harbour to the take-off spot, she remembered all this, and plunged her hands deep into the pocket in front of her to find her earplugs, only..." He had a hankie out by now, rubbing away tears. I waited for him to gather his composure, sensing the punchline coming quickly. "Anyway, my God... sorry, there was no pocket hung there on this plane, and she had plunged her hands right down the back of my trousers. Can you believe it? She said she realized just as she did it, but it was too late. I tried to leap out of my seat in shock but was pinned down by the lap-belt."

"That's too funny. She must have died of embarrassment!"

"At first. An interesting shade of red, to be sure. But we all saw the funny side of things. I so wanted to say that I had come over to protect your assets – and left my own exposed – but I couldn't, of course. I have her card, and she has mine. She was so much fun, we've agreed to meet for coffee. She's a vivacious, successful, international businesswoman with extensive property investments. Part time she is also an editor for a local author – more of a passion than a money maker I sensed. Sadly, she was recently married, or it would have been dinner I offered. But I left it that if I could ever help with any legal aspects of her work, I would *bend over backwards* to help!" We roared, again. If anyone were listening in, they would think we were crazy.

4: A HOLLOW SHELL

[Marcy] – When you study how to lead in a crisis, as I did as part of police emergency training, one clear message is to mentally separate yourself from the distractions; then assess, prioritize, collect and assign resources to their best effect, while avoiding the trap of putting additional people in harm's way.

As the detectives led Ethan out in handcuffs, Marcy-the-girlfriend was on her back, with Marcy-the-cop holding her down, preventing her from rewarding, but harmful, acts against the two detectives. I shook my head and reluctantly ceded control to my cop-self, recognizing it was she who Ethan needed right now. But she did whisper a promise after Bell and Webb that *the retribution train just left the station and you boys will be tied to the tracks.*

"Jake, well done," I began. "Now can you and Team Charlie maintain oversight of the search? Aiden will be with Ethan, so grab some people from the legal team to keep things honest. They get full access to the suites, and nothing else. OK?" He acknowledged, spun on his heels – his dreads whipping up and falling back to his shoulders – and pushed the two remaining uniformed officers back to the elevator lobby. Maurice closed the door behind them.

"Kelsie," I said, stepping closer so not everyone would hear the last part of my instructions, "organize full coverage of Ethan's locations – using drones or whatever – wherever he goes. And message SkyLoX; if she finds anything, it comes to me exclusively, got it?" I added the latter to offer Kelsie some cover. She is the best at what she does for us but is a little skittish when it comes to breaking any major laws – such as hacking into the police systems to see what they have on Ethan – unless it's a matter of life and death. The fewer people with that information, the better.

"Max, Gia, Jim. We need a contingency plan to extract Ethan. Jim, are you comfortable joining such an action?" I knew I would not have to check with the other two; their willingness to engage was a given.

"Marcy. It's nice of you to confirm but you won't be able to stop me from going if Ethan needs my help. Count on me, please."

"Great. We will keep this room. We can pull up anything we need on these terminals. Gwen, Naomi, and Moy Lei: Aiden slowed down the search of the building, but we have to plan on the assumption they will be back with the right warrants. Your job is to blow the dust off the contingency plan we put together to prevent anyone understanding what your laboratory does." To Moy Lei and Jim, I continued, "Ethan and I were sincere in our promise that anything we discover won't get out and risk having some government move to weaponize your race."

Fifteen minutes later, we had coffee instead of whisky in front of us. Kelsie was set up in the corner working with us, as well as keeping us informed of what she was organizing through her control room downstairs; our extraction planning was moving at an impressive pace.

"A critical question is, are we going in armed or unarmed?" said Max. I had never seen my little brother in soldier mode; I had forgotten he worked as a military-trained undercover operative for several years. My personal knowledge of the station and police procedures had him peppering me with questions and, in no time at all, he had sketched out all of the tactical features, risks, and interim objectives we would need to consider for our plan. Already we had moved to the second step: Human resources.

"If unarmed," he continued, "then it's Jim and Gia who go in. Armed, it's Jim and I. Jim gives us a tactical advantage, of course, and I would send him in alone if he were capable of carrying Ethan out on his own. He could neutralize everyone easily, but that would include Ethan, too."

"If we need to activate this plan," I said, "much bigger shit will have hit a bigger fan already. Plan on being armed. You are up, Max; plan accordingly." I was harking back to my last police role of task force commander. A familiar, if already rusty, feeling.

"Won't there be internal cameras? Do we want them to record my personal commando here, strolling through the station with a polite, older, black gentleman?" *Good point, Gia.*

"The data centre is in the basement. We would need to pop by and relieve them of some tapes, I guess?" I offered. "Kelsie. How are we coming with the floorplans and maps?"

Just as I asked, the windows – which she had already turned an opaque grey – turned white, and a bank of projectors dropped from the ceiling and tactical data started to appear on the window-turned-screen. She already had drones on site, discreetly circling the police facility, sending back real time, high definition video. Next to the three video screens, each showing different angles, popped up four layers of internal schematics, one per floor, that she was ready to zoom in on. All that, and a street map in satellite mode set up with a six-block radius. I knew from experience that she could overlay our assets on that map to enhance our situational awareness.

"Ready to go," Kelsie replied, already distracted with her next task. *Queen of understatement,* I chuckled to myself. Jim and Moy Lei began studying the maps; Max and I had grown up here, but they were fairly new to the city.

My phone buzzed. A message from Aiden. I passed on his message to the team, explaining about the fraud, money laundering, and body found at Deep Cove. I let Maurice know about the financial aspects of the alleged crime by Messenger – he was not party to our capabilities, therefore could not be here, in the room – while Kelsie swivelled her chair to access another console. I surmised she was tasking someone to research the Deep Cove area for tidal data, news articles, and whatever else might be helpful.

A small window silently opened on the screen I was using. Black with blocky green text.

SX: HELLO MARCY!

SkyLoX seemed to rejoice in subtly showing she could appear anywhere, at any time, regardless of how secure we thought we might be. But I was very pleased to hear from her today. I say 'her,' but we don't know their true identity or gender. I have a gut-feeling 'they' are female, but I can't say for sure.

SkyLoX has helped us many times. She was very impressed with our actions against the sex-trafficking criminals, who she apparently battles often. I clicked onto the small screen and began a chat session. When either of us typed, our messages had initials as a prefix.

MS: HI SKYLOX, THANK YOU FOR HELPING US

SX: KELSIE SAID TO ADVISE JUST YOU. NO ONE ELSE

MS: CORRECT. I HOPE TO ASK YOU TO DO SOMETHING ILLEGAL

SX: I ALREADY HAVE. IT'S VERY CURIOUS. THE VPD SYSTEM HAS NO RECORD OF A CRIME INVOLVING ETHAN

MS: NOTHING AT ALL? THEY BROUGHT SEARCH WARRANTS FROM A JUDGE AND HAVE ETHAN AT THE STATION NOW

SX: YES. BUT ASIDE FROM A RECORD CREATED IN THE LAST HOUR FROM THE BOOKING SARGEANT (HOLDING FOR QUESTIONING) THERE IS NOTHING

MS: THAT'S, WELL, CURIOUS. YES

SX: I EVEN CROSS-REFERENCED THAT MESSAGE FROM MR DOYLE JUST NOW. NO DEEP COVE MURDER. NO FRAUD

MS: HOLD ON. THAT MESSAGE WAS ON DARCY'S NEWEST STATE-OF-THE-ART ENCRYPTED PHONE

SX: YES, IT'S VERY GOOD. HER BEST ATTEMPT AT ENCRYPTION YET. ANYTHING ELSE I CAN HELP WITH? SORRY - HOLD ON...

My head was spinning. I didn't have much respect for Bell and Webb, but that's because I think they are weak, lazy idiots, not bent or corrupt.

SX: DETECTIVE BELL WAS JUST ON A CALL WITH THE CORONER. I TOOK THE LIBERTY OF HACKING HIS CELL PHONE WHEN KELSIE GAVE ME HIS DETAILS. ANOTHER CURIOUS ITEM. BELL DOESN'T SEEM TO KNOW HIS VICTIM'S NAME. HE SEEMED SURE HE HAD SEEN THE VICTIM AT THE AUTOPSY TWO MONTHS AGO, BUT HAS MISPLACED THE DETAILS

MS: SKYL0X. WHEN YOU SAY THERE IS NO RECORD IN THE SYSTEM, IS THAT BECAUSE YOU ALREADY WIPED EVERYTHING OUT?

SX: NO, MARCY. I COULD HAVE BUT DID NOT NEED TO. HOWEVER, I DID DOUBLE CHECK THAT NO ONE ELSE HAD, EITHER. I WOULD SEE A TRAIL IF IT HAD BEEN DELETED. IT WAS NEVER ENTERED. ANYTHING ELSE?

I considered what she had told me. Only one thought occurred.

MS: IS SUSPENDING OR DELETING THE INTERNAL VIDEO AT THE STATION WITHIN YOUR CAPABILTY?

SX: I WON'T TAKE THAT AS AN INSULT, MARCY –
LOL

As SkyLoX's clandestine message erased itself from my screen, and I suspect the fabric of space-time, too, I asked Kelsie to step out. She didn't need the burden of knowing we had just hacked the police. I brought Gia and Max up to speed. Then I texted Aiden and cryptically said that there was nothing in the police system about these crimes. I instructed him, in my best legal-texting, that: 1) he should keep that to himself and Ethan; 2) he should never ask how I came by that tidbit; and 3) he should delete this message using Darcy's purpose-built tool.

Then I called Kelsie back into the meeting.

As Kelsie settled back into her chair, seemingly unruffled by being excluded, Jim leapt out of his seat, as if something had stung him.

"We need to move. Now!" he yelled. No one moved. He stopped as he reached the door, incredulous that we were not hot on his heels. "Quickly! I'll fill you in on the way!"

"On the way to what, Jim?" asked Max, as shocked at Jim's sudden outburst and departure as me. "What's more urgent than completing this plan?"

"I sense another adept has just arrived in Vancouver, and looking at the map, I think she's heading towards Ethan! I don't think we want to get there in second place, do you?"

Despite his head start, Jim was last to the elevator.

*

Kelsie rode down with us and captured a description of the Adept. Jim was fairly sure he had felt her mind before. If he was correct, he would be surprised if she were hostile. I didn't want to take the risk that he was mistaken, so I made it clear we would treat her as hostile until proven otherwise. Kelsie would return to her control centre and have drones scanning the streets within minutes.

I texted Aiden with a cryptic message: "Tell Ethan the following, URGENTLY. Unidentified Adept approaching your location. Treating as hostile, although Jim skeptical. Activating Plan Po immediately. Aiden, don't try to interpret this – just relay it quickly."

Ian Po was killed last year by an Adept called Guance. Ian held the same position as Jake, but Ethan had grown close to him and his family over the years he had been employed as Team Leader. Plan Po is a contingency plan designed to defend against Adepts, and the best way to fight an Adept is from a distance. In addition to our four security teams, Max clandestinely had two of his ex-military-now-mercenary friends close by, wherever we travelled. Our four teams have handgun permits, carry when on duty, and are all rifle and shotgun trained. But none have killed anyone in cold blood. We didn't want to run the risk that they may freeze if asked to take down someone as harmless looking as, say, Jim. Max was already on his cell activating his snipers, discussing potential shot positions and angles, and relaying the description Jim had provided.

We rolled out of our secure parkade 30 seconds after the private elevator reached the basement. It was rush hour, and the 5 to 15-minute drive would seem like an eternity. I pulled out my phone and called my ex-boss Dennis Preece out of desperation.

"Marcy?" he answered, in his curt manner. "I heard Ethan was in custody. I don't think we can be having a conversation. You know that's a conflict of interest, right?"

"Dennis, shut up. I won't argue his case. This is an emergency. Remember last year? The assassin? The lengths we had to go to take him down? Right now, there is someone worse coming for Ethan. I think the VPD have been tricked into taking Ethan there, so he is vulnerable to attack. And believe me, you can put this station in lockdown but if what I think is coming at you arrives, most of the dead will be your colleagues."

"What are you talking about, Marcy? Who is coming?"

"No time to explain, Dennis. You need to get Ethan out of there. The assassin won't hit the station if Ethan is not there."

"I can't just go down there and set him free. You know that. And a prisoner movement order takes a while to arrange."

"Detectives Bell and Webb. They work for you now, right?"

"Yes, but..."

I cut him off. "Dennis. We've been through a lot together. I'm asking you to trust me, but not to ask too many questions. You don't have time. Pull up the files on Ethan's arrest. If you see anything amiss, find Bell or Webb and have them tell you who the murder victim is. If you notice anything unusual – and you will – get Ethan out of there immediately. I can have a chopper on the ground at Science World by the time you get him there, and we can airlift him and you out. That will nullify the threat to your people. You can handcuff yourself to Ethan if you need to keep him in custody. But hurry, Dennis. We are talking minutes, at most."

I hung up. Letting him respond would slow him down. He would either act or he wouldn't.

Gia was at the wheel, allowing Max and me to operate our phones freely. Max and I were both trained extensively in high-speed vehicle manoeuvres, but we left it to her, as Vancouver's rush hour would keep our speed in check – or so we thought; Gia drove like a maniac. We crossed sidewalks, medians, and even made a one-way street two-way for 20 seconds. Her protective drive for Ethan, her reflexes, and sheer balls got us near the station faster than my training would have. But two blocks away, on the Cambie Street Bridge, we were suddenly stymied: All lanes were blocked, and there was no way off the bridge in a vehicle. Jim jumped out onto the street first and took off like he knew where he was going. We abandoned the car and jogged – more of a frustrating fast walk for us younger folk – along side.

After my call to Preece, we had set our phones onto a common, open circuit, and were now all in touch through earpieces. Kelsie cut in.

"We have you on screen and have also picked up a potential target. A woman matching Jim's description just entered a coffee shop roughly 100 yards ahead of you; you are heading straight for it." I watched Max click onto a separate tactical channel and direct one of his snipers to cover that location.

"She's sensed us," gasped Jim. "She's stopped. We can slow down, before one of us has a coronary." We knew he meant himself. "Let me go in first," he said.

"Bullshit. Gia and Max will cover the back and the front, and I'm coming with you, Jim. The team will need a feed from inside." I pulled my phone out and activated its camera, adding a video feed to the line. I clipped it onto my tactical vest, taken from the supply we always kept in the SUV.

As we neared the coffee shop, Max sped up and shot down the alley to its side. Gia grabbed a newspaper from a free dispenser on the sidewalk, and took position casually reading out front. Jim and I walked through the door, and I paused to allow my eyes to adjust to the light.

A smartly dressed but plain looking woman stood at the front of the line placing her coffee order. She held a finger up to the barista and addressed Jim.

"Hello, James. I noticed you coming. Do you still take your coffee black? Is this one with you?" She nodded a jaunty welcome to me. "What can I get you, mademoiselle? My name is Courtney du Caron."

*

[Ethan] — When Aiden relayed Marcy's message, I leaped up and tried the door. It was locked and, being a security door in a police station, not something I could quickly break through. I started pounding to get attention, but no one answered. Aiden was shocked and confused but was handling himself well. I sat back down and racked my brains. I told Aiden to move his chair to the farthest corner of the room, and that whatever happened, he was not to move. He complied, probably because the look on my face terrified him. He reached into his pocket; his phone had buzzed again.

"Another message from Ms Stone, Ethan: 'Threat contained, probably false alarm. Remaining alert and close by, just in case. Hang in there. Hopefully, cavalry en route.'" I breathed a small sigh of relief.

"I don't know what to make of all this, Ethan. I thought I *was* the cavalry." Aiden seemed a bit miffed.

Just then, the door opened, and a red-faced Dennis Preece stormed in and dropped himself into the chair opposite me. He gave me a long, hard cop-stare. He seemed to be trying to decide how to approach something. After a long exhalation, he dived in.

"Can we talk without your legal representative present, Mr Booker?" said Dennis, nodding towards Aiden and the open doorway, indicating Aiden should leave.

"I don't think that's a good..." started Aiden, but I held up my hand. Preece and I had history – not all of it harmonious – but he is a good man.

"Aiden, thanks. Stay close in case I need you, but would you pop out and see if the station coffee has improved since your last visit?" Aiden and I exchanged looks, mine being, 'I've got this' and his expressing, 'I've worked for a number of idiots who thought they'd got this.' But as he headed out the door, Aiden shot me a final glance that conceded, 'OK, you are smarter than most of them and I like you.'

Preece and I stared at each other for a moment, my show of trust helping him make his decision.

"Ethan," he started, "I wanted to keep this between the two of us, as I find my team facing the wrong end of a potential lawsuit. You are free to go, with my sincere apologies for the stress and inconvenience – which I will not repeat in a public forum, for liability reasons. The team searching your suite has been pulled out. Rather than make them tidy up, I thought you would prefer they just leave." He paused for me to comment, letting the classic cop-trick of a long silence do his work for him. I was quite baffled.

"That would be fine, Dennis. Do you mind telling me what's going on?"

"I was hoping you could tell me, Ethan. Marcy called and asked me to check into what was going on. I looked at our system, and it was essentially blank, aside from us holding you for questioning on an unspecified money-laundering charge. The murder, and the other circumstances Bell and Webb accused you of, are not in the system. No record at all. I admit that at first it crossed my mind that you pulled some strings and had the system wiped clean. I had Bell and Webb standing at attention in my office trying to explain their actions for the past few minutes. They are one hundred percent convinced they entered details, went to the morgue, and interviewed witnesses. I called Judge Meredith, who recalls signing warrants; but now that I'm asking questions, he and my team are genuinely confused about the details. I quickly checked with the morgue staff and two of the witnesses, and they know nothing about any of it. There is no corpse, and no evidence."

"I don't know what to say, Dennis. I haven't killed anyone and haven't dumped bodies anywhere. This is all bizarre." Which was true.

"I've built a career around identifying liars, Ethan, and I don't think Bell and Webb are lying; they are convinced of their account of the situation. You, on the other hand...I sense you aren't telling me everything I should know."

A long silence followed.

I cracked and decided to give him something, hoping that his ability to detect lies is not as good as he thinks. I relied on his need to find a way to explain the unexplainable.

"Dennis, I don't know everything that is going on. But I can assure you I haven't murdered anyone – or dropped bodies into

Deep Cove – and have no knowledge of this victim; this whistleblower." I was careful not to mention the laundering aspect, thinking of the Silent Souls, or my shooting Guance dead which I see more as self defence as opposed to murder. "I was stunned when they came and served the warrants today."

Preece nodded for me to continue. All had been the truth so far. Now for the next part.

"I don't know what happened, but I am involved, in another jurisdiction, with some people who may want revenge. Did you ever see the movie with Denzel Washington, the *Manchurian Candidate*?"

"Bad guys feed him sleeping gas then brainwash him; he's not aware of his actions. That one?" Preece recalled, accurately.

"There are some folks who can do something a bit like that who are associated with the assassin who came after Marcy last year. They are into experimental chemicals. I don't understand it all, but I do know we pissed them off – royally. I don't need an apology from you or your team. If anything, perhaps it should be the other way around: Maybe I got Webb and Bell involved in something none of us understand. Get them checked out thoroughly, Dennis, but cut them some slack. That's my advice."

"That would explain some of what Marcy said when she called me to warn that someone deadly was headed to my station."

I could tell he wasn't 100% sold, but he walked me through to booking and returned my property. Aiden and I then stepped out of the building to one of the most welcome breaths of fresh air I have ever had.

"Was the coffee any better, Aiden?"

"Nope!" he said, dying to know where things stood. I pulled out my phone and messaged Gwen.

Gwen, could I ask a favour? I'd like you to buy fifteen of the top coffee machines and send them, along with a three-year supply of your best coffee, to Detectives Webb and Bell with my compliments and a note reading: *No hard feelings. I hope this makes you guys the station heroes.'*

*

Jim invited Courtney back to the meeting space in the Booker Building, where those of the team who knew about Adepts convened an hour later. This gave Marcy and me a moment – we needed to settle our fears and get in a hug – and allowed me to get a much-needed shower. I had sweated a lot in the last three hours.

Max was helping everyone to a generous shot of TD50 whisky as we walked in and closed the door behind us. Jim made the introductions.

"I've known Courtney for about thirty-five years, Ethan, and up until now she has always had my trust. I would dearly love to know her involvement in all of this, and she has promised to tell us."

"Mademoiselle du Caron," I said, as I shook her hand and sat down next to her. She made a point of insisting we call her Courtney. I noted Moy Lei had taken the seat on the other side of the new Adept and seemed very focused on her. Understandable, I guess. Courtney would be only the third of her species she had met and, I must admit, there was something compelling about her.

Courtney appeared to be in her late 50s – maybe even early 60s – though looks can be deceiving with Adepts. She had grey hair cut into a soft bob: a classic, if plain, style. Perhaps it's the accent, but I always feel French and Québécois people seem more chic, yet she didn't fit that profile: Courtney had a full, rounder nose, separating eyes full of wisdom from a wide mouth, which was flanked by sharply pronounced cheekbones. As I took her in, an awful thought crossed my mind: *With a bit of effort, she could look exceptional.* I felt ashamed of myself as I hate that sort of body-shaming. But it was as if she had gone out of her way to dress as plainly as possible, which we later found out she does quite intentionally. Like all Adepts, she can have humans turn a blind eye to her presence, but it turns out that her role in life puts her alongside political and government figures, where there are often media and security cameras that are immune to her mind tricks. It suits her to be as forgettable as possible.

"Courtney, I've had a trying afternoon," I began. "I'm not a big believer in coincidences. Can you shed any light on why Vancouver's finest think I murdered someone?"

"I'd be guessing at any specifics, but I am pretty sure I know who is behind it." She took a bracing sip of whisky and continued. "I'm head of my clan, one member of which left us some months ago. We have been looking for her since, and we know she has been here in Vancouver often over the last few months. I have a theory that she has targeted you specifically, Ethan, but her real purpose in leaving Le Perjure – my clan – is less clear. When she exerts herself to deploy her talents to influence a large crowd, she uses a great deal of mind-power, and we can sense her. Using this method we know she has been in many cities across Canada and, more often recently, the USA. It seems too organised to be random travel, but we don't know her motives."

"Can you shed any light on why the police were so adamant Ethan killed someone?" This from Naomi, who no doubt was speculating, as I was, as to how an Adept could achieve what we witnessed today. Our experience to date was that Adepts can scare and immobilize people, but not reprogram them.

"Ah, I'll let Court' explain," said Jim – I noted the use of the shortened name, in an affectionate tone – "but you will find that, like Moy Lei here, female Adepts operate quite differently from male Adepts."

"Talan, our missing Adept, built a hollow shell. That is what we call this method of attack. We even trained her in the technique. She will have spent many hours using her powers to convince people of your guilt, whom you've met, what you've done, and perhaps had them falsify information and create false evidence. But this shell of lies is weak – hollow – as she didn't spend the time to put the next layer of details in place, which would further substantiate her lies. This attack on you may have been just an attempt to weaken you, to remove access to your friends and resources so that she can return later and apply the *coup de grâce*. Although mercy is not one of her values."

"Hollow shell...that phrase sounds familiar," I said.

"The term hollow shell goes back to Napoleon III's days – Napoleon Bonaparte's nephew – the reigning monarch when the Second French Empire fell apart. His realm looked robust from the outside but collapsed quickly when beset by Russia in 1870 and no one came to their aid." She took another sip of her fine whisky, pushed her bangs away from her eyes, and was about to continue when Gwen interjected.

"Isn't he famous for the phrase, 'It is usually the man who attacks. As for me, I defend myself, and I often capitulate.'? That Napoleon?"

"Yes, that is him. History records his wife as detesting him and wanting nothing to do with him after giving him his heirs, and so he took a string of lovers. A colourful crowd: a spy; a cousin; the daughter of the hangman; the most famous actress in Europe at the time; a prison laundress; and the author of the book *Last Love of an Emperor*, who most certainly was not the last. Some say the man was as hollow as his empire."

"As interesting as all that may be," I said, not so subtly steering the conversation back to today's events, "why would Talan set her sights on me?"

"To answer that question, I first need to tell you some of our history; we may need another bottle of this wonderful whisky. A good place to pick up the story would be fall of 1835, in Montréal."

5: LE PERJURE

"Centuries ago, before the Europeans came to North America, a family of Nimbus, aghast at how petty politics of mostly power-hungry men caused so much waste and suffering, dedicated their efforts to interceding secretly in order to help steer the world to less violent, more egalitarian ends.

"They named themselves Le Perjure, derived from the Latin *perjurare*. Hopefully, none but perhaps Jim will have heard of that term." Courtney paused, and assessed the room before continuing.

"My clan members – my family really, as our talent flows through our bloodlines – are able to control what people believe. We are the bastions of truth, and the most subtle purveyors of 'fake news,' whichever we deem necessary to meet our goal: A better world."

Gwen cut into Courtney's story, bristling with suspicions and concerns. "Better by whose measure? We could all list dictators who have tried to impose their will with disastrous results for humanity. Hitler for one."

"We support no person or country and seek no lands..." started Courtney, but Gwen cut her off again.

"So, you are more like the Taliban? Or are your more like Spectre, the secret society in *James Bond* stories?"

"We try our best to respect all religions and atheism equally, and aside from some very modest funds for our quite basic lives, we take no financial benefit from our abilities. Like you, I believe," she said, looking at Gia and Max, "the funds we acquire typically come from the coffers of organised crime."

Naomi put her hand on Gwen's, to moderate her partner's interruptions, and said, "Courtney, forgive us. Some of our experience with Nimbuses has been painful, and anyone who admits to deliberately and routinely manipulating the truth doesn't sound trustworthy at all. Please tell us about your clan's purpose."

"Perfection is an impossibility of course, but we strive to minimize suffering and maximize prosperity for all of humanity, not just one race, country or faction. We believe this comes from geopolitical stability and scientific advances relating to improving health and global nutrition. Individual equality and freedoms are also important to us."

"So, you stand against crimes such as sex-trafficking?" asked Gia.

"Yes, absolutely. But in truth, there are very few of us and it is rare for us to have resources to interact at the criminal level. We focus more on national, government-level activity. If you'll allow me to get back to my story, it will provide some illustrations."

"Yes, please continue," asserted Ethan.

"In 1835, Esmé du Caron became head of our clan. Over the centuries our leadership has moved to France, England, Spain, or whichever country influenced the world most greatly at any given time. Le Perjure came to North America earlier, in the 1600's, to help shape this continent into a few larger countries rather than many smaller ones. We had observed how the many small countries on the European continent were always at war and too fragmented to address issues such as pandemics. We determined, rightly or wrongly, that North America as one nation would be too large and powerful, but would – on the other hand – be too fragmented if every European power retained a slice, which was how things were shaping up before we interceded. Le Perjure influenced events to form what is now the USA and Canada; that is, two large countries, each with their own power. The Hudson Bay Company was almost a third power, but we gradually tempered their purely fiscally driven influence so that local government by residents, as opposed to corporations, could flourish. This exemplifies the level of influence we typically focus on."

"That's mind blowing," interjected Max. "But, putting that aside for a second, how does this relate to Ethan's troubles?"

"Le Perjure is formed around a core of family members whose bloodlines have been delicately managed for as long as our records go back. Like most families, we have internal factions that don't always think the same way. I believe that until Talan, our rogue Nimbus, all of us believed in the goals I have stated. But my faction, which is in the majority, values the belief that powers should be used only for the good of others, and we see using these powers for personal advantage as evil. The other faction, while certainly wanting to help humanity, is less bothered if they benefit along the way and feel entitled to take want they want as long as it doesn't impact the broader mission."

"What would be an example?" I asked.

"Let me tell you a little of how our powers work, and then I'll give you a real-world example."

"I would love to know about your...our...powers," ventured Moy Lei. The room seemed to take a collective gulp. I guess it hadn't occurred to any of us that Moy Lei had learned what she knows exclusively from Jim, but that her own abilities and physiology would be more akin to Courtney's.

"I know you have seen Jim in action," Courtney continued. "He has lived an independent life, but his powers are similar to a clan I know you are familiar with, The Chord. Although their powers are similar, Jim is altruistic, and The Chord is the polar opposite." She was right about The Chord who, in our experience, were evil, vicious people who saw humans as beneath themselves on the food chain, and who killed for their own benefit or entertainment. I was interested in how much she seemed to know about our little gang's recent adventures.

"Like you humans, although our male and female physiology is similar, we experience differences along gender lines. For you, stereotypically at least, males have more aggressive traits and females are more nurturing. Perhaps it's testosterone, or some other chemical, but The Chord have always been hyper-aggressive, and their powers have only manifested through the males in their family line. Their late leader, Moy Lei's aunt, led their clan, but was from a different family altogether. She is a rarity in our species; a hyper-aggressive female."

"The Chord really only developed their fear-based talents as it was all they typically required. A blunt but very effective instrument to dominate and kill. Jim would be an example of a male with a much broader set of emotions he employs, but fear would still feature as it is so accessible in his core.

"But there are other powerful emotions that can be projected to great effect, too. Human females have weaponized sex since Adam and Eve, and so do we. Desire and denial are much more subtle influencers than fear. So, while The Chord uses fear like a hammer on a drum, Le Perjure use sexual persuasion more like a piano, with many keys, subtleties, and tones. A mature member of my clan can twist your minds, individually or as a group, and turn you onto our purpose, making you believe it was your idea all along.

"The schism in my clan goes back to the 1600s, when one of our novices seduced another novice's male partner, who was human. As it was impossible for the human to have resisted, most of us considered this as an act of rape. But our less moralistic faction, of which Talan would be a contemporary example, largely discount the feelings of humans. You are to them a species they are largely benevolent too, but for a more selfish purpose. They insert themselves into positions of great power and leverage, and skim benefits for their dynasty off the top so to speak, rather than see you as equals with different abilities."

"Ok, I understand, I think." ventured Max. "But I still don't see why Talan would go out of her way to hurt Ethan. What has he done to her?"

"Well, two reasons really," Replied Courtney. "For the first I must bore you with some history. In 1835 Esmé was of my faction, who saw humans as equals who have different powers, and her sister Shanelle, of the other faction, thought humans were a lesser species. Both had daughters, who each shared their own mother's values. Esmé and her daughter had to fend off a near rebellion from the Shanelle's faction, which made family's historical tensions worse. During this struggle, her daughter had help from a human called Timothée de Relieur. He essentially helped her thwart Talan's ancestors."

I noticed Ethan's posture change. Something in Courtney's story had struck a note with him, but I didn't know why.

"What happened to this Timothée?" asked Ethan.

"He ran off with Jaz. Jaz's desertion from Le Perjure was also considered a serious crime, but one that Esmé tolerated. She believed that Jaz and Timothée had killed one of The Chord members. Jaz's life was in grave danger, and to save it, Jaz was allowed to disappear into obscurity to the relatively wild, western parts of the continent."

"Ethan, what's bugging you, bud?" asked Max, softly. Max has known Ethan all of his life and was very attuned to him. He had also sensed Ethan's tension.

Ethan held his hand up, effectively silencing the room, while his mind raced; we could virtually see the cogs turning. Eventually, with a fleeting glance at Naomi, he addressed Courtney. "Would it be feasible that the runaway couple had children?"

"Oh, we know they did, Ethan," answered Courtney. Ethan looked at all of us, one at a time.

"I'm descended from them, aren't I? If I follow my family tree back far enough, I have a branch from France, with that same family name."

"In fact, Timothée changed your family name to Booker, Ethan, to help hide you from The Chord, after Jaz bore him a son. Luis Booker is a key member of your family tree, I'm sure. This was in 1836. In 1904, Le Perjure rediscovered this sub-branch of our family and as a result, The Bookers have always been on the radar of Talan's faction, but nothing has really come of it until now."

"Right," said Max, "it's old news. Why after nearly 180 years would it matter?"

"Ethan's lineage was the first reason but, as I said, there was a second reason. Talan has been a 'problem child' for a few years, gradually pulling away from her position in Le Perjure. We have caught her in several nefarious activities and mixing with – shall I say – the wrong sort. She has been reined in and punished often, and until a few months ago, we believed we had turned the corner with her. But apparently, she had just become more subtle, and learned some tricks we hadn't credited her with."

"So, what's changed?" pressed Max.

"The week Talan left, we discovered she had departed because someone killed her lover. We had no idea about her liaison with this person; it came out retroactively in our investigation to locate her. We think she believes Ethan killed the man she loved. A member of The Chord. A Nimbus called Guance."

My stomach lurched as the air was sucked out of the room. Will those terrible events not lie down and die? The room was silent for many moments before Max broke the tension: "Well I guess that would do it. Someone from a family she has hated since birth kills her lover. And that Ethan is human, a lower species in her eyes, is bound to make things worse."

We all nodded, except for Ethan, who was looking from Courtney to Naomi. Each nodded to him, Courtney with a smile, and Naomi with a look of worry, or perhaps sadness. Ethan looked at me, and he shared the look of worry.

"What's up, Ethan?" I asked him. He looked almost frightened. Not my kick-ass-in-any-scenario macho man at all.

"Well, that's just it. Naomi told the group earlier today someone else she has tested recently had the fourth super-neuron. Naomi, am I an Adept?"

"You don't exhibit any Nimbus characteristics, but yes, you have four super neurons," she replied.

6: ONE AISLE TOO MANY

Vancouver, November 2020

[Ethan] – It was Jim who interrupted the silence that filled the boardroom following my realization. I think we all needed time to digest what we had just learned.

"I'm sorry everyone, but I sense Courtney needs some nourishment. Adepts need their fuel, you know." He was referring to the fact that Adepts burn food some 40% faster than we do, and Courtney had stepped straight from a flight to come to find me at the police station and had been talking for hours without consuming anything more than whisky and nibbles. I suspected Jim, and probably Moy Lei, were ravenous. But I think he realized I needed to talk to Marcy. How would she feel discovering her lover isn't human?

"Hell yeah, I'm hungry. Heading up to the roof to barbeque some chicken if anyone wants in," growled Max.

"Where are my manners? Sorry, Courtney. I just got so wrapped up in the history." I said. Then I relied on some of my 'detective mojo' and took a leap. "Jim, would I be wrong in believing you and Courtney could use some time to catch up?" It was clear they had met before and watching the interaction between them at the table had me convinced there was a history greater than a mere passing acquaintance in their past.

"I would love to take Courtney for dinner, if she has no other plans and is willing to forgo Max's offer. But perhaps you would like to check in to a hotel first?" Jim directed the last remark at Courtney.

"I had my luggage sent directly to L'Hermitage on Richards Street. Is there somewhere near there we could meet? It's been too long, Jim."

"I've already put a car and driver at your disposal while you are here in Vancouver," interjected Kelsie, happy to be back to her usual five steps ahead of everyone's logistical needs. "It's outside the lobby now. The driver will give you her number so you can call her as needed."

We adjourned for the evening, with a plan to pick this up again in the morning over breakfast at 8 am. It had been quite the day. The room emptied, but I sat still. Marcy stood up and closed the door behind Jim as he left. This was potentially going to be a difficult and emotional discussion, and I felt myself bracing for it so hard that my heart and stomach ached. But Marcy surprised me again. Marcy pushed my chair backwards a foot or two from the table, straddled my lap facing me, leaned in, and hugged me.

"Marcy..." I started.

"I've been fucking an alien? How friggin' cool is that, Booker?" she giggled. "You know this makes no difference. I'd love you if you had three heads, you idiot."

"But..."

"Come on. If you just found out I had one of these extra neurons, would you feel differently about me? Should I be worried?" She stared deeply into my eyes and watched her words filter though me, and her smile broadened as the lightbulb came on.

"Of course, it wouldn't make a difference at all," I said.

I was shaking with relief. I needed to let off some steam and get my mojo back. The fear of things breaking apart between Marcy and me had turned me into an emotional wreck in seconds. *Get your shit together Booker; she wants a stud, not a sop.* I drew her in for a deep, long kiss. When we came up for air, Marcy anticipated my need to exercise and suggested we go for a run. I had been thinking about a different sort of exercise, but admitted she was probably right again.

"Love to, but I first need to drop downstairs and thank Aiden and see if Maurice needs anything. I'll see you shortly. Go stretch because you will need to be limber if you want to see anything but my dust trail." I cheekily spanked her butt, pushing her towards the elevator as I peeled off to take the stairs down to the business floor. She rolled her eyes and gave me an 'in-your-dreams' smile, as well as a subtle wiggle designed to hit me right in the groin. She knows I can't run with an erection.

*

Maurice and Fatima had spent the last two hours marshalling his army of business leaders to ensure Booker Enterprises recovered, as the judge's asset-freezing instructions were rescinded at the banks and other institutions. As I stepped quietly into the back of their meeting room it was evident Maurice was wrapping things up with a summary.

"Everyone clear? Our competition has been working hard to take advantage of this disruption, but they will not be expecting this sudden reversal. If we execute Fatima's aggressive plan correctly and in total secrecy, we should steal the market advantage back from our competitors. We can come out ahead of where we were before this storm hit us. Fatima will lead the teams working to buy up financial positions through anonymous brokers overnight; she barely sleeps anyway, as you all know. And before the competition realises...*we'll be back!*" These last three words were said in a convincing Schwarzenegger accent, showing a side of Maurice I hadn't seen before.

I chuckled, once again counting my blessings that he was doing all of these things I hate to do, so effectively. The attendees dispersed in a businesslike manner, and if they wondered what I had done to invite such legal actions, they showed no sign.

"Looks like you have everything in hand, Maurice, but is there anything you need from me?"

"No thanks, Ethan. I think we have everything under control. But I do have information you may be interested in. Sit down a moment." I complied, my mind wandering to Marcy squeezing into her running gear.

Maurice started. "To unwind the turmoil caused by the various warrants, it was important we thoroughly document every warrant, bank action, communication, and asset affected.

When we went through it all in detail, I noticed something odd. I haven't shared this with anyone but Aiden, though he couldn't add any insight, I'm afraid."

"What's up?"

"Well, Detectives Bell and Webb initiated all of the activity here in Vancouver and included seizure writs for non-Canadian assets. Imagine dominos being knocked down one by one. Like a ripple, if you like. Well, there was a separate set of writs hidden among the chaos that did not appear to originate from the Vancouver Police. Aiden called Bell and Mr Preece, and they could not account for this activity either."

"I'm not clear on what you are telling me, Maurice."

"Well, whoever started this nonsense here in Vancouver, also initiated something similar in the United States. Preece has already reached out to the FBI and talked to the investigating officers who were just in the process of issuing warrants for your arrest on a drugs charge, having been alerted to your alleged nefarious activities in Denver. He apparently suggested they take another look at their investigation and they were as surprised as Webb and Bell were that they had no evidence for their actions at all. Quite perplexing, Ethan. I hope one day to learn the back story from you, but I won't pry."

"Thanks, Maurice. If I thought you would believe me, I might tell you, but I have promised some good people to keep it confidential. Am I wanted in the States?"

"No, that's been dealt with already. And I understand and respect your need for confidentiality, of course." Maurice was as professional as always.

"Thanks for bringing this to my attention. Should I call Preece for details?"

"He sent over a file already. It should be in your personal inbox. He also mentioned he has made a tentative appointment for you and Ms Stone with a Denver PD Detective, Gilda Coop, for 6 pm tomorrow evening. Her phone number is in the package, too."

I patted his shoulder and said thanks once more, then walked down the corridor and properly thanked Aiden, too. As I left him, I was sure he was humming *Country Roads,* the John Denver song, under his breath.

As I rode the elevator back up to our suite, I sent one more message of thanks via a highly secure and secret application on my phone. 'Thanks, SkyLoX – I seem to always be in your debt. Let me know if I can ever pay you back.' There was a brief pause, and then a GIF of a fist with the little and the index fingers extended appeared on my screen. 'Just keep kicking these arseholes in the balls for us, Ethan. Rock on!'

The connection dropped as the image of the fist faded into an ethereal mist.

*

Marcy and I limbered up as we walked through Yaletown, down to the traffic circle at the end of Davie Street by the entrance to the marina. We stopped and stretched there before starting our run in earnest along Vancouver's stunning seawall. The sun was already dipping towards the ocean, and the first part of our run would be directly into what promised to be a stunning sunset. I balanced on my right leg, reached back, and grabbed my left ankle to stretch my left quads. Marcy pointed out a pair of pugs — these cute dogs are common among Yaletown's condo-population — and I looked over and smiled at their tough yet slightly silly bodies and faces. Her distraction successful, she ambushed while I was balanced on just one leg and shoved me hard into a shrub bed.

Marcy was a good 40 yards ahead by the time I pulled myself out of the bushes and set off in pursuit. I could hear her trash-talking and laughing at my expense. As runners, we are closely matched, although I'm a little faster over the shorter distances while she can maintain a faster pace in longer endurance races. The route would favour her slightly. I deduced she was trying to get me to push hard now, to make it easier for her to beat me over the long term, so I set a pace to catch her slowly, rather than playing into her hands by sprinting at full speed to catch her early.

We wound along the seawall and up onto the Burrard Bridge, and as we pulled over the crest, I had halved the distance between us. We were moving at a full run, not a jog, which meant our bodyguards in Team Delta tracked us from their Range Rover. Some of them may have kept up on foot, but then wouldn't have been in the best shape to defend us if anything occurred that needed their intervention. They knew our route in advance and leapfrogged from spot to spot as we sprinted around the course. As they passed me, I heard them yell for me to "pick it up;" and as they passed Marcy, I'm pretty sure they yelled "kick his ass, girl!" but I wasn't sure, as the blood was pumping hard in my ears by this time.

We made our way down to Granville Island and turned east, tracking in the opposite direction along the bank on the other side of False Creek, back to where we started. Our plan was to continue on past Science World before looping back to our start point. A complete circle of five miles and we aimed to set a record each time we did it. The world record for five miles is a shade over 21 minutes. We are both hyper fit but not runners first and foremost, and given the terrain, if we can beat twenty-seven minutes, we consider it a solid achievement. Having started the day in a bike race, I felt I would struggle to hit the target.

Yet the burning in my legs was rapidly consuming some of the worries of the day and the remainder were being left in my wake. I elected to go for it. As great looking as Marcy's ass is, I decided it was time to stop looking at it and pull ahead. I eased up a gear, as did she when she saw me gaining faster. I drew level as we reached Science World and added a few strides to try to break her spirit. I raised a finger in salute and poured on the power. As we reached the site of the old Edgewater Casino, I had a good twenty-yard advantage and was well into my stride.

Passing under the Cambie Bridge and entering the final leg, I had already rehearsed several witty put-downs and had even decided on which I would greet her with at the finish line. I thought I imagined something at my shoulder and glanced around, only to see Marcy sailing past, having found some extra reservoir of energy from who knows where.

"If you catch me, you can have me any way you like tonight, Ethan. But if you don't, I have kinky plans for that slack ass of yours. Slave-Boy." I was so tempted to slow down, but I didn't. I committed to leaving nothing in the tank, gritted my teeth, and pulled out every last stop.

As we walked back through Yaletown, gasping, panting, and sweating profusely, I pointed out to her that had she not cheated at the start, I would have overtaken her and won. I had been closing in on her and she had been out of juice as she smacked the sign for the False Creek Ferry Terminal that marked our finish line. If only the course were 20 yards longer. But, twenty-seven minutes flat; not too shabby.

As we walked up Davie street, Elvis was rolling on his back outside our hair salon, Blonde Apple, enjoying a belly rub from Hanif, a trendy and salt-of-the earth, stylist-cum-friend who cuts both of our hair. Hanif is a regular stop for Elvis when he escapes The Bean, as Hanif spoils him rotten. We spent five minutes enjoying Hanif's banter and hearing the latest shop-gossip, before taking Elvis back with us for his dinner. Elvis has a knack for knowing when we go for a run, and where to stand to intercept us on our return to take care of his many culinary needs.

Team Delta met us at the entrance to the garage and handed us our towels and some water. As they headed inside, I saw money being exchanged. Where was the respect?

"Wait here, Slave-Boy. I have to collect a few things and drop Elvis into Gwen and Naomi's." Marcy ducked inside, returning five minutes later with a small leather bag. "This way," she beckoned, heading into the service area that the Booker Building relies on for deliveries, trash collection, and the like. She led me through some security doors and then down several concrete staircases, which I hadn't seen for years. She seemed to be familiar with the sub-ground labyrinth and stalked confidently towards her destination.

We went down two more levels, our steps echoing in the stairwells. At the foot of the stairs, at the P4 level, Marcy turned and pressed me against the stone wall, kissing me passionately. She ran her hands over my neck and down my arms, and then caressed my butt cheeks. I reciprocated, and we enjoyed five minutes of increasingly close, sexy canoodling. I could do this all night but hoped I would get to rip her clothes off soon; a fire was building within me.

With a last, long rub of my groin, she pulled away and led me by the hand through a security door into our business archives section of the building. The lights were off. She pointed up at the security camera set just above the doorway; the light signifying it was active was extinguished.

"I told Kelsie we wanted to do some private research and to turn off the security cameras until we let her know otherwise." She led me forward, and overhead lights automatically illuminated each aisle of the archives just as we walked up to it. There were large pools of darkness, but we could see the path behind us, and a just little further ahead. I knew that if we stopped moving, within a few minutes the lights would switch off once more, a measure in place to save electricity and maintain the humidity levels.

At the far end of the space, Marcy pulled me to the right and took me fifteen feet into the second-to-last row. She reached into her bag and pulled out a pair of handcuffs and a combination lock.

"Hands up," she ordered, and cuffed my hands together, using the lock to fasten them to a steel brace overhead. She then proceeded to kiss and tease me for a few minutes. I was getting pretty worked up. Then she reached into her bag once more and pulled out some kitchen scissors. She slowly cut away all of my clothes until I stood naked, unable to use my hands to cover my blushes or move from this spot.

She pulled a bulb gag from her bag of tricks, pushed the soft, rubber orb into my mouth, and fastened the leather straps behind my head. She then slowly began to squeeze a small bulb that connected to the ball inside my mouth, which forced air in to inflate it. My mouth filled slowly, to the point where no sound could escape until the air was let out by a small valve. She detached the inflation bulb and pipe so the gag looked like just a rubber strap across my mouth. Ball gags are fun, but you can make a lot of noise through them; a bulb gag was a true silencer.

Next came a paddle and a short, leather whip, with tails only about nine inches in length. She circled me like a panther, striking without warning at strategic spots. No part was safe from her attention. She started softly and unhurriedly but, over time, wound up the speed and pressure. After five minutes of this, she had me panting through my nose, wincing – and loving every second of it. If my erection looked like it might flag, she used her hand or mouth to bring it back to full attention.

She suddenly stopped and stepped back.

"This is thirsty work," she complained. "Wait here. I'm going for a couple of beers." She started to walk away, then turned and came back. She reached into the pocket of my shredded shorts, pulled out my phone, and thrust it into my hands, which were still locked together over my head.

"You should be fine here. The only person I haven't told that the room is off limits is Maggie. I couldn't find her. I think she is off today. But, if you have any concerns, text me, and I will send you the combination for the lock and you can escape. Of course, you will have to run around and hide, as you are a little under-dressed. Again." With a quick squeeze of my testicles, she picked up my shredded clothing and dumped them in the bag, hefting it onto her shoulder before gaily marching off down the aisle, humming something I didn't quite catch. A few seconds later, I heard the archive-room door slam behind her, and a few minutes after that, the lights began to click out.

I stood in the dark, contemplating my lot. I was actually surprised Marcy had left me like this; we had read it was quite dangerous to leave someone tied up alone, especially if they had their breathing restricted, as I had. I could breathe well through my nose at the moment, but what if I sneezed or had a reaction to the dusty boxes here? Still, it was fucking hot.

It suddenly got lighter as my phone's screen lit up with a text from Marcy. 'All OK? I bumped into Maggie's boss and she is here today. He is going to track her down and let her know to stay clear. I've decided I'm smelly, so taking a quick shower. It's hot thinking of you naked down there. I might get a toy and take my time showering, thinking of you. But I will remember to take my phone in the shower, in case you have any problems.' It was hard to text back in this position, but I managed a 'Don't take too long...'

Maggie was something of a character, known for being scared down here in the archives on her own. If she couldn't lure a colleague down for company, she always brought down a Bluetooth speaker and blared 80s rock music loudly, to ward off the bogeyman. Her other claim to fame was making perfumes. She tried to sell them to anyone who would listen. They were quite nice, but a little too strong for most people's liking.

I heard the door bang open and saw the light by the door flick on. Just as I identified Maggie's bouncy blonde hair in the distance, I was assailed by Def Leopard's *Pour Some Sugar On Me. Shit!* I froze. Then my cool-in-a-crisis, private-detective side kicked in and I texted Marcy, 'Shit! Maggie's down here. Send me the code.'

I was a bit worried that when Marcy texted back, the screen lighting up would alert Maggie and she would come to investigate. Hopefully, she would run scared into the other direction. Oh, but then she might bring people to investigate. Jeez, what a fuck-up!

Maggie moved two aisles closer, pushing a trolley stacked with small filing boxes. She paused and took one into the aisle and presumably placed it on a shelf. She moved the trolley again and repeated the activity on the next aisle, the music growing louder each time and each aisle's light's flicking on as she stepped into its sensor range. Where was Marcy with this code? God, I bet she was in the shower and couldn't hear the texts. I sent a new text. 'Hurry up, or I will have to hire a new filing clerk.'

Maggie skipped a couple of aisles before stopping once more. I realized I had been holding my breath, and slowly and quietly took in a lung full of air. Vanilla and coconut! Maggie's perfume is unmistakable.

With only six rows to go before Maggie reached my location, and no code from Marcy, I decided I needed an alternative escape plan. I examined the metal brace, the cuffs, and the combo lock. All solid. Without the right combination, I was going nowhere. What code would Marcy use? It was exceedingly difficult to manipulate the lock's wheels while holding my phone, and I couldn't give that up in case Marcy came through for me. My brain was working through birthdays, anniversaries, her police badge number – anything I could think of that she might have used.

Maggie had moved to within two rows now, and the lights flickered on so that the row just in front of me lit up. Some light was thrown through the shelving and I was partially highlighted, though still largely hidden. Peeking through the racks, I could see that Maggie only had three boxes left on her trolley. She took one to the row to her right. I sent Marcy another urgent text. 'It's now or never!' Maggie picked up another box, walked down the aisle to her left, and I heard her drop it on a shelf and turn back again. One box left. Def Leopard had given way to Rush, who now gave up the stage to Bon Jovi's *You Give Love, A Bad Name!*

Maggie picked up the last box. Hopefully, she was going to place it on that same row and turn back. She studied the label, then looked around, before finally deciding the row I was standing in was the right place. She began to walk towards me. I tried to yell, but the gag was completely effective: Not a sound. The lights flicked on and she stepped into my row, turning towards me. Our eyes met. For some absurd reason, she was grinning like a lunatic. She reached up, grabbed at her hair, and pulled off the blond wig. And turned into Marcy. What a cow! She hadn't left me at all but had let the door slam and changed into her 'Maggie costume.'

Marcy was laughing so much it took a few tries to reach up and release me from my predicament. I was stressed, angry, starting to laugh, and horny as hell – all at once. I had to admit, this was the closest she had come to creating that feeling of my being trapped naked and about to be discovered. She deflated the gag and pulled it out. I stretched my jaw.

"You OK, baby? I had planned this for a few weeks' time, but you had such a fucked-up day, I decided you needed some kinky therapy." She asked a little sheepishly, looking deeply into my eyes.

"Fuck, yeah!" I said, as we sank down onto the floor. It didn't take long. Things were so pent up. When we sat there giggling and panting afterwards, she pushed the last box from the trolley across to me with her foot. Inside was a fresh set of clothes for me.

"Just how long have you been planning all of this, Marcy?" I asked, in awe of her creativity.

"It's one of many I've been concocting since St Tropez, Slave-Boy. And you will never know what is coming next."

7: THE HUNT BEGINS

I left the suite at 7:30 the next morning, stepped across the corridor to Gwen and Naomi's suite, and picked up Elvis – who I swear had slept with us but Houdinied himself to Gwen's in the night – and took him for a walk to help me think.

Next, I saw Jim, whom I had messaged to meet me in The Crazy Bean coffee shop at the street level of our building. I wanted a moment alone with him. As always, 'The Bean' was packed with locals and very few tourists. Gwen has always had this ability to create a family atmosphere that brought in the locals but, like Diagon Alley in *Harry Potter*, seemed to not allow outsiders to find their way in. Elvis dumped me as we entered and made his way over to his place by the open fire, to be welcomed by regular patrons who shamelessly catered to his needs: scratches behind the ears and doggy treats. I spotted Jim reserving some overstuffed leather wingbacks and holding a spare caramel latte for me.

After some pleasantries, I got straight to the point, as our meeting with the gang was about to start.

"Jim, it's clear you and Courtney have some history. I'm not going to pry, as it's your business. Unless it isn't, if you know what I mean. Is there anything I need to know that could affect Marcy or the team's safety – or my business interests?"

"Not that I'm aware of, Ethan. And there is nothing to hide, either. Courtney and I had a thing once and have kept in touch since. Her vocation doesn't really allow for long-term romantic partners, sadly. She's one of the best people I know, and I've often thought...well, you know, if things were different.

"We've stayed casually in touch and enjoy catching up if in the same part of the world. If it helps you any, I trust her completely as a person, but I know to keep in mind that she will always put her clan's survival above all else, followed by what they think is right for humanity. Everything else, including you, me, and her personal needs, come after those two priorities."

"Fair enough, but I need to know if she's determined that either Booker Enterprises or I are a threat to either of those priorities." I could see he was balancing his loyalties, but I needed to press him.

"Courtney repeated last night that she has a rogue clan member who has come after you. She knows you will act to protect what you love. Hear her out. She is the sort of person who will be clear about how she sees the rules of engagement for you towards her clan. Then you can decide your course of action."

"OK, but one last question," I said, as we stood to leave. "We've learned that Le Perjure Adepts gain the most control of their targets by subtly influencing them in long conversations. That's different from you: You increase control by sharing food or fragrances from a common source. Would you be able to sense if Courtney were influencing us in these meetings? And if so, would you warn us? Sorry to put you on the spot, Jim."

"Yes to both, Ethan. But now that you know what to look for, I think you would see it, too. If during or after the meeting you are horny as hell, or abnormally un-horny for that matter, it might have been Courtney." *That's what I was afraid of,* I thought. Was I hot for Marcy last night, just because I always am, or was it Courtney? I would have to trust Jim.

As we walked towards the door, Bennet – one of the baristas – handed us a tray of coffee and food that Gwen had ordered for our meeting. I whistled to Elvis and he looked up, yawned, and lay back down. It's clear who his pack leader *isn't.* The staff look after him like family, and Gwen would collect him when she came to check on her store later in the morning.

Back in the meeting room, breakfast goodies and coffee distributed, I briefed the team on what Maurice had shared last evening. You always know when Kelsie is listening, because the speed of her keystrokes varies as she translates what she hears into searches or actions. I could almost imagine a large, virtual searchlight swivelling around to the southeast, illuminating Denver.

"I think we should meet this Denver detective that Preece spoke to in person, Ethan. We will pick up more and will be on the ground if there is anything we want to follow up on." Marcy the cop, right as always. It crossed my mind to mention I didn't want her entering a potentially dangerous situation, at least until we knew what we were up against, but I was smart enough to keep my mouth shut. Marcy, Gia, Gwen, Moy Lei, and Naomi would tear me apart while Max enjoyed the show. Instead, I nodded in agreement and noted Kelsie's fingers clacking out instructions to have cars, a plane, and clothing readied for us, and probably an advance team of protection and surveillance toys in place for when we arrived.

We turned our attention to locating Talan. The obvious question was why Courtney couldn't just locate the missing Adept using the uncanny internal radar that Adepts seemingly possessed. We had learned there are limitations to the ability. In England last year, Moy Lei had only been able to track the assassins – who had been sent by The Chord – once those individuals had taken an interest in her. We think that Adepts can't maintain a connection to all seven billion people for sanity reasons, and so their physiology filters out everything except people taking an acute interest in them, and with whom they've had some sort of significant interaction.

Jim explained that a rare few Adepts had the ability to minimize their mental footprint, and so become mostly invisible to their brethren. According to Courtney, Talan had never shown such a talent before but conceded she must have acquired it in the months she appeared to have been brought to heel, before escaping the clan. This reinforced Courtney's sense that Talan planned to leave anyway, and our takedown of The Chord had been perhaps a final straw of sorts. Only the occasional higher-powered use of her Adept 'influencing talents' had escaped from this mental invisibility Talan had evidently developed.

Courtney shared the timing and rough locations of Talan's mental broadcasts over the past few months. Adepts only sense direction and a rough range, and so two or more clan members had to work together to triangulate the locations. Kelsie plotted these on a map, which she then projected onto the big screen in our makeshift war-room. We could see Talan's visits to Vancouver, and others to Denver and LA. Courtney explained these bursts were barely discernible, so a lower power blast. By contrast, bigger surges of power lasting for up to 30 minutes at a time came from Québec City, Montréal, Ottawa, Toronto, and Detroit.

We puzzled over this and other data for 20 minutes, but it was only when Kelsie added the time overlay to the big wall screen that an obvious pattern emerged. If you drew a line through those five cities, it was pretty much a straight line, and the blasts travelled along that line in order, appearing at the next location roughly a week after the preceding blast.

"It's as if Talan is driving between each city, letting off a blast of energy, then visiting the next city, travelling east to west," observed Kelsie. "If she maintains that pattern, she might be in either Chicago or Indianapolis in two to three days' time." Neither of these cities were exactly on the line we had plotted – Chicago was slightly north of it, and Indianapolis slightly south – but they were the next two major cities to the west that looked most likely.

We kicked several other ideas around but couldn't come up with anything more promising than those two being the target locations in the next few days. We decided Marcy and I would take team Charlie to Denver to interview the Denver PD officer, Gilda Coop. That meeting was already set for 6 pm tonight. Max and Gia would go with Team Beta to Chicago to scout around for a few days, and Jim and Moy Lei would visit Indianapolis with Team Alpha and do the same there. We toyed with pairing up so that each team had both an Adept and a non-Adept who was a good fighter, like Moi Lei and Gia, or Jim with Max; in the the end, we stuck with the first thought.

If either scouting party picked up a clue, then everyone would converge on that spot. Courtney would return to

Montréal. We figured Talan would sense me, Courtney, and maybe Marcy approaching, and so we would stay away until the last moment. We hoped Talan's Vancouver sorties had not made her supernatural radar aware of Marcy, Gia, and the rest of the gang.

Max and Gia had an additional reason for being the ones to go to Chicago. Silent Souls, the charity that helps sex-traffic victims, was holding a fundraiser event there this week, led by David Brearley, one of the recent additions to their team. They could assist David, as well as see him in action for the first time, and it would be a natural cover for their clandestine search. In reality, Kelsie and her technology wizardry would be the most effective at searching for any breadcrumbs Talan may have dropped, but we would all do what we could on the ground in the various locations to which we were dispersing.

We drove out to Vancouver International Airport in convoy. Marcy and I to the south terminal to take a private jet; Kelsie had booked the others first class commercial. Most airports have ultra-VIP channels that hide the rich, famous, and occasionally royal travellers from the public and Kelsie used one of our shell companies to book the team through that service. It offers a non-public route through customs and immigration, a discrete lounge, and the right to board and alight from the plane ahead of other passengers. If the plane has a separate area, such as the top deck of a 747, quite often no one even knows the privileged are there at all.

There are lots of flights direct to Chicago's O'Hare and Indianapolis's Weir Cook airports, so it is easy to save a little of the climate and fly commercial. Marcy and I nearly always go private as our wealth makes us kidnapping targets – especially now with Talan in the fray – plus in this case, we needed our private jet handy in Denver to be sure we could zip to the other locations without delay should the need arise.

We all felt some trepidation as the groups split up, but also a sense of relief to be taking action. Having fought through two battles together, this attack on me was like a switch that controlled us all, and once activated, compelled us to track and take down the enemy. Sitting in the meeting room hearing the story and making our plan was necessary, but throughout we had an uncomfortable itch, due to the urge to pursue and put down the threat. Aside from interviewing Gilda Coop, none of us had much of a real plan of action once we hit the ground, but we were primed, focused, and ready. Or so we thought.

8: DENVER

Denver is one of my favourite cities and feels like an inland version of Vancouver. You can be drinking some amazing craft beer in the River North – or RiNo – district surrounded by fabulous and officially sponsored graffiti one minute, and skiing or hiking in Aspen or Vale's trails within an hour or two. It is a clean city with a fitness culture and a creative soul.

I would typically stay at The Crawford Hotel, a boutique, wonderfully appointed establishment built right inside Union Street Train Station. It is centrally located and the eclectic bars and stores inside the heritage building create a cool atmosphere. You can sit in one of the character pubs or bistros, or in The Crawford's exclusive hotel bar, nestled in the rafters of the building, and soak up the goings on below.

But being on alert as we were, Kelsie had us booked into a neat AirBnB ranch tucked into the sparsely populated rolling hills within ten minutes' scramble to the airport and our jet.

Two of our four-person protection team were camped out on separate local hills where they could overlook both our property and each other's positions. For good measure, Kelsie remotely launched and stationed a drone above the ranch so no one would sneak up on us.

Detective Coop was kind enough to drive out for the interview. We spotted her Tesla on the overhead camera when it was still a mile out, and after verifying her identity from pictures sent by Preece, Marcy met her as she pulled into the driveway in front of the building. We felt that leading with Marcy, both a female and an ex-cop, would be the best option to establish a trusting forum for information sharing. Marcy brought Detective Coop into the ranch's kitchen and grabbed refreshments. Then they sat and shared a beer in the well-appointed den, framed by twelve-foot-tall picture windows that looked out across the hills to the west; the setting sun was busy painting the few clouds a dusky rose.

Once the women were three quarters of a beer into getting to know each other, I joined them.

Denver is a health-oriented town and Coop was a good example of the fitter-than-average population. She looked very athletic, and I asked if she did triathlons, but she surprised me by explaining ice hockey was her sport. Ice hockey is the fifth or sixth most popular sport in the USA, unlike in Canada where it is almost our religion. If anything, Coop was more forthcoming because we were Canadian and enjoyed some of her hockey stories, rather than because of the initial female-cop connection. But all of this helped, and Coop was very easy to talk to, especially since detectives are understandably suspicious and slow to trust others.

"Down to business," started Marcy. "We are really appreciative of your time and any information you can share."

"Honestly, I want answers as much as you do, Marcy." Coop's gaze had been lingering on me as if she knew me from somewhere but wasn't sure, and she went on to explain why. "Mr Booker…"

"Ethan, please…" I interjected.

"Ethan, then. It's so strange. I have a clear recollection of meeting you, and your face is familiar, yet not, at the same time. It's hard to explain, but you seem so much more three dimensional than I recall. I feel we have met, but…it's like I've only seen a photograph of you. I am so confused. I have almost an eidetic memory, and this is such an unfamiliar experience."

"Go on," I prompted. "We can offer you some answers later but prefer not to influence your recall. Tell it as you remember it, first. But as I understand it, your experience matches that of other people in this case."

"Three days ago, I was leaving my gym, which is in a strip mall in LoDo…oh, that's Lower Downtown. It's a pretty nice area, but has an edgy club there called the Mile-High Bar. Known for drugs and lap dances which go much further if you get my drift. It was late, I had come off duty at 10 pm, and had had a good workout and cooldown. It was 12:08, according to my notes, when you left the club and were getting into the car next to mine as I was leaving. When you opened the trunk to deposit your sports bag, it slipped, and some bags of white powder spilled onto the ground. I identified myself and challenged you. You started to resist, so I pulled my piece and cuffed you. I called for back-up, and a squad car and my partner attended. She took your car to the pound, and the officers in the black and white arrested you and took you to the station, where you were formally booked."

"So at least five or six people would have seen Ethan, if you count the arresting officers and booking sergeants?" confirmed Marcy.

"You would think that, but while my partner remembers it, she is fuzzy on the details. The two back-up officers have no recollection of it at all, in fact one wasn't even on duty as he was off sick that day. The booking sergeant can't recall it, either, but he sees about thirty people per night, so that's not too weird. We have your photo and prints on file, and a record of your kilo of cocaine being entered into evidence."

"That's pretty compelling..." I spluttered. "Why are you now having doubts?"

"Well, your Canadian chief called my chief and said to sift through it all with a fine-tooth comb. The first clue something was off was your release record, which states that you lawyered up and that there was a witness brought in who claims I didn't identify myself correctly. You were released during the night, while I was at home, due to technicalities. That wouldn't have happened."

"Why not?" I asked, although I suspected Marcy would know.

"If that had happened, I would have been called back in before you were released to straighten things out. Anyway, next I discovered Officer Bailey had been sick, and hadn't even been on duty. I went to check the evidence locker, and the drugs were not only missing, but had they been there in the first place, there would have been additional records, which hadn't been created. And the clincher? I went over the arrest record and noticed your booking photo looked off. Took me a while, but I realized it was because we had recently updated the backgrounds for our photos, which show height and other information, and your picture had the old background. So, I checked your fingerprints...and this really spooked me...to find out they were mine. I took it all to my chief and am now facing some sessions with Internal Affairs. What the heck is going on, you guys?"

"Wow, that's tough," consoled Marcy. She looked at me to continue.

"We don't know all the details ourselves, detective, but if it helps, I will fully cooperate with IA. It appears that someone has tried to discredit me, both here and in Vancouver. There are two detectives up there in the same situation. I think that alone would give your IA team pause. There are a number of completely honest people with fake memories who have acted on them. A Vancouver judge signed search warrants without many of the normal checks and balances, for example."

"As near as we can tell," interjected Marcy, "someone with incomplete knowledge of proper procedure influenced a number of people to frame Ethan. He has been a pain in the arse to a group who we think has access to neurotoxins, or poisons, which make people open to suggestion. But that's a theory and we can't substantiate it." We had agreed Marcy would deliver this white lie as it would be more credible coming from her. "Can I show you some pictures and see if any of the faces ring a bell?"

Courtney had supplied a picture of Talan, and we had selected some similar faces from the internet to create our own suspect line-up on a page. Coop scanned them and recognized Talan immediately.

"What is this? Why would you show me a picture of Debbie? She's got nothing to do with this; I do yoga with her. I've known her forever. What does she have to do with this?"

"If she ever went to yoga with you, I would be surprised. I hate to make you question everything, but we think she is the creator of these fake memories. I think if you do some digging, you will find you hardly know her at all."

We sat there quietly as Detective Coop processed this. It must be so hard to comprehend that what you remember from just a couple of days ago is false, especially when you have a memory so sharp you rely heavily on it.

"Detective Coop, how would you two contact each other?" Marcy asked. I guessed she expected Coop to draw a blank. The detective pulled out her phone and scrolled through her contacts.

"Look, call me Gilda, please. Here's her number," she said, holding up her phone. "And there is a call log, too..." She was relieved for a moment, but then her face darkened again. "Hold on...there are several calls, incoming and outgoing, but each only lasts s few seconds. That's really weird." Before we could stop her, she dialled the number. "I'll tell her I've had something come up at work and won't be at yoga this week. I've done that before so it shouldn't be suspicious. Oh, the number is disconnected. Crap."

"Perhaps it's like hypnotism," ventured Marcy. "Maybe the quick calls are just to relay a trigger word or relay a short instruction. Gilda, we don't really know, sorry! Can we take that number?"

We went over the sequence of events several times and undertook to have Aiden put together a summary of what we knew, and were prepared to share, which would help her sort out the mess Talan had created in her life. I gave her the number of a talented private detective acquaintance of mine. She was also based here in Denver, and we had helped each other out on a few of our respective cases on occasion. I suggested a second pair of eyes would be useful to Coop to pick through her life to see which details she could trust, and which were suspect.

THE NUD<u>EST</u> DETECTIVE

I told her that I was picking up the bill for any private-eye or counselling services. She said no at first, pride getting in the way of smart, but Marcy persuaded her. We sent a summary, including Talan's number, back to Vancouver and sat and drank a few beers with this really nice woman who up until now had been confident and complete, and now was falling apart. We eventually put her in an Uber and arranged for her car to be driven home the following day. What a mess.

9: CHICAGO

[Gia] – The Silent Souls' event was set for just two hours after we touched down, so Max and I decided to make that our initial focus, while letting Team Beta do some legwork. While Kelsie worked her online magic, Roxy Storm, Team Beta's leader, would split her group up and put them to work. Roxy would stay close to us in case of need while she set up our mobile operations centre in her hotel room. Recent events had us put together 'go bags' full of drones and other gadgets we could carry and quickly deploy in the field. Roxy's always seemed to have some additional, personalized tools; she was a creative planner. She even carried her own shower head, to temporarily replace the hotel shower heads she frequently felt was not to her high standard.

When we travelled commercial, the large drone batteries had to come in hand luggage while the specially packed custom-cases went into the hold; even VIPs have to follow that rule. But we do get extra overhead space, of course. The other three Team Beta members each took a sector of the city and hoofed it from hotel to hotel showing photos of Talan, using their Booker-Stone Detective Agency credentials to facilitate access. Long shot, but sometimes simple works best.

The Silent Souls event was at The Folly hotel. The hotel is first class, and we use it when in Chicago because Ethan loves the aviation backstory. The hotel was originally opened as Daley's Folly Hotel, but that name was soon shortened to avoid litigation. If you are into flying, at some point you've used Microsoft's famous flight simulator. For years, the default and arguably most fun airport in the simulator was Chicago's Meigs Field, a small airport on a tiny island at the downtown waterfront, surrounded by Lake Michigan. It is very similar to Toronto's Billy Bishop airport, except that it was closed in 2003 in controversial circumstances. Chicago's mayor, Richard Daley, had fought hard to close the airport to make it into the tourist zone it has since become. The local aviation enthusiasts fought to preserve it and appeared to be winning. Then one day, they woke to find the bulldozers had moved in overnight – some say illegally – to begin ripping up the runways, marking the end of the aviation landmark, since the damage could not be cost-effectively repaired. One of the most vocal advocates of keeping Meigs Field open was a local hotelier, and he renamed his waterfront hotel in protest.

We took three adjoining suites: one for Max and me, one for Roxy, and the other – a two bedroom – her three male counterparts shared. I admired Roxy enormously; she is a fiery redhead and a true warrior. We spar and train together often and, while I might be the more skilled, her strength and ferociousness are a handful. You only need to drive in her car with her to sense her competitive nature. Neither of us are girly-girls, and we get along with few words. We have a strong connection, and with just a glance, we know how the other is sizing up a situation or person; deciding if they are they admirable or stupid.

When we took off from Vancouver, we had let David Brearley know that we would be dropping in on the event he was staging for us, and that he should act as if we were not there. We were happy to meet anyone he wanted to trot us out to glad-hand, if that would increase donations, but otherwise it was all his show. He messaged back, acutely embarrassed, that he suddenly had a 30 percent dropout rate from the invited donors. A few normally don't show, but this was highly unusual and there was no obvious cause. We later found out that word of mouth among North America's rich philanthropists and hangers-on was warning many to stay away from such events. But only with hindsight could one have noticed that first sign that something was amiss.

Max and I dressed black tie. He looked so sexy in his tux. It's not the way his muscles filled it out perfectly; and it's not the way his triangular frame was highlighted in the suit's sharp, fitted lines. Max is rarely in anything other than workout gear, jeans and T-shirt, hoodie, sometimes lumberjack plaid shirts;

his clothing line would be Mr Rough-n-Ready. A sexy 'very ready,' not grungy, but super-clean and cocky as hell. The tux was a layer of sophistication that transformed his cocky charm, and his rugged sexiness, into a cheeky handsomeness. He carried off the transformation well, but I just wanted to unwrap him and get my Tarzan back.

Having an athlete's physique makes 'cocktail attire' easy for me in one sense. My fit, muscular frame allows me to look great in almost any cocktail dress, and I feel admiring eyes on me right up until I try to walk in high heels. I'm like a Versace-Bambi. During my young years as a prostitute, I wore my fair share of heels, but in the decade since, it's like my feet are the ex-smokers of shoe wearers. *We won't! We can't!* They complain bitterly. So, I compromised. My outfit demanded four-inch heels, but I chose one and a half-inch booties, where the material was lace, not leather, and wrapped and swirled up over my ankles to showcase my calf muscles, distracting onlookers from my lack of stiletto heels.

Max and I are always set to hot. Hot to fight, hot to adventure, hot to make out. There is no warm or cold for either of us. Today was sexy hot. However, even for us, we were feeling unusually horny, and we put it down to dressing up. This was 'missed clue' number two. This one was arguably one we might have recognized.

The party was under way as we arrived, fashionably late. Round tables, chandeliers, and glitz. With classy cocktails in hand, we mingled and made small talk, enjoying the friendly atmosphere. Many in the crowd were tactile, in a charming sort of way, but a little too invasive of physical boundaries. I know I am very protective of my personal space, so I put this down to me just being too 'me,' and the culture of a different city than our own. Clue number three: we missed another. They were racking up, but we were oblivious.

Max and I both noticed the security was off, too. Men and women dressed like the crowd, but of a lower socio-economic position class. There were bulges where they were hiding weapons and curly wires looping into their ears, making them easy to spot to experts like us. Being obvious is not unusual in itself, but what made them seem off was their posture and positioning. Professionals always look relaxed to blend in, but there is a formalness and alertness that sets them apart. Eyes seeking threats all around the room, and not, like the security team here, on cleavage or butts. Professionals tend to position themselves strategically around the space, ready to act. The biggest warning that Max and I should have picked up on was not that the security was too casual, wrongly spaced, and easily distracted by the abundance of cocktail-dress-flesh, the alarm bell should have wrung loudly that neither of us cared. We noticed things were off but were swept up in events when instead we should have been alarmed or at least highly suspicious. The fourth missed clue.

The auction started and was lively, the surprising level of enthusiasm making up for the lower numbers. David was thrilled he had surpassed his donation target long before the end of the event. As the fundraiser wound up, a server passed through the group and gave a select few an envelope each, inviting us to a short, private function to thank us personally. Max and I both got one and, although we hadn't known David had planned this, agreed it was a great idea. Oddly, by now we would normally be keen to slip away, but today we were curious and keen to attend the extra gathering.

David wrapped up the formal event with a wonderful speech, which was warmly received, and we met him as he stepped off the stage. He, too, had an envelope, and we congratulated him on the initiative. He looked puzzled, and explained he thought we had organized the post-event reception. Looking back, I could hear the alarm bells in my head ringing loudly, but...so what, right? It sounded fun. I linked arms with David and Max, feeling very sexy between two hunks, and we pressed through the departing crowd to discover what was in store.

THE NUD<u>EST</u> DETECTIVE

*

I woke up with a pounding headache and a sinking feeling I couldn't put my finger on. I went instantly on guard and sat up, looking for threats. I was in our suite, Max beside me. My sudden movement woke him, but I didn't care. Something was very wrong. He sensed it, too, and, as if we had choreographed it, we rolled out of bed and took up defensive stances. We were not armed, but our bodies are lethal in most circumstances, so we confidently moved through the suite and confirmed we were alone. I checked the hallway and saw no threats.

In the seating area of the suite was a desk, and on it was a bright yellow envelope positioned prominently so it could not be overlooked. I went to open it while Max picked up his phone to message Roxy to check all was well. I stopped in my tracks when he reacted to what he saw on his phone.

"Crap, Gia. There are missed messages from Ethan. He and Marcy are en route and will be here in about two and a half hours. It appears Talan was active here in Chicago last night."

"Why didn't anyone notify us?" I asked, puzzled.

"They did, here you go. There is a string of messages. In fact, one is from you, Gia. You confirmed that all was quiet at the event, and that we shouldn't be disturbed."

"I didn't send that. Or...?" I stopped. I couldn't remember much past about halfway through the auction. I recalled that I had nibbled at a few vegetables and had some polite sips of a cocktail and some bubbly, but nothing in a quantity that could have been drugged or cause this gap in memory. I certainly didn't get drunk. How did we get to bed?

"Do you remember the end of the event, or coming to bed?"

"I'm blank. Nothing!" declared Max, racking his brains, too.

An urgent bang on the door interrupted us. We pulled on housecoats, then I checked the peephole and let a very worried-looking David into the suite. He looked more than worried, in fact: he seemed terrified, especially of Max, whom he was giving a very wide berth. He had a yellow envelope like the one on our desk in his hands. He tore his eyes away from Max, scanned the room, and spotted our unopened yellow package on the desk. I thought he might bolt at that point, but to his credit he didn't.

"What's up, David? You're in such a state," I said, doing my best to reassure him.

"Jesus guys, I have no explanation. You've gotta believe me. Last night's a blank, but... well... for what I apparently did, I apologise profusely, with all my heart. Not that you are not both good looking, but... it's not my thing, you know? Jane, that's my wife... well, she's going to kill me. What will I tell her?"

Max took a step towards David to reassure him and get him to calm down, but it had the opposite effect. David jumped away and put his hands up in a defensive posture. Did he think Max was going to hit him?

"No, man, no. Stop! I think we are all being blackmailed. I could be mad at you guys, but really I just want answers," he said, almost yelling it in panicked desperation.

"David," I barked, to shock him a little and get his attention. "We have no idea what you are talking about. Just slow down. The event was apparently a huge success. Relax!"

"Look, just open your envelope and watch the video. Just know I didn't do anything... well, apparently, I did, but...we all did..." David trailed off and hung his head, clearly awaiting execution.

Max retrieved the yellow package, slid out the tablet it contained, and turned it on. It obediently lit up, and a video started. It took a while to comprehend what we were seeing, although it was simple enough really. It was a small subset of the auction attendees, including David, Max, and me, entering a suite adjacent to the ballroom where the main event was held. I recognized some faces I had chatted to earlier in the evening. Two judges, some bankers, senior police officials, including the chief, the owner of the city's paper, and a member of the local TV station. There were a couple of security folks, and at least two other camera operators, plus the one whose camera captured this scene.

THE NUDEST DETECTIVE

We watched ourselves on this small screen, totally mesmerized and in disbelief at what we witnessed ourselves doing over the next moments: The video showed us falling into each other's arms, right there in public. And it wasn't just us. We were joined by all of the guests, who lost all inhibitions, pawing at each other, removing each other's clothing, and initiating...an instant orgy?

Max and I swapped horrified glances. Nobody seemed to have any doubts or reservations. Everyone just dove in. Max and I stayed as partners throughout, intent on each other, but certainly didn't seem to object when others joined us. Several did, including poor David. All of us were willing – enthusiastic, even somewhat rabid – participants. Part of my mind was trying to see how this video was faked, but my stomach churned as I sensed this was all too real. No wonder David seemed terrified of Max. He is one scary dude to look at, and there David was, on screen beside us.

I wretched, gagging vomit back, and shrank into myself, transported back to earlier days. I looked at Max and he was white as a sheet, too. I could see he was filled with a jealous rage but stymied because his onscreen self had David's cock in his hand, helping him mount a woman I think might have arrived with the Governor.

The screen switched to another, broader camera view of the room, away from our little part of the sick orgy. In the back of the room, we could see the only three people who remained dressed: two security guards and a woman, whom I recognized as Talan, from the pictures Courtney gave us. She was using her powers to drive the room crazy. Why?

The orgy scene faded out. We had apparently seen enough. I checked the movie's time counter in the corner. It was just 55 seconds of footage, but it felt like my whole life had ended. I burned with shame at myself, and rage at Max, David, and everyone in the room. Fuck it – even at Ethan and Marcy, though they would have been thousands of miles away. Rape is rape, even if I appeared to be an active participant and even though in the short segment, only Max had his hands on me. I felt deep shame, as my hands had been reaching out to others. Tears welled up.

As we watched with mounting horror, a slim, plain-looking man, lounging comfortably behind a desk in an office, appeared on the screen. He could have been a friendly teacher or doctor. Early sixties perhaps, with fair skin and white hair with a slight grey patch on the short side of his part. Small mouth, bulbous nose, and chunky black spectacles. Bushy eyebrows. When he realized the camera had started, his innocent expression changed into a slightly judgemental and disapproving look, tinged with a sly knowing. Underneath this apparently normal, casual, old guy was a predator. I had dealt with so many, it was easy for me to tell.

"Mr Stone. Ms Braekhus. My name is Jakub. I should tell you the little show you just saw was just warming up. Experience has taught me that if I show people much more of themselves, shall we say, misbehaving," he smiled at his own rehearsed wit, "that they don't pay attention to what I tell them next. In fact, one poor Senator was so upset, she smashed the tablet and I had to send her another.

"About now, it dawns on people that this is probably about blackmail. And let me reassure you, it is. Plain and simple. You haven't gone mad, which might be worse. We chose you both because you, like the other stars in the montage, have wives, husbands, bosses, voters, or others you can't let us show this stuff to, and you have something we want. In your case, two things: Money from your well-funded charity; and your contacts – those whores and twinks you are trying to save, along with the pigs...the police you work with to save them."

As these last words filtered through the red haze that my mind had become, everything changed. The haze dissipated sharply and my pulse settled, the killer in me taking over from the shocked, frightened victim. He would never get that list. I felt Max beside me become aware of my changed state. I sensed him swallow back the bile and rage. I felt him mentally join me;

our kinder selves put aside for now, and our inner killers unleashed. We could be patient, but we would find a target. Jakub and his cronies were top of that list.

The man on the screen continued, unaware that his death had just been moved up. "I represent a syndicate of organized crime that operates across the north of the continent, on both the US and Canadian sides of the border. We have recently acquired so much leverage, over so many people, there is nowhere for you to turn. We have police, judges, government officials at all levels, the FBI – even three Generals – all in our pockets. We will know if you try to act against us. Mild infractions will just cause us to share your portion of the movies with people you care about. Anything more significant will cause your death, and that of those you love."

He paused for effect, then signed off with, "I'll be in touch."

10: CODE RED

39,000ft over Omaha, Nebraska, May 2020

[Ethan] – I was glad our link to Gia and Max was audio only, so that they couldn't see our expressions of disgust and revulsion. They hadn't given us the graphic details, but their overview was horrifying enough.

Disgust is an ugly and powerfully mobilizing emotion, and I saw it on Marcy's face, which I'm sure mirrored mine. Disgust is one of the brain's methods for invoking instant and profound separation. It is one of the hardest emotions to conceal. Its social purpose is to loudly broadcast the message to "get away from me" or, better yet, "get away from my group or clan."

It is so strong an emotion that it can often misfire terribly. I might feel disgust at an individual act, and it might show on my face, despite my trying to conceal it. The person committing the disgusting act often will assume – consciously or subconsciously – that my disgust is with much more than the act; that it's with their character and identity, too. A third party witnessing my expression of disgust will also have a strong negative reaction about the transgressor, and their act, but also to me, to the same degree, whatever the merits of the event. The alarm bell of disgust rings so strongly that nobody wants to be near it, and everybody withdraws and distances from it.

I deliberately spoke my mind in an attempt to counter this effect, and although Gia and Max were victims, I didn't want them to feel we saw them as weak or victimized, or conversely, in any way being willing participants.

"We love you guys. Let us know if you need anything. This was already personal, but doubly so now. What do you want to do next?"

"We've parked David with Roxy in the adjacent suite for now, but we should expect to hear from Jakub soon, so we need a plan," said Max, signalling their intent to move forward rather than wallow in self-pity, however understandable that would be.

Max had signalled 'code red' from his phone, which is our prearranged signal to bring teams up to full readiness and lock down our buildings and assets. As soon as practical, we all connect to a pre-set conference bridge and start dealing with the emergency at hand. Max's briefing showed his military training: Concise and unemotional, keeping facts and speculation clearly separate and objective. He had fallen back to his soldier-self to mask his feelings. My heart went out to my best friend.

"I know this feels like a continuation of Talan's attack on Ethan," speculated Marcy, "but could her attack on the event, and the fact we are linked to it, be a bizarre coincidence?"

"I don't believe in coincidences," said Max.

"I don't typically, either," replied Marcy, "but hear me out. This seems too organized to be an opportunistic attack. We didn't know you were going until that morning, and you didn't let David know until a few hours ahead. He added you to the event only about an hour beforehand. If Talan wanted to attack you, why not do so alone in your suite? Why obtain a side room, involve strangers, print stationery, and send messages on tablets, all in record time? Why not just kill you, or worse in some ways, secretly turn you against Ethan and send you back to stab him in the back?"

"The woman makes a good point," said Gia. She hadn't said much so far. "Marcy is seeing this more objectively than I can. It just feels so... so... personal." Contrary to Max's overly professional tone, Gia's voice was uncharacteristically emotional; some bizarre cocktail of bitterness, grief, and shame. "It would make more sense that Talan was targeting the event, and we just walked in and she saw us as opportune targets for her blackmail scheme."

"Perhaps we can use that," offered Kelsie.

"Another point," interjected Courtney, whom we had added to our code red call, "I'm sure David is sincere, and may be exactly what he appears to be, but if I wanted to infiltrate your event, I would have suborned him a week ago. He may not be aware that he has been controlled for some time – and maybe he hasn't been – but we should assume the worst."

"On the assumption Talan still hasn't linked Gia and Max to me," I said, "and we assume she can track my whereabouts, then I shouldn't land in Chicago. Marcy and I should stay apart from you two and not tip her off. I don't want her walking into your suite and using her powers to get that list, either."

"But if we're not here when Jakub comes looking for us, he could release the videos. We would allow that to protect the list, of course, but it would be a last resort," said Max.

"Look guys," cut in Kelsie, "if we assume that Talan has teamed up with gangsters with the objective of blackmailing a network of people in positions of power, there are some avenues we can clandestinely explore that are not directly tied to David, Max, or Gia. I want to kick off the following lines of investigation, immediately. I think they could generate good information, but you need to buy us some time."

"What are you thinking, Kelsie?"

"One, quietly reach out to our FBI and RCMP contacts to see which criminal gangs appear to have ascended rapidly in the areas where Talan's mental energy was detected. Don't mention sex or blackmail, as that might sound alarm bells. Perhaps they could be Polish mafia if the name Jakub is a clue.

"Two, research what charity events or similar gatherings of influential people were in progress in each of those cities when Courtney detected the mental energy bursts. Track down guest lists and cross reference them with what attendees do for a living, to make an inventory of Talan's potential network. I can ask SkyLoX if she could do some background checking of the people on that list, looking for unusual activity such as charity funds getting drained."

"Great ideas, Kelsie. What else?" I encouraged.

"Three, prepare to use Jakub's next communication as a way to hack back into their network. Analyse the tablets, tap phones of the attendees who have also been – er...um – involved in the video."

"Don't worry, Kelsie. It's awkward, but just keep going, please. This is brilliant," reassured Gia. Kelsie was moving us forward and Gia appreciated that greatly. The sense of momentum helped, it seemed.

"I'll have Roxy set up covert internal and external surveillance and think about ways to follow anyone who approaches us in person. As well, to set up scenarios to plant trackers and bugs on people."

"Yes, and how about we send Team Alpha to support them? Even if we are guessing that Indianapolis might be Talan's next target, let's fully focus on the chance we have in Chicago," added Kelsie. "Oh, and I should research events in major cities west of Chicago. Perhaps we can identify Talan's next target. Should we ask Courtney to fly to Chicago?"

"For what purpose?" This from Gia. Both Marcy and her brother – both tactically trained and motivated – started to answer together, until Marcy deferred to Max to answer.

"It's natural to think Courtney would have sensed the activity and come to investigate. There is a good chance this would motivate Talan to leave town, if she hasn't already done so. Jakub might come and try to take the list of names from us and we can stop him. We can't stop Talan, at least with the set-up in the hotel. So, separating Talan from us is tactically smart."

"I think that's a great idea. I will make my way there promptly," offered Courtney.

"Thanks, Courtney," I said. "OK, while we were talking, I checked with our pilot, and we can extend our range and just about reach Detroit. Marcy and I heading to Denver and then Detroit actually makes some sense, based on our interview with the Denver PD officer, Detective Coop."

"Yes, what did she have to say?" asked Max.

"The story was much as you'd expect. She felt certain about the reasons for filing drug and fraud charges, but when her sense of it was challenged, she found there were massive holes in her own story. We showed her Talan's picture, and were surprised that Coop recognized her. She thinks Talen is a friend named Debbie that she does yoga with on Sunday mornings. But we got her to go through her phone and email records, and at about the time I was getting arrested, there were several calls from the Detroit number to Coop's cell, and she doesn't recognize the number. We think Talan has Coop so under her spell by this point that she was able to direct her action via phone instructions. Kelsie has already confirmed the phone was a burner, which has since been deactivated."

"Then your going to Detroit makes perfect sense," agreed Max.

"OK, well done Kelsie. Awesome situational evaluation and action plan. Anything else, anyone?" I asked.

"Just one thing," Naomi chimed in. "Darcy and I have been working on our project to create an Adept blocking device. When we last talked, we had it working, but it required a suitcase-sized cabinet of electronics to operate it. Darcy hasn't slept in 48 hours, but we now have a design that is more of a lunchbox size and fits into a backpack. I want to test it out, but our lab-rats – I mean Moy Lei and Jim – are off chasing bad guys. If you are not using them, could I get one or both back here? This device might come in handy, given the circumstances."

"Jim, how would you feel about staying in Indianapolis, in case Talan shows up there, while Moy Lei heads back to help Naomi?"

"I was about to suggest it, Ethan," replied Jim.

11: DETROIT

We had already started our descent into the Chicago area when we decided to reroute to Detroit. We descended from our 37,000-foot cruise altitude to 24,000 feet and changed course well to the north of the city, where we believed Talan to be. We had to assume she could sense me approaching and was perhaps even preparing an unfriendly reception. Jim and Courtney felt confident Talan would know by the speed of approach towards her that I was airborne, and as we landed in Detroit that the sudden slow down would suggest we had landed.

There were several airports where our Challenger jet could land in Detroit and we picked Willow Run. It had two 7,000-foot runways and an active helicopter rental operation. It was also close to Oakland, Wayne County, and Windsor airports, which we hoped Talan would assume we might use – should she even be tracking me. This would reduce her chances of preparing a nasty surprise when we landed. It seemed a little paranoid, but if she were linked to the mob, and perhaps blackmailing people in Detroit, our arrival would be a natural opportunity to attack, should she so desire. She had very little warning to set anything up, but she'd know we would have to land at one of the city's eight airports.

Kelsie had used one of our shell companies to arrange an Airbus EC135 helicopter rental, fully fuelled and ready on our arrival. This variant could hold seven passengers and a pilot. We decided we could be tracked too easily on the ground, so this way we could land and immediately fly out again with the complete protection team plus cargo, and soon disappear into the countryside. I would pilot us, so that a third-party pilot would not be drawn into our mess. I would also be willing to fly lower than the rules would allow to keep us – literally – off the radar.

As the Challenger pulled off the runway and rolled towards the prearranged hangar, Jeff, our captain, called me up to the flight deck.

"There are three police cruisers at the FBO. We thought that as you fly with bodyguards, you might want to avoid whatever trouble they are tackling."

"Actually, Jeff, I hate to say it, but they might even be here for us. It's a long story, but can you taxi right past that ramp and drop us past the hangars farther down the field? Just tell them your eccentric passenger requested it if they come knocking."

Jeff did even better. As we neared the hangars, one was open, and he rolled right inside, obscuring our plane from the police, who we could see running down the flight line towards us. Leaving everything behind except our handguns, we ran out through the hangar's rear exit. Jeff pulled the cabin door closed behind us and said he would delay opening it as long as he could without getting arrested.

On the far side of the hangars, opposite the police, we doubled back past where we were supposed to have stopped and kept going until we came to the helicopter rental company. True to their word, our EC135 was on the pad and with a quick photocopy of my licence, they handed the keys over.

A typical EC135 start-up would take nearly ten minutes, but by cutting quite a few corners we were ready to lift in two. Marcy was in the co-pilot seat, and the team was strapped into the passenger seats behind us.

While I got the engine fired up and the basic navigation online, Marcy updated Kelsie on our welcoming committee. Kelsie pointed out that the police could gain cell-tracking capability with a warrant – even perhaps without – and asked if we had thought to grab our emergency burner phones from our 'to go' kits: We had not. Kelsie advised there was a Walmart Supercentre 16 miles west of Willow Run and gave us the coordinates; then we shut off our cell phones and removed the SIMs from them. For good measure, Marcy raided the helicopter's emergency kit for a metallic survival blanket and wrapped the phones within it to block any passive signals. Of course, the helicopter might have a GPS tracker, but we would deal with that once away from the immediate threat.

I keyed the mic and sought clearance to take off. "Willow Run Clearance, this is Helicopter EC135 November 120 Delta Sierra on the ramp with Hotel, requesting VFR departure to west, over." Including the word 'Hotel' notified them I had the latest airport information, and VFR told them we did not require the more time-consuming Instrument Flight Rules process, which would have required a flight plan and other things we didn't have time to complete.

"November 120 Delta Sierra hold position. We've just been advised the airport is locked down and no departures are permitted. We will advise when we have additional information."

I acknowledged their instructions via the radio, but to those in the cabin I said, "screw that." I raised the collective control and added power, lifting us off the pad, spun us right towards the fence line, and departed as low to the ground as the terrain would allow. The control tower evidently hadn't been told to watch for us specifically and didn't notice our stealthy departure, or at least, they didn't call us on the radio again if they had.

We swung south across some fields and crossed highway 94 low enough that had a semi-trailer been coming, we could have hit it. We then turned a sharp right to follow a narrow body of water, which the GPS identified as Ford Lake. Within forty seconds from liftoff, we were over a golf course and skimming across rural farmland, heading southwest.

"How did the police know we would be there?" asked Marcy now that we could catch our breath.

"I don't think Talan's radar could have pinpointed us," I replied. "I have to assume she had someone working with air traffic control who was monitoring flight plans. It wouldn't be too hard to work out which planes departing from Denver were inbound to the Detroit airspace. Our updated plan would have listed the airport and the company we would use to refuel and service the jet. I should have anticipated that. We just learned something about the level of operational capability we are facing."

"I'm pretty sure ignoring the tower's instructions would be a federal offence. I'll text Aiden so he can start planning your defence once we get comms back," Marcy laughed. "Twice in 24 hours. He is earning his keep this week."

We wove our way at treetop level or lower through the rural countryside to the Walmart location where, after circling a couple of times, I put us down in a field roughly three hundred yards east of the megastore. Two of the protection team jogged off with a hurriedly prepared shopping list while I kept the engines spinning. Within ten minutes, we were airborne again with communications equipment and sandwiches, among other items.

We didn't have a final destination in mind. The land was very flat, so I kept us well away from roads and down on the deck as much as possible, lifting higher than 30 feet or so only to clear powerlines and the occasional tree line. After about 25 miles, we spotted a narrow and heavily treed ravine with a river winding through it. The nearest road was half a mile away and there were no houses or signs of people moving around. I dropped low between the trees and set us down on the gravelly bank of the lazily meandering river. After confirming we had cell service so we could talk to Kelsie and the team, I shut down the engines.

The protection team fanned out in different directions, each climbing up through the ravine to the far side of the trees to keep watch for anyone following. Even with Talan's radar, we felt fairly safe from pursuit, but didn't want to take any chances. Marcy had the burner phones unpacked and had loaded in a few useful numbers. We called Kelsie to let her know our situation, which she would relay to the team. There were no other updates of note from anyone, so scheduled a conference call for that evening.

It was a good time to catch our breath and discuss something that had been on my mind for the last couple of hours, something I expected was bothering Marcy, too.

"What we didn't talk about on the code red call was what we do with Talan if and when we find her," I began. "I know Courtney wanted us to bring Talan back to her clan, but I think Max and Gia might be looking for a more... permanent solution. I'm not sure I disagree with them. What do you think, Marcy?"

"We are not killers, Ethan," she said, quietly, although even she didn't sound wholly convinced. "None of us would hesitate to do whatever it takes to protect our own, but if we have her contained, killing her in cold blood is a line we mustn't cross." She thought for a moment, and I let the silence settle.

"But it may be a moot point," she continued once she had her thoughts together. "Our contingency planning against Adepts has options like a long rifle shot, which is obviously deadly, or knocking them out in some way. This will be really hard to do with their internal radar picking up on anyone with such specific intent to do them harm."

"If we can track and contain her long enough for Le Perjure to get close, Courtney hopes they can subdue her mentally, but it would appear Talan has acquired some new tricks, so Courtney isn't even certain that approach would still work," I chimed in.

"I think I worry about Gia and Max most," Marcy said, giving me a meaningful look. "Max and I have both fought crime as a profession and we've witnessed abuse, murder, and a string of horrific acts, and neither of us felt compelled to take a life unless deadly force was necessary to save others. But forcing them into an orgy is incredibly personal. Max will see it as someone raping Gia, and vice versa. Neither would kill for themselves, but I bet both are close to wanting to after seeing the orgy video. What would you do if someone raped me?"

Good point.

"I'd want to kill them, of course. And I don't think any of us really know if we would follow through until we are put in that position. Hell, I want to kill Talan for what she and her group did to our friends and family as it is. Shit, we all need time to process this."

"Are you going to talk to Max and Gia about it?" asked Marcy.

"Not yet. They know the score, and I think Max will let us know his intentions ahead of taking any unilateral action," I replied.

"And Gia?" We both just looked at each other. Gia is much more independent and unpredictable.

My burner phone chirped, and I answered. One of the protection team could see a military chopper, low-level and way off to the south in what looked like a search pattern. He estimated the chopper would be near us in about ten minutes; I told him to call back with updates every two minutes. I called the others back to the helicopter. It seemed a stretch to think Team Talan were searching for us this quickly, but I didn't want to take the chance. We would be spotted immediately if we tried to take off and make a run for it.

I raided the emergency kit Marcy had located and found an additional five metallic, weatherproof blankets – the insulated kind that are designed to keep your body heat from escaping when you are cold.

"I doubt the searchers will spot us through the trees with their naked eyes, but on an infrared our helicopter's engine will be a beacon. We need to cool it and mask it, quickly," I said, handing out the blankets. We made several quick runs to the stream and back, using the waterproof blankets to ferry water we then poured over the engine's exhaust, which was still hot enough for steam to billow off with an angry hiss. The steam quickly dissipated and wouldn't add to our problems

Our lookout reported a second chopper – an AH-64 Apache, he thought. It was off in the distance and appeared to parallel the first helicopter, which was slowly and diligently moving our way.

When we estimated the choppers were a few minutes out, we gave up trying to cool the engine and used the blankets to cover the exhaust and engine's cowling. I called the lookout back to join us, and we all stripped to our underwear and slipped into the water. It was damn cold. We submerged ourselves as much as possible. We had minimized our heat signature as well as we could and held our breath, figuratively and literally.

We gave it fifteen minutes, according to the CX Swiss Military watch I had selected for this trip. Then, shivering mightily, I slipped out of the water and could hear the choppers way off to the north, having moved past our position. I waved the others out, and while they trembled from the cold and dried off, I threaded my way through the trees to check the choppers were moving away. They were, in fact, AH-64s.

Talan certainly had some resources at her disposal.

12: FOLLOW THE PHONE

[Max] – After the code red call, we got busy. Roxy called her team members back to The Folly Hotel and using expertise Kelsie and Darcy fed us via phone, we accomplished a lot quickly. From our 'go bag,' we set up two drones: a small spying unit, and a larger communications platform drone. The latter we typically used as a hub to allow the team in Vancouver to remotely control whatever drones we deployed in situ, but it also had additional capabilities, one being able to pose as a cellphone tower. It intercepted the signals between cell phones and the official cell towers, then relayed the traffic seamlessly and we could hack the voice and text traffic easily if it not heavily encrypted.

We also visited the hotel's telecommunication room in the basement. When cell signals don't penetrate deep into a building, the providers put repeaters and relays in corridors and basements to improve coverage. These signals route out via a landline, which we also intercepted, federal laws be damned!

Back in our room, we hacked into the tablet computers the blackmail video messages came on, but we found nothing that allowed us to trace back into the mafia's network. We were, however, able to load our own secret applications in the background so that if they were taken back from us later, we could track them if they were online, as well as clandestinely snoop any audio and video within range of each device.

Lastly, we set up several cameras and listening devices around the interior and exterior of the hotel. Then Roxy's team split up, with two in separate cars that could follow any targets of interest, and the others on foot with the same role.

It was still a couple of hours until our next conference call, so we grabbed some food and settled back to wait.

"Gia," I started, somewhat tentatively. "How would you feel about getting out of Dodge and leaving this with me?" She started to bristle, thinking I was worried about her safety – the very cheek – so I rushed on. "Of course, you are tougher than me, babe. That's not my worry. I worked undercover in Europe for two years, so I have some experience in these situations. And to be honest, I don't think I will react very constructively if one of them tries to do anything to you. If these thugs think they own us and do something like trying to cop a feel – or worse – the smart thing would be to let them, until we reel them in and can take down their network. But if they do it with you? I don't think I have the control not to rip them a new asshole."

"You can. You will. I appreciate the thought, but deal with it, cowboy," Gia said, with mixed emotions rippling over her face. "Remember, I used to do a lot worse for money, right?"

"Different lifetime, different woman, Gia. You know that." I put my hand on her shoulder, and she let me gather her into a hug. She was OK with such displays of affection, as long as no one was looking and might think she was too soft.

"Besides," she grinned, "what makes you think they won't make a play for you? You are so last century. They have gay mafia now."

"Too soon! Last night was enough to be sure that stuff's not for me."

"You won't entertain my threesome fantasy, then? Two hunky men at the same time?" She was smiling and making light of things, but I could feel waves of distress under the surface. They resonated with me, as I felt the same.

We were interrupted by Roxy, signalling a likely looking target had exited the elevator and was approaching the suite. Game time!

We waited for the knock on the door, but it didn't come. Instead the lock clicked, the door opened, and a huge man entered, pocketing his skeleton-key card in the jacket of his expensive, tailored suit. He closed the door behind him, turned, looming expectantly, as if he had been invited to tea and was waiting to be offered a seat.

He was several inches taller than me, perhaps six-eight. No fat in sight, but he was very wide. Not just his body, but his head was blocky and wide, too. If he was a little more handsome, he might have doubled for an oversized Ron Perlman. He was overly large, but he wasn't ugly. Not like the *Hell Boy* Perlman, or *Name of the Rose* Perlman. More like the paradoxically classy Perlman leading *SAM CROW* in *Sons of Anarchy*. A little rough yet polished, too.

He finished his assessment of us with a long, slow sigh, and said, "I suggest we sit, and get this over with." He seemed bored. This invasion of our privacy and blackmail just an everyday a chore to him. He took the couch, and filled most of it, while we each took a on either side of him. We said nothing, determined to wait him out.

"You watched the video. You know what you did, and what we want. So, any questions?"

"How did you make us do that?" asked Gia, at the same moment as I asked, "What if we don't care if you release that video?" He turned to Gia first. Old fashioned, perhaps.

"How we got you to do it doesn't matter. You did it. Pick whatever helps you make peace with yourself. Big libido? We drugged your food. Whatever. But it's done, right? And the sooner you get used to it, the easier this goes, trust me. I've done this many times now."

Then he turned to me.

"If you don't comply, then we kill you. And, if we feel like it, your loved ones, too, as we explained on the video. I know it's unpleasant, but it's also simple. We own you, and we get what we need, or you die."

"I don't get it though," said Gia. "If you really can just have us killed, why bother with the sex thing? Why not just threaten us?"

"Well, it's a curious thing. If we threaten to kill you, and you balk, then we have to... well, kill you. Not great business. It seems people are more compliant when they have things to lose in stages. They understand how serious we are when we release a few seconds of footage and they realise the death threats are real. Psychology I guess, but that's above my pay grade."

"So, what happens next?" I asked.

"My role is to give you someone to shout and complain at. Some folks like to get that out of their system. Once that's done, I tell you to take a few days to process how fucked you truly are, and that to help you along we will provide a demo in a day or two. Something that shows just how many other people in power we are blackmailing, who can reach out and do our dirty work for us. Then I come back in a few days, once it's all sunk in, and tell you how to transfer the money to us, at which time you also give us the details of all of the sex workers you are trying to help. We will want that on a thumb drive, by the way." He pulled one out of his pocket and set it on the table between us. Mr Organised.

"You have a name?" I asked.

"Clay," he said. "I've been told I look like that Perlman guy in *Sons of Anarchy*, so I go by the lead character's name for these nefarious purposes. Do you have any other questions?"

We just stared at him, boring a hole through him with angry eyes, not really trusting ourselves to fully engage.

"I need the tablets," he said.

Gia stepped into the bedroom and returned with them, putting them on the hallstand before walking back into the bedroom and slamming the door. I sensed she was close to letting her feelings and fists fly, but that wasn't why she left. She went to check her texts from Roxy to see if they had hijacked Clay's phone. She would come right back out if not, and I was pleased to see the door stayed closed.

Clay stood and straightened his jacket, then nodded affably before turning and letting himself out.

*

We watched Clay enter one more suite on our floor via the cameras Roxy had put up earlier. Another victim, we deduced. When he left and entered the elevator, it went down two floors and stopped. Thirty minutes later we tracked Clay to another floor, and then another. It took him three and half hours to visit his victims before leaving the hotel.

We had managed to hijack the signal to his phone, but not crack into it and take it over. If security were lax, it would have been possible, but his cell was better protected.

The next trick was to get him to download some malware. Using the hijacked link, we watched him send a few texts in what appeared to be code written in Eastern European phrases. We sent him a phishing message, posing as one of the addresses he had just messaged with. We didn't understand their code, so we made the message appear like it was corrupted. Bingo! He clicked on it, and our malware downloaded and infected his phone. We could not do much more than download additional viruses, but it was a start. Over the next few hours, we would increase our grip and soon would be able to track his phone, listen through his mic, look through his camera, and steal data and contact information.

When he stepped onto the street, a Town Car pulled up and whisked him away. The protection team set up a two-car tail, keeping way back, out of sight. Our two drones were following him, watching from 400 feet above as he moved slowly through the traffic. We viewed the feed from one drone, while the second tagged along, maintaining our hold on his phone, still posing as his nearest cell tower.

Twenty-five minutes later, we started to bring the tailing cars in closer; the batteries on the drones were nearing critically low levels and would have to pull off and land soon. Just then, the Town Car pulled into a warehouse. The drones drifted down to a ledge halfway up the opposite building and, using solar cells that covered their upper surfaces, began to recharge.

Over the following two hours, our team set up various remote cameras and replaced the batteries in the drones. Based on the constant stream of messages from 18 different phones emitting from warehouse so far, we figured we had found a major operations centre.

*

Two hours later, we retreated to our rooms at The Folly and dialed into the scheduled code red follow-up call. We would have such a call every three hours – or as made sense – until the crisis concluded. Ethan and Marcy were still on the ground in rural Detroit and a little hard to hear due to the burner phone and their location, so they let Kelsie direct the update and she asked for our report first. We gave the group a summary of Clay's visit and the discovery of the suspected operations centre, and uploaded photos and other intelligence captured so far.

"We own Clay's phone now and have some SkyLoXS provided tools installed," chipped in Darcy, who had taken on this element from Kelsie. "We're sending malware messages from Clay's phone to his contacts that appear of interest. We have been successful in seven cases, and we are slowly deepening our penetration of their network. What we really need is to jump from a phone onto their computer network and get into their cloud or other systems where they keep their blackmail content."

"The tablets they sent to David and us were identical, except for our specific footage, and were presumably set up quite quickly. It would follow they have a repeatable template set up that processes the video and distributes it onto the tablets. The location we are monitoring would be an obvious place to start. Should we go inside?" asked Gia.

"We hacked those tablets to contact us if they were ever reconnected to the internet, but nothing has surfaced yet. They might use a VPN, or perhaps they are just thrown on a shelf until needed for their next victim. Is there any sign that this location is just for this operation or is it a more permanent facility?" asked Marcy. We had not been able to determine that information and said as much.

"Let's hear what else we have, before making a decision on going in," cut in Ethan.

"We are currently tracking the military helicopters that are up looking for you, Ethan."

"Amazing. How can you track the military, Darcy?" asked Gwen.

"Easier than you would expect," Darcy chuckled. "When involved in legitimate military actions, military aircraft don't participate in the commercial and general aviation air traffic monitoring system. But the rest of the time, such as transiting between bases and on training exercises, they use ADSB like everyone else, which is the mandatory radar transponder system, for safety reasons. I guess whoever dispatched these aircraft wanted it to look like a routine training mission. There are several ways we can capture their ADSB data and follow their movements."

"Where are they now?" asked Ethan.

"The two you saw are roughly 40 miles north of your position, Ethan, but that is not the interesting part. We expanded our view and discerned there are actually eight AH-64s in the air at various locations surrounding you. The closest is 15 miles and the farthest, 85 miles. We think we can tell something interesting from their search pattern."

I've known Darcy for long enough to know when she's feeling pleased with herself.

"The search aircraft's pattern is in an oblong box," she said, with a dramatic pause. I twigged immediately to her point, but not everyone has our military training.

"Why is that significant?" asked Jim.

"If you needed to search for someone, and had no idea which way they are heading, the protocol would be to search a circle, which expanded at the maximum speed you thought they would travel. You might alter the circular shape with some guesses. Perhaps the target is unlikely to fly over built-up areas for instance, but it would basically still be a circle.

"A box-search is used when you know the track or direction a target was to follow. In this case, we can tell that two groups of four aircraft were dispatched within 15 minutes of your taking off from Willow Run. One group to your north, the other to the south. They went to the opposite ends of the box, spread out, and started working their way towards the centre." She paused to let us picture what she was saying.

"Can one assume the orientation of the box had one end pointing to the Chicago area?" asked Courtney. I saw where she was going. Being an Adept herself, she would assume Talan, with her radar, would sense the direction Ethan would be in, but not the distance. She would have the search conducted along the track she could sense him on but be guessing at the distance.

"That's exactly what we expected, Courtney, but surprisingly no. If the search was divined from Talan's radar sense of Ethan, and she was in Chicago, the box would lie roughly west to east. But in this case, the box lies roughly 70 degrees off that line, more southeast to northwest. It's just a theory, of course, but extending the centreline of the box northwest, the only major centre would be Winnipeg in Canada."

"What about the other direction?" asked Ethan.

"Pittsburgh, or if you go farther, then Washington, DC."

"Where are you, Courtney?" I asked.

"Just landed in Chicago. If she is in DC or Pittsburgh, it's not like she fled because she sensed my approach. She likely left right after the reception last evening."

"She used her power, then left her minions to pursue the blackmail," said Gia. I saw disappointment on her face and squeezed her hand.

"If only we could get another directional line on her location, perhaps we could triangulate. What else do we have?" prompted Ethan.

"We are starting to form a better picture of what's transpired," put in Kelsie. "We've identified between eight and ten events that we suspect were compromised. We based this on the cities and the profiles of the attendees and cross-referenced against what the attendees have done since. We are a long way from checking everyone, but spot checking a few attendees at each event, we see some business and banking anomalies and, sadly, some mysterious deaths." She paused, as we digested the likely meaning of the deaths: Non-compliance of the blackmail demands. "In two cases the deaths were linked to some apparent sex scandal. But it is not all bad news. Some of the attendees – a mayor and two police chiefs – have had sudden and unexpected successes taking down criminal organizations in various cities."

"That's interesting," said Marcy.

"Indeed, and it aligns with other news from our delicate inquiries into the police intelligence community. In the locations we are interested in, there has been a surge of Polish Crime syndicates moving into the territories of competing organized crime factions. There are inter-gang wars in progress, but the balance has more than tipped; it's a complete landslide apparently. No one can explain it, but given what we know, I suspect Talan's using her victims in influential positions to get behind the Polish mafia, and setting other gangs at each other's throats so that the Poles can mop up. All conjecture at this point, but it fits nicely."

"If this is true," put in Marcy, "then we are up against an organized crime group that owns most of the eastern part of North America, coupled with...how many?... a few dozen powerful leaders in positions to direct law enforcement, to their own ends. We are in deep shit."

At that moment, Courtney screamed through the phone line. I thought someone at O'Hare had attacked her at first, but then Moy Lei exclaimed, "I felt that, too. What happened?"

"Courtney has dropped off the conference bridge," reported Kelsie.

"Moy Lei," said Jim, his voice shaky. "You know what it feels like when a Nimbus dies? Well, what we felt was the passing of many Nimbus simultaneously. Something tragic has happened."

13: THE CULLING

Just under 50 miles northeast of Las Vegas, the sun beat down relentlessly on the ever-expanding row of trailers that control the US Airforce's MQ-1 Predator drones in the Middle East and elsewhere. The drones are launched and recovered under local control in theatre, but once airborne, 'pilots' at Creech Airforce Base, Nevada, take control for the duration of the mission.

Predators based at the US base in Incirlik, Turkey, have been launching missions to the south and east for over two decades, observing and attacking targets in Syria, Iraq, and Northern Iran. But the drone currently being remotely controlled by Captain Ed Bains hummed over quite a different target, in the opposite direction. Like the USAF, Turkey's government operates MQ-1s, and even a sharp-eyed observer, who somehow managed to spot the drone above Istanbul, could be forgiven for believing it was one of theirs; but it wasn't.

Bains was often called upon to work these more secretive 'off- book' missions and had clearances most of the other pilots did not. He had worked with most of the CIA and military intelligence folks who came to Creech to direct missions, but the anonymous man at his shoulder was a new face, whose credentials and orders had been validated through encrypted keys. He knew how to direct a drone attack and its capabilities.

A Predator drone can stay aloft for nearly 24 hours, eight of which were used on this mission to launch towards Iraq, then circle slowly back to the current location. Another five hours were consumed circling over a lone building at the drone's maximum height of 25,000 feet. Bains and another pilot had worked three hours on, three off, mostly monitoring the that the autopilot of the drone was correctly executing the program given to Bains by the mysterious spy.

In the last hour, five cars had arrived bringing 12 women to the target location just outside Istanbul's suburbs on the European side of the Bosphorus. It was already the early hours in the morning on the other side of the world, and as each had a small overnight case, Bains speculated that the women would be on site for at least 36 hours. The mystery intelligence man had Bains zoom in closely to each face on arrival and, referring to an iPad, seemed to match each face to an entry on a list. Most of the targets were Caucasian, and a few appeared to be mixed race. But there was a similarity to them all, as if this were a family gathering.

Another car led its dust trail, visible on the vision-enhancing, infrared camera, down the nearby hillside, where it pulled up in front of a house. Bains dutifully zoomed in on the car's lone occupant as the car door opened. The spy pulled out a phone and dialled a number.

"All targets on site. Request confirmation Gamma 3. OK. Yes. OK." He hung up and waited a beat, then his phone chimed and he looked at the incoming message.

"Captain Bains, authenticate Bravo, Bravo, Delta, Foxtrot!"

Bains typed BBDF into his computer and waited. The computer accessed a central database once every four hours and downloaded a set of codes, which changed frequently. If the spy's code matched one in the database, and decoded correctly with a locally-held set of unique keys, the computer would advise him how to act with respect to instructions from the holder of the code he had input. If the sequence were invalid, drone control would automatically switch to another trailer, the doors would lock on this trailer, and MPs would take all occupants into custody without questions asked.

The codes matched, and the screen displayed "AAYM: Attack Sequence valid; WEAPONS HOT Approved; DESTROY TARGET as instructed by BBDF; TIME 15 MIC." The latter phrase indicated that Bains was allowed only to follow these instructions for 15 minutes, after which further authenticated codes would be required to continue the attack.

Bains sat back in his chair. He had not expected an attack order. Not on a dozen women in a friendly nation. But there was no doubting the authenticity of the order. He entered the commands to warm up the drone's laser designator, which would ensure the accuracy of any attack and arm two of the six AGM-176 Griffin air-to-surface missiles attached to the drone's hardpoints under its wings.

"All six Griffins, Captain Bains. Three in the initial volley, then following a battle-damage assessment, the remaining three in the most effective follow-up locations. Execute when the weapons are ready and trajectory nominal."

Thirty seconds later, as Bains sent the first weapons release codes to the satellite that would relay them almost instantly to the drone and launch the attack, he wondered if his soul was now forfeited; years of belief he was doing right for his country suddenly in enormous doubt, gone up in smoke with the building exploding on the screen before him.

*

Dave Gibbons sat in his hotel room in London's still-trendy Knightsbridge neighbourhood, watching the local derby match between Arsenal and Chelsea being replayed from the previous day. He was slowly sipping on the second beer of the evening. His CIA handler wouldn't accept any more than that, or any behaviour which would jeopardize a mission.

Dave's instructions had come via the usual dark-web route and were explicit, if unusual. Entering the target's house when a specific text arrived confirming the target was elsewhere, was not unusual; neither was finding a location to plant the remote-controlled explosive, enough C4 to demolish the building and damage those near by; nor was using the prescribed bomb design and components, which would lead investigators to think it had originated from Middle-Eastern sources. The unusual part was the strict instruction to avoid looking at anything that would identify the victim in any way. He should avoid photographs on the mantel and letters on the hallstand. Dave was to leave without a clue of who he was about to murder, and that suited him just fine. He took another hit of his beer.

His phone lit up and buzzed, and the display had but one word: 'NOW.' Using a different phone, obtained just four hours ago from Dixon's, Dave dialled the phone attached to the device in the target's house. As he heard the ringtone jingled in his left ear, the window on his hotel room rattled and he felt a tremor through the floor. He texted back one word. 'COMPLETE.'

*

Tadamasa Jo used his left hand to drink tea from his bowl. On the table in front of him his meal sat untouched. To the right of his plate sat his phone, face up. Under the table, in his right hand, was a silenced Sig Sauer P226 TB with one bullet in the barrel and 15 more in the clip.

Tadamasa's Yakuza boss had been explicit about this strange hit, in two respects. Firstly, Tadamasa would have no knowledge of the target until their picture was sent to his phone. They would be nearby when the picture arrived, it was explained, and he must be ready to act.

Secondly, that target must be dead within three seconds of the picture arriving. He had already memorized every face and knew where they all sat or, in the case it was a server, where they were at each moment. There would be no time to put down his chopsticks and pull out his gun, which is why he hadn't started his meal, despite the odd looks he was beginning to receive. He had been scanning the room and sipping his drink for ten minutes, and barely looked at the server when giving his order and receiving his meal.

A promotion to the gang's inner circle was the reward if he succeeded. He didn't want to consider what awaited if he failed. His boss had made it clear that this hit was a favour for his business partner in Toronto – a local triad leader – and there would be much face lost if things screwed up.

Tadamasa's phone lit up and a picture of a Caucasian woman appeared on the screen. In Tokyo, this close to the Emperor's palace, there were many *gaijin* – foreigners – but this exclusive restaurant was well off the tourist trail and patronized mostly by government officials, so there were only two. His target couldn't have been easier to locate and sat just 15 feet away.

Tadamasa stood, aimed, and fired four times without hesitation. As he did, in his peripheral vision he saw that two other diners did exactly the same thing. As she died, torn apart by at least a dozen bullets where she sat, Tadamasa replayed the two seconds leading up to her death in his mind. She had looked up before he stood and glanced at him and the other two assassins. How strange. It was like she had a premonition.

All three assassins, unknown to each other, walked out through the kitchen, unscrewing and pocketing their silencers and pistols as they went. Nervously glancing at each other as they exited the rear of the restaurant, they went their separate ways.

*

Courtney du Caron listened to the conference call with Ethan's team as she walked out of O'Hare's Terminal 2, cutting towards the Uber pick-up area and speeding up. As she took in Kelsie's information about organized crime, her mind was really on the earlier discussion about Pittsburgh and Washington DC. Pittsburgh was not on the track Talan seemed to be following but would be a natural addition to the empire she seemed intent on building. But it was DC that was more of a concern. Suborning a mayor or police chief was bad enough, but the power mongers in DC were on another level. Courtney spent 60% of her time there influencing the mega-influential.

Courtney stopped dead in her tracks. Partly due to the sudden realization that Talan may have a bigger plan than anyone suspected, but mostly because she became abruptly aware of two minds close by that intended her harm. Whatever the reason, jerking to a halt saved her life. A bus shelter window to her right exploded, and the shoulder of a man to her left jerked, spraying blood over her, as the bullet intended for her clipped him instead. If she had taken another step, both bullets would have hit her head.

Although Le Perjure prefer the subtle use of sex-related emotions to influence others, it didn't mean that Courtney couldn't project fear. Right that second, fear was an emotion she had no need to manufacture. The most powerful Le Perjure mind on the planet pumped all of that fear out as hard as she could on a reflex as she ran, leaving her bags where they fell. People nearest to her just went down, unconscious before they landed. At perhaps 50 yards away, people stopped and swayed in a daze. At 100 yards, people were confused and started running away from the area, even if they hadn't noticed the twin shots that just missed Courtney, or the three shots that followed her as she zigzagged back to the terminal.

As she ran, Courtney extended her senses and felt for the assassins she had become aware of immediately before the shots. One was towards the hotel on the far side of the drop-off zone, and up high. The other was farther out and in the other direction, towards Terminal 3. A perfect crossfire ambush. She narrowed her focus onto those two minds and pushed with everything she had. The distance was too far for control, but it would certainly spoil their aim.

As she barrelled through the terminal door, out of sight of the snipers, she dropped to her knees as a new and terrible sensation hit her: The severing from her mind, and therefore the world, of many members of her clan. Mental linkages she had shared for a lifetime evaporating in a moment. First a large cluster, and over the next few minutes as she stumbled unchallenged back into the customs-controlled area, several others in singles and pairs.

In the space of five minutes, as far as she could sense, Le Perjure had reduced from 32 Nimbus, to perhaps eight or nine;

it was hard to tell. Some of her clan she'd only met in a pseudo-work context, but many were her closest family, and she was beset by strangely personal memories. A favourite cousin who stole her favourite miniskirt in 1966 to date a boy. An aunt who nursed her through the terrifying change as she became a Nimbus, and the comfort food she brought to ease the anxiety of transformation.

Courtney found a janitorial closet, locked herself in, and sat in the dark, tears rolling soundlessly down her cheeks. She yearned for her lost family and became worried sick about the fate of the world without the guidance that had for centuries tempered the destructive nature of humans.

14: NEW BEGINNINGS

[Talan] – For my 57 years of adulthood, the oppressive weight of Le Perjure subjugation had been suffocating. If I'm honest, my dissatisfaction began as teenage rebellion at having my life's purpose preordained, with no hope of parole. The calling of others, who died centuries ago, in service to a lesser species. My feelings hardened with age as I didn't agree with most of the decisions on how to steer humanity, which I found too altruistic, and overly protective of the weak at the expense of the strong. I may have embraced this forced vocation had I been allowed to pursue my own policies and take opportunities to amass some benefits and wealth, as do The Chord. By the age of 28 I had decided that this clan either needed to be repurposed, which meant new leadership, or put out of its misery.

As the reports rolled in from my misappropriated army of Polish mafia and US intelligence assets, that stifling blanket evaporated. I should have felt elated; the dream that had fuelled me through my life was realized after years of careful planning. The centuries-old Le Perjure clan was gone. Culled from the face of the planet. Yet I felt empty and strangely vulnerable.

The 1928 Krug Champagne sat unopened in the ice bucket next to two exquisite crystal coupes, which were my preference to the taller flutes. My plan was to pop the $21,000 cork to celebrate this moment, pouring two glasses. While I savoured this rare liquid treat from one coupe, the other would sit untouched, a tribute to my dead lover, Guance. He had helped me plan for this moment, and before Booker killed him, was my partner in building the Polish mafia into the predominant organized crime syndicate in the north. Now the moment felt empty. The bottle would go back into storage for the day Booker died. That would be better. But there was no rush. I was now effectively queen of the world, so I could take my time with Booker – and his loved ones – savouring his demise as much as I would the Champagne once he was in the ground.

THE NUD*EST* DETECTIVE

We had killed all but nine of Le Perjure but missed the cherry on the top: the head bitch du Caron. She was still my top priority, but it was only a matter of time. My advantage was knowing which of her government puppets she held in her thrall, and I had used my assets to sequester them out of her reach. Without the clan and her network of power mongers, she was done. I would have to tread carefully, given her powerful mind, but she was now isolated and without help, whereas I now have a mighty, albeit unusual, army. And on top of that, I could track her movements, while she could not see me behind my barrier.

Being able to mask myself from the Nimbus had been a gift from Guance, too. He had found Lindi on a mission to Namibia ten years ago. He couldn't control her, but over time, I found a way. Lindi's name was given to her by the shaman of her birth village in the southern African nation. Her name has roots in a number of languages, ranging from Germanic and Neo-Latin to IsiXhosa, with meanings as diverse as serpent and shield of wood from the Linden tree, to beautiful and gentle. From an early age, the shaman discovered that Lindi could hide, like a snake, from the shaman's scrying, as well as shield others' presence, all the while with grace and beauty. The meanings of her name suited Lindi perfectly.

It took me months to insinuate myself into Lindi's mind, but I gradually seduced her and now she accepts me. She is a simple creature of little needs. I've kept her close, within 40 feet, every minute since escaping Le Perjure. She is quiet and sweet, but it will be a relief to not require her. *Should I let her go now? No, when Courtney is gone, I think.*

I looked at the ornate four-post bed, the silk sheets turned back invitingly. Exhaustion was upon me, but before I could rest, I thought it best to check the situation one last time.

I had used this house in Fort Belvoir as my base of operations for four months. The land was purchased by Lord Halifax in 1738 and he moved here eleven years later to establish businesses and plantations, which spring out from the

Potomac inland. His original mansion burned down in 1783 after Fairfax's heir had returned to England, but there were still many colonial- style buildings on the peninsula.

William Cochrane, Deputy Director of the CIA's Directorate of Operations, allocated this beautiful building to me when I bent him to my will last year. Fort Belvoir is home to a number of significant army organizations, and as such has the benefit of not appearing on Street View or any of the public search tools in any detail. If you compare public satellite pictures with reality and there are some similarities, but many differences. Being part of the air traffic control zone for Davison Army Airfield, no casual overflight is permitted. On the ground, only those presenting the correct credentials are allowed into the base. The irony of the military protecting my little hideaway is delicious.

Within the compound are areas of increased sensitivity and security, and my temporary colonial residence enjoys being shielded further by an electrified and guarded fence, tastefully hidden behind the rows of trees. I have a maid and a chef in the residential side of the house but can walk through to a wing that is set up as an operations centre. There I have loyal staff who liaise with those in the military, CIA, and mafia.

I pulled my weary bones from the wingback I was slowly sinking into and trudged through to operations, pausing only to pour a nightcap in the form of a 30-year-old single malt.

Cochrane typically left his underlings to run the facility, but as this night was the final step in my mission, he was here to oversee it personally.

"How do things stand, Cochrane?" I asked, taking a sip of the amber liquid and enjoying the burn as it slipped down.

"I can confirm 23 of the clan are dead, along with many of their staff and retainers. A ground assessment confirms no one escaped the meeting in Istanbul, and most of the separate actions were successful. In addition to du Caron, two others escaped and are being pursued. The remaining six were not in a position for us to attack when you gave the 'go' order, but remain targets of opportunity."

"Any update on Courtney? We must finish her quickly," I pressed. I could sense she hadn't moved far from O'Hare but, at this distance, that meant she could be anywhere within a 40-50 mile radius.

"Our agents are hunting her on the ground, and an APB is out with the police. Her credit cards, known phones, financial assets, passports, and communications channels we are aware of are all shut down as you requested. She is cut off from help and from reaching out to the survivors, so it is just a matter of time. She will be dead within 24 hours."

"Remember, she is to be killed on sight. Don't let anyone engage with her. What about Booker?"

"We haven't launched another salvo on his finances given the hornets nest we stirred up in the first attempt. He is off the grid, but we have set up a tight net." I took another sip and considered matters.

"If you catch him with the assets you have in play already, great. Bring him here. But if he slips past you, let us not be too overt. We have plenty of time to play with Booker now that the main threat of Le Perjure is destroyed. We can play a patient game. We have some bigger priorities, du Caron being the most pressing."

"Yes ma'am. Anything else?" he asked, with a hopeful look. Cochrane is a handsome and fit man, and I had satisfied my urges with him on occasion.

"Nothing for tonight. I think you can leave the mop-up to your staff and head home." His expression dropped, but he said nothing. "I am hoping to sleep for 24 hours, so disturb me only if you kill du Caron or if there is a major development you need my input on."

I took a moment to thank all present, stroking their minds with positive reinforcement, then I swept out of the room and back to the residential part of the house. I opened the door to the small room adjacent to my bedroom and checked in on Lindi. She was dozing fitfully, as she sometimes does if she senses I am agitated. I formed thoughts of reassurance and the need to shield me, then pressed them into her sleeping mind. She sighed and rolled over, settling deeper under the duvet. I walked next door, dropped my clothes in a heap, slid under the covers. I wondered for a moment if my current feelings of anxiety and vulnerability would keep me awake, but as I sank into the mattress, confidence that I now had the winning hand bloomed within me. Sheer exhaustion took over and was asleep within moments.

*

[Cochrane] – Nikki Strauss hummed Bob Marley's "Buffalo Soldier," a song he didn't love but did enjoy using to antagonize Antoni, the man sitting to his right, who was a blatant a racist. This unholy marriage of the CIA, the best foreign intelligence service in the world, with organised crime scum like Antoni was bad enough, but the mafia man was just too much.

Nikki – Nicolas Strauss Jr, Harvard's 2010 valedictorian – had begun their relationship offering polite professionalism, which was crudely rebuffed, due to his African American heritage. Matters deteriorated through several levels until the two were not speaking. Cochrane read Nikki the riot act, which produced minimal and curt cooperation, and things didn't rise to the level of barely tolerable until the mysterious Talan talked to both men. From that point on they hadn't warmed to each other but felt compelled to ensure the team was successful. But if Nikki could needle Antoni, he would.

The two men had shared repeated 12 hours on, 12 hours off shifts together for nearly three months without a break. Both shared only what was required about the activities of their respective organizations but had become an efficient unit, nonetheless. Their shift had started nine hours ago, just as the operation to take down the female-only terrorist group Le Perjure reached its climax. For a two-hour period, both they and their counterpart shift overlapped to ensure maximum effort for the coordinated execution of a plan that required the collaboration with organised crime, reasons for which he was not fully briefed about. He hoped this mission would be over shortly, and he could return to Langley and his career.

The operations room held ten computer stations, six manned by CIA personnel and the remainder by mafia. The analysts – and goons – at each station liaised with their respective intelligence and operational units. In the CIA contingent were representatives of Homeland Security, who could direct both domestic police and military activity, as well as the Canadian Military Forces through a NATO arrangement. Access to Canadian police resources was enabled by the mafia counterparts, who also had leverage on many US and Canadian government functionaries. This arrangement wasn't ethical, to Nikki's way of thinking, but it certainly allowed them to cut through red tape.

"Sir!" barked one of the CIA analysts. "Subject Booker alert. A small company that is part of his business empire just opened a flight plan for four people: Gerald R Ford Airport, Grand Rapids, to Vancouver International, Canada. Grand Rapids is about 80 miles from Booker's last-known location and well within range of his stolen helicopter. They are taking off shortly."

Flight plans must be lodged 30 minutes before departure as the norm, but a pilot in the air can also open a plan on-the-fly, while in the air. Nikki pulled up a map and studied the likely route.

"There is no point in a military intercept at this point. Let's monitor their flight and have a reception ready for them in Vancouver, but also along their planned track. They could alter the route at any point," I instructed. "Antoni, can you handle the Canadian end? We made a mistake at Willow Run, positioning the police so overtly that they were spotted, allowing Booker to evade them. We will feed you updates on their progress, and you arrange for a more discrete – but deadly – reception, yes?"

Within ten minutes, the telemetry and radar images of the flight were being relayed to Nikki's station, and he watched with interest as the plane took off: Instead of heading west over Minneapolis, it turned north and well below its planned altitude. He listened in as successive controllers attempted to contact the wayward flight. Several minutes later, with the Phenom passing through 15,000 feet, its transponder code – a four-digit code assigned to every flight so radar can distinguish it from others – changed from the specified code to 7600, which is the international code for a plane with a communications failure.

The plane crossed into Canada minutes later at 19,000 feet and started a slow turn westward, its course becoming increasingly erratic. As the flight reached 30,000 feet over the most northern point of Lake Superior, the pilot upgraded the transponder code to 7700, signalling to air traffic control that he was declaring an emergency. When the radar system detects these predetermined codes, it raises alarms and ensures attention is brought to the radar image on every controller's screen by highlighting the data block, so it can't be overlooked.

The plane made a sharp turn towards Thunder Bay, the pilot presumably attracted by the long runway the town's airport would have. All eyes were now glued to the unfolding drama, which someone had arranged to be projected on the large screen at the front of the room. The silence was broken only by a calm and professional air traffic controller patiently repeating calls to the the struggling flight. Suddenly there was an answer.

"Mayday, Mayday, Mayday...Phenom Charlie Golf November India Bravo has a complete hydraulics and partial electrical failure. Severe control problems, attempting Thunder Bay, ETA 18 minutes. Five souls on board, fuel 4800 pounds..." The message was distorted and crackly and cut off abruptly. Nikki, who had researched Booker for the mission and watched several youtube videos of him speaking at various charitable events recognized the pilot's voice as Booker's.

"Look...!" gasped Antoni, gripping the table. On the screen with the relayed radar image, where previously there had been a dot overlaid with a block of text denoting the code 7700, the failing plane's tail number, the altitude, speed, and direction of the Phenom, was now just a smudge. The plane's transponder had stopped transmitting, and the smudge was the low-tech radar return. In modern flight, radars paint the aircraft with a beam of radio waves and capture whatever bounces back, a technique dating back to World War II. A transponder in the plane detects that beam, and transmits the plane's details, which are overlaid onto the radar operator's screen, providing a stronger and more accurate position of the plane. This transponder transmission had ceased, leaving only the radar reflection.

The silence was broken by the pilot of another plane in that area. "Centre, this is Speedflight 891, at 34,000 feet, 12 miles north west of Thunder Bay. I'm monitoring the Mayday and am now observing bright lights and explosions approximately six miles south and well below me, over." This call was echoed by two other flights in the area, but no further contact from the Phenom was received.

"Mr Cochrane, should I wake Talan?" asked Nikki.

"No, let her sleep. I'll break the news when she wakes up. She said not to be disturbed unless we catch him or need input from her. Monitor search and rescue to ensure it is thorough but keep the pressure on finding Courtney. She is the priority."

15: EVIL MAIDS AND SPICE

[Marcy] – "Rest assured, Ethan, it looks like a plane exploding," I declared, wondering if we had overdone the pyrotechnics. Ethan was not able to look back out of the window at the fireworks we had unleashed as he was preoccupied with holding our position as close as he dared to Speedflight 891. The plane we were snuggled up to was helping us mask our radar return and was flown by one of Max's friends from the forces, who now flies private jets for a living. A second and third friend in two other planes we had chartered were conducting flights nearby and were helping us to maintain the deception.

Courtney had been silent for several hours before making contact. She was devastated as she relayed her feeling that her clan had been all but wiped out. She had stayed hidden, then used her talent to obtain a cellphone from a passing tourist but couldn't recall our numbers. She ended up calling the switchboard, and then security at Ethan Booker Detective Agency, eventually reaching Jim. There was little doubt Talan was behind the sickening events, the target of the attack being a rare gathering of most of the clan's country-level leadership; the upper echelon of Le Perjure. Courtney would have been there, too, had she not been working with us to find Talan.

One of Ethan's many toys was the Phenom 300e jet, which had been heavily modified by Darcy's team. Last year, we had to flee from an assassin called the Kingman, for which we had been quite unprepared. So, this time, one of Darcy's projects had been to coat Ethan's jet in similar material used on military stealth aircraft, which she obtained through her contacts to whom she supplied hi-tech, clandestine electronic assets. The radar signature was dramatically reduced, albeit not to the level of military jets, which are also shaped to scatter radar beams rather than return them. But this radar-absorbent coating certainly helped.

Another modification completed in just the last few hours was the ability to drop a package while in flight. The package contained a duplicate transponder, a parachute, some pyrotechnics, and masses of tin foil. As we neared the course flown by Speedflight 891 we had turned off our plane's transponder, dropped the package, and joined formation with the passing plane. The package had exploded and scattered the foil, which would do a fair imitation of the radar return of a plane exploding in mid air. Or at least we hoped it had. Our make-shift decoy had dropped quickly down into Lake Superior as we headed for Istanbul, tucked in so close behind a legitimate flight that we should appear as a single aircraft to anyone monitoring on radar.

We were gambling our lives on the assumptions that Jim was correct, that if Talan were in DC tracking Ethan, the distance would make us hard to pinpoint with any accuracy. She might know we hadn't died in the crash, and that perhaps we were in flight heading west, but we could be anywhere within hundreds of miles.

We launched seven chartered planes in addition to ours, all on a similar course but spaced out. These planes were mixed in with regular commercial flights. We were banking on Talan not launching attacks amidst civilian planes, just in the hope of hitting us. We felt if we could get to Europe in the confusion of the faked crash, we would be out of her paranormal radar's useful range. The Phenom on full fuel could cover 2,300 miles and so we would stop in Iceland to refuel.

Ethan stayed tucked in close behind our decoy until we were well over Northern Canada before separating to a more comfortable 500 yards and letting the autopilot take over.

Our escape was part of a plan put together over several calls while we hid in the woods in the helicopter. The first part was for Kelsie to organize the various charters and pilots, and for Ethan's plane to be flown out from Vancouver to Grand Rapids, Michigan, stopping in Calgary where the modifications were made and the decoy package was loaded. We timed our run in the Eurocopter to arrive in Grand Rapids as the plane was being refuelled, so we could take off immediately. We left the protection team behind in case we were intercepted, which had caused protests from just about everyone. Kelsie had another team en route to Istanbul, using commercial airlines, who would meet us on the ground.

We were on our way to Istanbul and several other locations to investigate what happened to the clan. It helped to keep us out of Talan's orbit, too.

Part two of our plan was to infiltrate the warehouse in Chicago to which Clay had been tracked. The objective was to gather intelligence and, if possible, extend our electronic reach into the gang's network. Jim flew up to Chicago and joined Gia and Max in the entry team. We received a text to say they were back safe and set up a call to hear how it had gone. There was a slight delay through the satellite phone, but once everyone was dialled in, Ethan asked Max to bring us up to date.

"It went about as well as we could expect, but I must say it was very unsettling seeing Jim do his thing."

"How did the delta-blockers work?" asked Gwen, keen to hear how Naomi and Darcy's invention had fared outside of the laboratory. Moy Lei had flown back to Vancouver the day before to help test the prototype. Naomi and Darcy had brought two units out to Chicago, to be worn by Max and Gia. The intention was for Jim to use his Adept talents to subdue the warehouse occupants. The blockers were to prevent Jim subduing his own team in the process.

"Gia and I felt pretty normal most of the time, but we both experienced some bursts of unexpected moodiness during the penetration."

"I'm just reading through the telemetry logs now," cut in Darcy, sounding a little distant with her head buried in a laptop, no doubt. "There are some frequency spikes. If I had to guess, you walked by some heavy-duty electrical motors or machinery, which caused interference. I can increase the shielding."

"If you can, but it wasn't much of a problem, really," replied Gia. I would focus on miniaturization and extending the battery life first." The units drew a lot of power and, with batteries, needed a small backpack to be carried around in.

"We also need to refine the drug delivery process," Explained Moy Lei. There is too much risk to use our current process again. We need a solution that allows our drug to breach the blood-brain barrier. That way we can inject a slow-release micro-capsule in an artery in the chest to administer the drug, and Darcy's device to refine and direct the dosage. For today's test, we needed a surgeon to make a microscopic hole through the skull to deliver a smaller capsule to the required site on the brain side of the barrier. Aside from the risk from the surgery, it limits how much drug we can load in, and there is a risk of infection. The surgeon is one more person we have to come up with a story to hide what we are up to, which is another risk we can shed. But I must say I am pleased with this step's results."

"That's a complex and risky procedure. I hate that we are asking people to take chances, even under these circumstances. But, well done everyone." Ethan's voice a mix of concern and pride, both.

"But you got in and out without detection?" I asked.

"As far as we can tell," said Max. "We know there are cameras outside of the building for their security, as well as those used by other businesses nearby. We were banking on, but didn't find, any on the inside. Crooks don't typically warm to their activities being recorded, even by their own team. We chose an infiltration spot where only one external camera could see us. As we approached, looking like we were on the way home from a club, Darcy dropped a drone down close to the camera and scrambled its electronics while we cut past it."

"We did a thorough search for interior cameras and saw nothing," said Gia.

"Conditions were good for me, too," cut in Jim. "As you know, for my emotional transference to be most effective it helps if we can seed the target environment with a chemical that I've previously ingested to enhance my mental link. We've stockpiled and conditioned various plant-stock in Vancouver which I've connected myself chemically to and flew some in for the mission. We drone-dropped some into the building's air-conditioning intake to ensure everyone inhaled some of the scent, and I definitely felt I had a good grip on the minds throughout the complex. But even so, 15 minutes was about all I could manage, and I'm exhausted now."

"OK, so entry and egress went smoothly, and the occupants were put into a trance so hopefully won't have noticed 15 minutes of their lives slip by unaccounted for. What did you find in there?" asked Ethan.

"It's mostly a chop shop for cars, with a back room with cash and cocaine," I recounted. "But we found the office that Jakub recorded his video in, with a cupboard full of computer tablets and wires. There were also several cameras and laptops. We tested some of the cameras' memory cards, but they'd been wiped. Presumably by the laptops we found. It could be that the blackmail videos are transported on separate memory cards, but there was a lot of Wi-Fi there, so we think they are uploaded to a server, which we didn't find on site, so presumably is at another location. We completed a total of six Evil Maid hacks on the computers we found, and dongle'd the routers, too."

"OK, back up. You lost me," said Gwen. "Does the dongle make the maid angry? What are you talking about for us humans?" We all had a chuckle. Darcy explained.

"The dongle is one of those little USB sticks that, in this case, we've loaded with a suite of autonomous cyber-nasties. Putting it in the Wi-Fi router lets it monitor and then crack into the traffic flowing in and out. It phones home to momma and tells me what it finds.

"Evil, not angry, Maid attacks get their name from the hotel context. Most computers are encrypted, password protected, and well screened from attacks from the internet. But if you can get your hands on them physically, unplug the hard drive from the laptop, and plug it into your own, you can definitely copy it and decrypt it later; or, if you have the right tools, you can actually crack into it then and there and load your own software. The maid part comes from the idea that you lock your encrypted computer in your hotel safe when you leave it, thinking it is protected. But an 'evil maid' can get in, open the safe, crack your drive, and have her way with your digits. It's common."

Max chimed in. "Darcy showed us each how to perform this attack and we took the tools in with us. We found 11 computers, hacked six, couldn't break through two – but copied them – and didn't have time to get into the others. We wanted to stick to the 15-minute window, as the drugs and Jim's stamina wouldn't last longer than that."

"SkyLoX and I have already established contact with the router tools, and with two of the computers. The next 24 hours will be intelligence gathering, password capture, mapping out the local and cloud networks, as well as attempting to compromise any other local or remote system we find if we think it is low risk. We will see where that gets us and keep you all updated." Max finished and sat back.

"What's next?" I asked.

"Clay's been in touch," put in Gia. The tension in her voice kicked up several notches. "He told us to be in our hotel room at 8 pm tonight our time. That's about 16 hours from now."

"If all goes smoothly, Marcy and I will be in Istanbul by then," said Ethan, in his directive voice. "As communications via satellite could be spotty, and this is an undercover op, please take direction from Max if you can't raise us. Courtney, how are you doing?" This in a softer tone. There was a pause, and we all waited respectfully.

"To be honest, I'm adrift. I don't know what to do now. I'm having trouble keeping everything straight. It's the shock of course. I must find the missing members of my clan, and I can't thank you enough for the work you are already doing for me to locate and protect them." Kelsie had a team already dedicated to tracking down the contacts Courtney had supplied.

"My duty to the world is clear. I must deploy what is left of the clan to help humanity as best we can, albeit with diminished effectiveness. But what I really want to do is focus on destroying Talan. Of course, I need to neutralize her so Le Perjure can carry on, but it's more than that. I feel this rage..." She drifted into silence, and we waited quietly for her to gather herself.

"Anyway, there are so few of us left. I will have to rethink how we go forward."

A small, fearful voice put in, "I'll help..." It took a while for me to place the voice; it sounded so timid.

"Pardon?" asked Courtney.

"I'd like to join Le Perjure. I can help." Moy Lei sounded more confident this time, as if the decision had sounded better having heard it from her own lips. "I have been considering it since I met you. You are the only female Nimbus I've met, so there is that. But between my aunt, leader of The Chord, and my mother, Queen of Assassins, my family owes a debt to society. Ethan, Marcy, and Jim have been wonderful, of course. All of you have. But I feel I could have a more meaningful purpose helping Le Perjure. If you will have me."

*

The descent into Kangerlussuaq, Greenland was particularly gruelling and, technically, illegal. The turbulent air bounced us around, and the combination of Ethan's current proficiency and the equipment on the plane required that we emerge from cloud and see the runway while still 200 feet above the ground. Ethan fibbed to the tower claiming he could see the runway as we hit 200ft but didn't truly see it until we were at 110 ft high. Our tanks were on fumes, so diverting wasn't an option in any event.

Due to the high risks and illegal flying manoeuvres throughout the first leg of the flight, just Ethan and I had left on the Phenom from Grand Rapids. When we landed in Kangerlussuaq we took on board a relief pilot so that Ethan could get some much-needed rest.

We reclined our chairs in the rear as far as possible, and slept until Dublin, where we refuelled again and checked in with the team. The penetration of Talan's network was progressing, but not much else had happened other than Courtney had been picked up by Roxy and was now sharing a room with her at The Folly in relative safety.

I felt Ethan and I would be more effective if we took a short break from the drama to clear our minds. I had an idea and texted Kelsie to make some additional arrangements for us in Istanbul, then we closed our eyes for the next few hours as we flew over Europe. Turkey required advanced notice of passengers arriving, so we had assumed fake identities through a source of Max's from his time undercover; we were now John and Jane Delaware.

We met up with our new protection team when we landed in Istanbul, who had two black SUV's as near to the terminal doors as one could get. They had us checked in at the Four Seasons, complete with our clothes from Vancouver – thank you again, Kelsie – and we ate and then showered quickly. Ethan had been frisky on arrival, but I had other plans for him.

"Don't we have an arrangement whereby I get to play with you if you solve a case?" I said, with what was supposed to be a sexy laugh but came out more like a shy giggle.

"What case is that?" he replied, clearly interested.

"The case of the missing airport. Only you could have found that runway though all that cloud, honey," I said, in a mock-adoring tone. "Get dressed, Slave-Boy, and you will find out."

We were back in the SUV and down to the docks in short order, where per my text to Kelsie a large speedboat awaited. We all piled on, and were soon bouncing across the Bosporus, with Ethan and I alone at the front of the launch and the protection team at the rear.

"See that island with the domed tower?" I pointed. "Look familiar?"

"I've been there once," my well-travelled man admitted.

"Does my personal James Bond know what happened there in *The World is Not Enough?*"

"I believe I do," he said, with that cute look he has when accessing his memory banks. "Didn't Elektra King tie Pierce Brosnan to a chair and have sex with him, while she tortured and tried to kill him by snapping his neck in a medieval torture device?"

I reached into my coat pocket and flashed the two bathrobe belts from the hotel room at him with mischievous intent.

The Maiden's Tower was designed by architect Damat Ibrahim Pasa in 1725, and sits on a flat, low island I could jog around in less than a minute. There are five levels: two in its small, oblong base, and three more in the 59-foot tower. A wrought-iron Juliet balcony circles the top level. It is a very attractive addition to this wonderful city.

In addition to occasionally being used as a movie set, the site is mostly used for corporate events and tourism today. Over the years, it has been a quarantine station, watch tower, garrison and canon site, lighthouse, and is part of the *Hero and Leander* legend.

As we pulled up at the small jetty, we were met by the facility's operations manager. Inside the tower base is a restaurant and café; the manager assured us it had been cleared and that we had the island to ourselves for two hours, before he hopped into his own boat and departed for the evening.

"Ethan and I are going to explore the Byzantine architecture and take some photos from the top of the tower. Set up a perimeter defence and phone me if there is any threat, but otherwise remain outside," I instructed the team.

We stepped inside the ancient doors, and into another time. We spent 20 minutes marvelling at the building and its contents, eventually arriving at a large, circular room just under the dome, where we admired the 360-degree view through the floor-to-ceiling arched windows. The floor, made with 12-inch, polished hardwood planks, had been cleared of its furniture, which had been stacked at the far end of the room.

"Move that one big chair to the centre of the room," I commanded, finding my Phoenix-bossy voice at last. The chair was an authentic period-piece with a high wingback and ornate carving, quite heavy, and Ethan had to strain as he dragged it across the floor. Watching the muscles in his arms and thighs flex through his clothing helped build the erotic momentum that was taking hold of me.

"Now strip and put your clothes out on the balcony." He dropped his kit with amazing enthusiasm and, after folding it – he is such a tidy man and I love that – was less enthusiastic about depositing it where instructed. I toyed with demanding he step out onto the little balcony, and I knew that threat was crossing his mind after the Vancouver bike ride, but I let him just reach out with one arm in the end.

"Come over here and kneel by this chair!" He turned and found me sitting in the chair, with my best posture, making it as throne-like an image as I could. When he was at my feet, I slowly removed the head scarf I wore in respect of the local customs and blindfolded him. I stood and walked around him, making sure my high heels clicked sexily on the hardwood so that he could track my movements.

I slowly circled him until I stood right in front of him again, and I teased little Ethan, our pet name for his penis, with the point of my shoe. He was all appreciation and energy. Little Marcy was answering him, eager to dance, but I wanted to savour this moment.

"Stand." He did, and I kissed him, stroking him slowly.

"Sit, and don't complain if the chair is cold. I was just warming it up for you," I said, guiding him to the seat. I pulled both his wrists up to the top of the tall back of the chair, which was about an inch higher than his head. Then, using the housecoat belts I brought from the hotel room, I tied his hands to the top of the chair.

I removed two more scarves from my pocket and tied his ankles together with one, then used the other to secure his feet to the centre of the rail spanning the bottom of the chair.

I dipped back into my magical coat-pocket and pulled out several small paper packages I had acquired earlier from the gift shop in the hotel. Istanbul is known for the famous Spice Market and, being the gateway from the Middle East to Europe, and has an endless capacity to offer the tastiest and spiciest wares. I had selected an interesting assortment from the hotel's gift shop.

Sitting astride his straining and bulky thighs, I open the first spice packet and, wetting my finger, dipped it in and swirled it around, to coat it with the contents. I tasted it; a mild, minty spice. I pressed my finger into Ethan's mouth and watched his face as he caught up with my game. He liked that spice, but there were more. We slowly worked our way through them, alternating kisses with spices, honey, and other treats I fed him with my fingers.

I got to the last packet and took a little of the red dust-like substance and told him to stick out his tongue, then rubbed some of the powder on it. He tasted it, and then coughed gently.

"Wow, that's got a kick," he said. I kissed him quiet. Then I leaned back and reached down, emptying the remainder of the packet onto his engorged cock and around his sack, which had already condensed down into a tight, purposeful ball. He started to squirm, but just a little. I knew that over the next few minutes, that burn would slowly increase as the paprika and ginger mix got to work.

I kissed him again and removed the scarf that covered his eyes, draping it around his neck.

Stepping back, I admired my handywork while he blinked to readjust to the sunlight streaming in through the windows. Taking out my phone, I selected "Earned It," by The Weeknd, and turned up the volume so it echoed nicely through the cavernous space. I pulled a small chair over, so it was six feet in front of him, then I did my best tantalizing striptease for his entertainment. I could tell I had his full attention; his breathing was elevated, his mouth moved like it was dry, and little Ethan pranced, happy but on fire, while Big E pulled at his bindings.

When down to my lingerie and heels, I did my best sashay over, climbed astride Ethan, and tried my hand at lap dancing. We were both really getting into it when the song ended, so I stepped off and changed the tune. As Miley's "Adore You" began, the first song of a longer, sensuous playlist I had prepared for the occasion, I removed my bra and panties and mounted him again. The heels stayed on.

"This is getting really hot," he said, gruffly.

"The dance or the spice?" I whispered, cheekily.

"Well, both actually." He tried to kiss me, and I teased him by keeping just out of range. I wrapped the blindfold-scarf around his neck twice, bringing the ends to the front, and holding them like reins. We are not really into choking or breath play, but it was very erotic to symbolize it gently. Ethan certainly responded.

Suddenly, I wanted his hands on me, so I reached over, thrusting my breasts into his face, and untied his wrists. His lips and hands were on me in a second as I lowered myself down onto his shaft, intent on sharing his spiced-up experience. It was hot, he was right about that. We lost ourselves from the world for the next half hour.

When we finished, I carefully washed off the worst of the hot spice using the contents of the water bottle I had brought. It was harder for me to clean hot-little-Marcy, and I would suffer greatly all of the way back to the bidet in our hotel bathroom, my new best friend. It was certainly worth it once, but I was not sure it was a 'do again' experience. I looked forward to hearing what 'Ethan Bond' thought of the diversion.

16: BAITING A HOOK

[Gia] – Max, Courtney, Moy Lei, and I spent the afternoon rehearsing for the upcoming discussion with Clay, but my tummy did an uncharacteristic cartwheel when Roxy messaged to say Clay was exiting the elevator and approaching our suite. He had company, she warned us. We had prepared for the possibility that Clay might bring some muscle or a superior, and we were not too worried about things getting physical; our concern was the negotiation we were about to embark on going sideways. Sure enough, he brought his goon.

I was not armed, but Max had a gun tucked behind a cushion on the couch he was sitting on. In the confined space, I felt comfortable that if it came to it, I could move fast enough to do a lot of damage, while Max stood back and covered me.

Clay let himself in as before – rudeness that was surprisingly annoying – and smiled at us like we were old friends. He didn't introduce the goon, who leered at me openly. The goon was short and all muscle but looked quick on his feet. He reminded me of someone from the TV show *Gladiators*, so I nicknamed him Gladys, which I distantly recall meaning 'small sword,' so it seemed doubly fitting. His jacket's armpit bulged rather obviously, but he made no effort to intimidate me with his gun. He seemed supremely confident in his physical prowess.

Gladys began to walk towards me, and I worried our game plan was about to tank, but Clay explained Gladys was only going to check that the bedroom behind me was clear. I stepped around and stood nearer to Clay, careful not to block Max's line of fire. Gladys took his time but emerged indicating we were alone, and he took station just in front of the bedroom door in the classic bouncer pose: squared up, arms crossed at the waist and flexed to define his muscles fully. His legs were shoulder width apart.

"You've had enough time to comprehend your predicament," began Clay. "I understand you had a visitor this morning to convince you?" He was referring to the brief visit we received from none other than Chicago's Commissioner of Police, who had arrived at our door earlier in the day. He had been at the fundraiser and had also been an unwilling participant in the mind games that went on there. He made it clear he felt he had no choice but to comply with the blackmail. He seemed like a great man and hadn't been swayed by the threat of exposure to his career. He had even already confessed and explained events to his wife, who hadn't been at the event. That was a hard conversation. The real pressure for him, however, was that his superiors, the mayor and the District Attorney, were also compromised. For all three, the mafia had doubled down and shown them each candidly taken pictures of their families and made various death, maim, and torture threats. Typically, such threats were handled through federal witness protection programs while the issue was dealt with, but apparently, in this case, even that organization had been compromised.

We commiserated with him and pretended we also had no idea why we all did what we did that night. His visit was a clear demonstration of the powerful grip of the extortion gang. He left after ten minutes - message delivered – moving onto the next victim with cold efficiency that clearly didn't sit will with him.

"Commissioner Blake explained things to us, yes," answered Max.

"You have the list on the thumb drive?" asked Clay, holding out his hand, expecting full compliance.

No one in Ethan's team had any intention of handing over the list, but we had spent a long time discussing how to handle the situation. A fake list had been the favourite idea to buy time until Marcy had come up with the brilliant but risky idea we were about to attempt.

"I'm sorry, but we will never give up that list, Clay," said Max, "but we have a proposal you should listen to before jumping to any conclusions."

Two things happened as Max offered this defiance: Gladys pulled himself taller and took a menacing half step forward; and a strong feeling of calmness flooded the room, mitigating the confusion and anger Clay and Gladys had started to feel. Courtney and Roxy were stationed in an adjoining room and were watching events via a camera hidden on top of our minibar; as planned, Courtney was attempting to influence the blackmailers to consider our proposal.

Courtney's job was difficult, and she had to dial things down since her manipulations were also impacting Roxy, Max, and me. We had considered wearing the delta-blockers, but due to their bulky nature and our desire not to have our skulls painfully penetrated a second time, we gambled on this sub-optimal alternative. She was somewhat effective, seeing that Gladys paused – almost stumbling from confusion – and settled back to his original stance.

"If you need a further demonstration..." Clay faltered mid-sentence, as an overpowering feeling of Adept-generated guilt pressed down on us all. It certainly helped that I was prepared for Courtney's attack, but it was still hard to not be influenced by it. After a long and dangerous pause, Clay cracked and asked us to explain our counter proposal. As Max laid things out, the room felt warmer and his wisdom, compelling.

"Look, our lives are dedicated to this charity and helping our clients. We will die before putting them through more suffering. So, Gia and I have had our rights to the database revoked, effectively locking ourselves out of that part of the system for the next sixty days. Kill us if you need to but hear us out first."

"Go on," said Clay, signalling to Gladys, who had begun to move towards us again, to hold fast.

"We won't give you the names, but we will give you the charity's money. I will wire you 15 million Canadian dollars today, which will leave us 3 million to continue our work." Thanks to Courtney, this felt like the best thing since sliced bread to me, but Clay was still hesitating, no doubt wondering how he would explain this to his superiors.

"But that's not all," put in Max, quickly. "We can offer you something else, too. We already have the next fundraiser planned to take place in Vancouver in ten days. We put a draft of the guest list here on your thumb drive." Max held up the drive for inspection, as he continued. "The Mayor, the Premier, and the Provincial leader of the RCMP are on the list. And we have invited some of our richer citizens, whose money you could get access to." Ethan's name was on the list, but we didn't name him now. We thought that might be too obvious as bait.

"What's to stop us taking up your offer and taking the other list in 60 days?" My emotions flipped... and Clay's suggestion sounded like a terrible idea. I could see the same emotion flitter across the faces of the blackmailers, too.

"Do what you want to us, Clay," said Max levelly, "but you will never get that list of sex-trade workers."

"You have a sister, don't you? Marcy Stone. And a brother and parents. You care so little for their lives?" We had expected this from Clay, assuming he had done his homework. I felt Courtney's influence once more, revulsion at the idea.

"Personally," said Clay, changing tack in response to his manipulated feelings, "I think your idea is doable, but I know my boss won't go for it.' He raised his voice. "I need the list of whore-names, and I think you need a further demonstration." He nodded at Gladys, who took a step towards me, reaching into his jacket for his pistol. Crap. "Shoot the woman!" demanded Clay.

Out of nowhere, Roxy's booted foot appeared between Gladys's legs, landing so brutally hard that it lifted Gladys an inch into the air. She stepped further out of the bedroom as he crumbled to the floor and tasered him. Clay had obviously become complacent, having met little resistance from other victims. His hand only made it halfway to his holster before Max was across the room with his own pistol pressed to Clay's temple.

The door to the adjoining room with Roxy and Courtney had been locked when Gladys had searched the bedroom, but once that was done, Roxy had quietly let herself into ours with the key.

Five minutes later, we had both blackmailers zip-tied to chairs. We left Courtney with them and went to get a bite to eat, while she used her full powers to convince them of our proposal and wipe the memory of events from their minds. Max and I didn't want to experience any more mind tricks, as fascinating as they were academically.

It was still a big gamble that Clay would be able to sell the bait to his boss. He would be programmed to look at the list and ensure he pointed out several wealthy targets – Ethan foremost among them – and that the idea would reach Talan. The clincher, we hoped, was that we transferred fifteen million dollars to the account specified by Clay, just before sending them back to their organization. Ethan didn't blink at returning the funds stolen from the Toussaints and replacing it with some of his own money. The brush with Detectives Bell and Webb made him want to divest himself of any crooked funds.

17: ISTANBUL AND LONDON

[Ethan] — We kept the update call with the gang short, as we had dinner plans with an ex-colleague of Max who we hoped could give us some insight into the deaths of Le Perjure's leadership team. Max and Gia recounted the visit with Clay and his sidekick, and we agreed that Courtney's reinforcement of our story was probably the best tactic.

Kelsie's report on the penetration of the mafia network showed progress. On the one hand, it seemed to take ages, but when we thought about the massive amount of work it required, it was actually racing along. She felt she and SkyLoX were closing in on the cloud location of the blackmail material and hoped to have confirmation shortly. The next step would be to locate any back-ups or duplicates. She also shared that the list of confirmed blackmail victims was expanding. We felt we had identified the majority of the victims and were doing our due diligence to substantiate it.

We were now in contact with all of the remaining Le Perjure members, who were making their way to safehouse 'airplanes.' With Talan's ability to track her clanmates, keeping them on the move in the air and travelling under assumed names seemed lower risk than sitting in one place in an actual house.

On the downside, Courtney was able to confirm all of her financial assets had been frozen and, more worrying, that her various North American government contacts she used to influence world events were not returning her calls. She was barely holding herself together but was gushingly grateful for our support. We decided it would be prudent for her to leave Chicago quickly and also become a moving target for Talan. Roxy's team would accompany her, as would Moy Lei. Darcy was returning to Vancouver. Max and Gia would remain at the Folly to stay connected with Clay and await developments. I didn't like them not having the additional benefit of a protection team, but it would only be for a short while as the men who had been with me in Detroit were already en route to them.

With our protection team scouting ahead of and behind us, we left the hotel on foot and walked south along the river for two miles to the Galata Bridge and through a small park of the same name. We had both been to this city before, but like tourists with no concerns, we stopped for a few minutes to stare at the wondrous scenery that took our minds back to what it must have been like in the Ottoman period of the 15th century.

Once through the park, we swung right and entered a series of smaller streets that bustled with commerce and bloomed with the aroma of exotic spices. Our mouths were watering as we pushed through a small, charming door into a darkened restaurant. Max's contact, Ms Asuman Demir, was already seated, and we joined her. Two of our team sat by the door, while the other two were outside monitoring for trouble. Max's undercover adventures had had him working with various agencies across the Middle East and Europe. Ms Demir was one of his trusted contacts.

Asuman was born in Kuwait and was 19 years old when Iraq invaded in August of 1990. Her parents were neurologists and were arrested and taken to Baghdad to help with Saddam's biological weapons program researching nerve agents and neurotoxins. Asuman's uncle smuggled her to England in the dead of night where she frantically awaited news of her parents throughout the allied invasion. Her mother was killed for refusing to cooperate with Saddam's officials, and her father took his own life soon after. This was discovered after the fact once the US re-established stability in the region.

MI6, Britain's foreign intelligence service – similar to the US CIA – was never slow to jump on such opportunities and approached Asuman on her 21st birthday. Within the year, she was inserted back into the region and has been an intelligence asset for the British ever since. In 2014, now aged 43, Asuman requested a less strenuous task and was moved to Istanbul to clandestinely gain information on Kurdish activity. Over the last five years, she worked her way into a senior analyst position within the Millî İstihbarat Teşkilâtı, or MİT, which is responsible for intelligence and counterintelligence. She had worked with Max on several weapons-trafficking investigations and, as a personal favour to him, had driven the five hours from her home base in Ankara for today's meeting.

"Merhaba, bize gösterdiğiniz gayret için teşekkür ederiz," I attempted. I hoped it meant *Hello and thank you for the effort you have undertaken.* Asuman laughed, her face lighting up at my gesture, and replied in a perfect Oxford English accent that rolled slowly and clearly off her tongue.

"Welcome, please be seated. Tea? Something stronger?" I blushed and pushed in behind the small table, letting Marcy sit opposite Asuman. We declined alcohol sensing Asuman was offering out of courtesy but wasn't wholly at ease around it.

Both women were the same height sitting down, had black hair, but the resemblance ended there. The extra 20 years and far harsher life lived by Asuman left her looking well into her sixties instead of being just shy of her fiftieth birthday. Her face was big-boned and her features large and prominent. She was more handsome than pretty. The years dissolved somewhat when she made small talk asking after Max, who she was still clearly very fond of.

Small talk continued while drinks and then several courses of food arrived, and we learned much we didn't know about the political and religious rollercoaster Turkey had been through in the last decade.

Marcy – got to love her – deadpanned as she kept asking about several of the spices, we had gained intimate knowledge of these spices very recently and she was making puns only we would get. As we tucked into a delicious lamb meatloaf – a main course I couldn't pronounce but would love to eat again – the subject came around to the event we had travelled there to discuss. Asuman had been thorough and provided a professional level briefing that was missing only a few PowerPoint slides to make it complete.

"The media are reporting the destruction of the residence to the south as being the work of a Kurdish terrorist cell; a bomb- factory accident. They will be fed additional information that supports that theory as the investigation unfolds, but as Max implied to me, you are already aware that the site was not being used by terrorists at all.

"There were just over twenty people at the site, mostly women, and although there are very little human remains to study due to the intensity of the explosion and resulting fire, it is clear none of the deceased are from this region. Most of the remains appear to be from Northern Europe."

"Then why the pretense?" asked Marcy.

"The residence, which you might call a lodge retreat, routinely hosted large gatherings, usually corporate team-builders and the like. The occasional wedding, too. It was exclusive and had enough bedrooms on site to shame a small hotel. As you know, the Turkish-American relationship is complicated. They collaborate, and sometimes they have conflict. In this case, our 'allies' from across the sea reached out as 'friends' and offered us intelligence that one of their assets had smuggled a bomb into the building to take out a clear and present danger to US interests."

"At a retreat in Turkey?" I put in.

"The Americans furnished us with documents showing how this all-female organization had been buying chemical weapons from ISIS and were preparing to transport them across Europe and even as far as to the USA. Each would carry a small amount of the substances and travel using different routes to their respective destinations. The US claimed they acted at the only point they could, namely when the chemicals were all in one place. They kept this intelligence to themselves and conducted an operation on our sovereign soil to limit the risk of a leak, which might have put the chemicals out of reach entirely."

"And MIT believes them?"

"Not in the least, no. But it's not a battle we want to pick. No Turkish nationals were hurt, and the US has even provided funding to replace the damaged building. Last year, several incidents at the hands of MIT happened elsewhere in the world, and the US chose to remain silent. We consider the slate clean. I think that's the right phrase, no?"

"And what became of the person who supposedly smuggled in the bomb?" inquired Marcy.

"Well, that's another interesting aspect. The damage is completely incompatible with a single blast. There are at least four and perhaps six detonation points, and we don't think there was anything on site more dangerous than an egg sandwich to create secondary explosions. And if there had been, it wouldn't explain the three eyewitness reports that would make it appear as if the destruction came from missiles."

"The US sent planes or cruise missiles into your airspace to do this?" I asked, incredulously.

"We think a drone. We have ears in Incirlik, where the US drones launch from, and there was one drone in the air at about the right timeframe that left with six missiles and returned with none; a fuel burn that did not match the declared mission profile was also detected. It was claimed that the drone operated over the ocean on a training mission, loitering and firing missiles for the US fleet to knock down to test their own defences. If true, the drone would have returned with twice the fuel it actually still had left. We think it came to Istanbul instead and left its payload in the residence."

"Someone at Incirlik conducted a mission inside Turkey? That's incredible."

"Actually, the mission would have been launched from there but remotely piloted from Creech Airforce Base, in Nevada. But yes, it's hard to believe. But it has happened before and is not unique."

"And the agency that fed you the bullshit about chemical weapons?"

"It's not always easy to tell with these things, but if I had my guess, I think the CIA."

We stayed for another hour and genuinely enjoyed the hospitality of the restaurant and Asuman. We thanked her and took taxis back to the Four Seasons Hotel.

We reported what we discovered to the gang and started making plans to visit London to follow up on the deaths there. We didn't want to stay in one place too long. On the call, Max suggested Courtney and Moy Lei might detour to Nevada to see what could be discovered there, and we agreed. An hour later, we were rolling down the runway, headed north."

*

Although Jeff, our relief pilot, sat beside me, I wanted to personally fly us into London's City Airport. It wasn't technically on my bucket list of *difficult landings of the world*, but it was interesting, especially when the wind was from the east as it was today, under a low overcast sky and moderate rain. The approach is low over City Airport – so, awesome sight seeing – resulting in a much steeper and slower descent than typical, staring down to a very short-looking runway. We only really needed 3,000 of the 5,000 feet available to stop, but the steep approach made the runway look much shorter than it was in reality.

Our team disembarked, and while we took a very short helicopter trip along the Thames to Battersea for our quick meeting, Jeff refuelled the plane and took a very short flight to Biggin Hill Airport, where we would meet him and head back to North America. I didn't know if working this hard to be a moving target was worth it, but I didn't see how it could hurt us.

Two red Range Rovers met us at Battersea Heliport, which was once owned by Harrods but is now a public facility and London's only licenced heliport. Our ground transportation was arranged by Cornell Boyle, Permanent Secretary of the Security Service MI5, from his personal protection unit. Cornell is proudly gay and an outspoken LGBTQ ally. He would have rainbow-coloured cars if they made them, or if he could sneak their respraying costs through the government finances.

Cornell's parents and mine have been lifelong friends. Our fathers fought together in the Falklands during the ten-week, undeclared war between the UK and Argentina over tiny islands in the South Atlantic. Richard 'Tricky' Boyle, Cornell's dad, flew Sea Harriers from HMS *Ark Royal,* and my father flew search and rescue helicopters in support. You would be mistaken for thinking the lifelong bond between the two stemmed from some dramatic rescue from the frozen waters; the pair's friendship had blossomed when dad defended 'Trick' – Richard's pilot nickname was 'Tricky-dicky' as he was black and gay which eventually was shortened to 'Tricky,' then Trick – at a time when the Air Force were particularly unwelcoming about both colour and sexual identity diversity. As Dad had spent four of his eight years with the Canadian Forces in military intelligence and had personal knowledge of the Falklands from a prospecting trip in his teens, he was seconded to the RAF as an advisor. Dad intervened in a hate related incident on Cornell's behalf and the pair spent the rest of the trip watching each other's 'six.'

Trick married his life-long friend Janice in 1986 just so that he and his true love James could adopt a child. Same-sex adoption was not legal in the UK until 2002, yet by 2016, 9.6% of adoptions were to same sex parents. So, Cornell was raised by a mom and two dads, which might account for his flamboyant confidence in all things; yet, surprisingly, this 'irregular' arrangement didn't raise flags on the intensive screening required to allow Cornell to climb the career ladder in the intelligence services.

Cornell and his family spent a lot of their vacation time at our cabin on Gambier Island near Vancouver, and he and I shared many adventures over the years. So, it was nice to see him on the doorstep of his Chelsea Mews flat to greet us on arrival. We left our respective bodyguards outside, and the three of us had a quick but delicious meal prepared by James while we caught up.

"Isn't red a rather conspicuous colour for the MI5 chief's motorcade?" asked Marcy, only half joking.

"Of course, it is, dear. That's why I have them. Half the time I'm not even in the cars, but they are tailed anyway while I am elsewhere getting things done. I'm happy to say not all of our enemies are as smart as they think they are," he laughed and winked. With Cornell, you rarely knew when he was completely serious.

"Ethan, you said on the phone you were interested in our little explosion. It's just a mile from here and we think we felt it, didn't we, James?"

"God, you're not going to make one of your we-felt-the-earth-moving jokes, are you?" replied James, spooning a second helping of his blue cheese gnocchi onto everyone's plates as he spoke and then refreshed our glasses.

"What's your interest, if you don't mind my professional curiosity?" asked Cornell, leaning in for effect.

"I'd like to keep some of my cards to myself," I started, "but I can say that someone framed me for some crimes in Canada. It was quickly cleared up, we are happy to say, and we think it might be both a personal matter and possibly industrial espionage." I hated lying to my friend but didn't want to risk exposing other friends' secrets and getting into the Adept part of our lives with this lovely but intrinsically curious man. "When following up, there was a suggestion that it was related to a bomb here in London, and an explosion in Turkey, too. We are interested to find out whatever we can." I didn't press him for specific information, as he was a master at deflection and would have decided what he would share and what he wouldn't long ago. He took a few moments to enjoy his food and mouthed a compliment at James, while he pretended to ponder. Such a ham.

"Curious case, actually. The occupant wasn't on our radar before the blast, but now that we are looking into her, there is something off. She has a business that runs well, and her staff talk fondly of her as if she is there every day, but we pulled her cell history and she is there once a quarter, at most. She is also a member of clubs where – shall we say – the government's mighty leaders also hang out, yet no one I've spoken to has seen her, let alone knows her name. Despite the fact she has signed into my own club at least once a week, which conforms to her cell records, none of the staff recognize her as far as my short and discrete inquiries have revealed." That all jived with what I understood would be typical of an Adept at work, but I said nothing on that aspect and was keen to shift his focus.

"That's odd, certainly, but anything about the bombers? I think that would be my area of interest rather than the victim," I said.

"It's part of an active investigation, and so I am bound by the Official Secrets Act on what I can say, dear boy." He paused. I deduced he was telling me things by speaking in code and that he was waiting for me to catch up. A gas leak or lovers tiff wouldn't be a state secret.

I thought about what he was saying, and his unusually formal tone. When Cornell vacationed with us three years ago, he brought me an early edition of Michael Dobbs' trilogy, *House of Cards*, on which the UK show of the same name was based. We watched some of the US adaptations, too. Cornell admits he likens himself to the main character, Francis Urquhart, in affectations but not in morals.

Dobbs stated in an interview that the inspiration behind Urquhart came during a drinking session at a swimming pool after a tense encounter with Margaret Thatcher, resulting in his deliberately creating a character moulded around the initials 'FU.' The protagonist started as the chief whip, and through questionable means manoeuvred his way to the top and refused to leave office until he had beaten Thatcher's record of 11 years as longest serving, post-war prime minister. Urquhart was famous for several catch phrases, one of which he used often when seeking plausible deniability when leaking information. I hoped Cornell and I were on the same page when I asked my next question.

"Our contact in Istanbul confirmed that there was a rocket attack at the site we were interested in and hinted that the US military had a hand in it, probably at the behest of the CIA. Anything resonate with the incident here?"

Cornell beamed at me and said, "You might very well think that, but I couldn't possibly comment."

18: CORRUPT WITCH

[Lindi] – The *nakele umthakthi*, or as Uma would have said, the 'corrupt witch,' was yelling at Mr Cochrane, again. While she yelled, I felt her twist his thoughts at the same time and, as is often the case, she was unaware that she was even doing so.

Uma and I were ripped from our village by another of the tainted, the witch-sorcerer Guance. He travelled with missionaries through our lands seeking Iquinso, *The True.* Namibia is a land of many languages and, as usual, the elders require that I sit and listen to the talk of the missionaries and other visitors and correct their words. I am not a translator, and cannot speak in their tongue, but thought has one language across all people, and I can understand their thoughts when they talk in their many different languages. I can understand everything Talan says, but can only answer with the words Uma taught me.

There have been an increasing number of missionaries in recent times, with the self-appointed task of finding our witches and helping them. They would stop at the one store in our area and ask people, "Do you have a witch in your family or village?" As everyone does, the answer is invariably "yes." They explain to us that our witches are what they call people with dementia, a sickness of the brain. It can come with age, or from the HIV curse, or from another witch or sorcerer, they say.

Those they find lost in their dementia are not considered by the missionaries as having a magical power, and I agree they don't have much, but most of my folk believe that the scattered thoughts and words of these 'dementia-witches' are evidence that they are speaking to spirits. Others, who appear saner, deliberately use their power for a purpose, which might be to fulfil their own need, or for a task purchased by another. Mostly, we believe witches use their powers to take the life force of others, and so we fear those closest to us. After all, witches are arrogant and lazy and would not travel far for their needs.

Those who seem confused and less purposeful have equal power through their spirit talk to those witches who are sane, yet their objective is harder to divine.

In either case – in fact, in nearly all cases observed – this magic is just the tickle of a breeze on a rock; it holds very little influence over the people of the world. Yet among the many, we few hide. Our magic is a windstorm on a flower. We few are the Iquinso, *The True*. We have real power, whether we know it or not.

A witch in my homeland is someone who has a power and needs no objects or things to employ it; they just apply their will to make their magic. A sorcerer has a power, too, but needs things – crushed cow horn, sheep innards, or human blood – to use their gift. This is the reverse of the way the people who surround me here in this strange land would explain it.

Guance was Iquinso, though he is now with the spirits. I felt him die, and I saw the rage and hate it inspired in Talan. Talan is a true witch. Guance had small magic, which increased many-fold if he used nature to enhance it. A full sorcerer has no power without props, and so Guance was a mix; a witch-sorcerer. But his witch power alone was sufficient to sense that I had something he desired, and I refer not only to my young flesh. He knew I was Iquinso, too.

Guance spoke to Mufi, our elder witch, who hated me for my greater potential. She knew one day I would displace her. One night I went to sleep and awoke here in this land, to a new and strange life with only Uma as a friend. Uma could speak the words of this land so was stolen and brought here, too, as Guance believed he needed her to explain what was required of me. He was unaware I could already understand him, and so her suffering was a tragedy. She was not a witch and held no power, although had a way with plants and animals, who obeyed her to an unnatural degree.

Soon after Guance died, Talan brought us here. She is hiding from others and insists that I keep her mind *inside*. Mostly our minds are *outside*, where people can see them, but they can be hidden *inside*, too, where the magic lives. Now I travel wherever Talan goes, to keep her hidden, and often must also take the minds of others *inside* for short periods, too. It is a simple task, and just one of my several magics; the only one Talan is aware of. Although she experiences my ability to understand her words through her thoughts, she thinks I understand her because I can speak her tongue. The fact I can only answer her with a very few words frustrates her greatly. She thinks me badly behaved.

Uma made me swear on 'The Mother' not to reveal my other magics as Talan would force me to do great evil. When Talan was angry at me, Uma would stand between us and was beaten often for doing so. I intended to send Talan's mind back to The Mother, where the spirits live, and end her time here on the earth, but Uma made me swear not to. She said I would then be *nakele umthakthi*, too.

Three weeks ago, Talan entwined Mr Antoni in her power and took him to bed. They writhed and sweated an afternoon away, feeding her needs. Antoni had a desire to bring me into their bed, too, and although she was sated, Talan thought it amusing to allow his request. She reached her mind for mine but, as usual, her efforts were pointless; I let her wind blow around and past me. She resorted to calling for me, and Uma again stood between us. Affronted, Talan told Antoni to force me physically into their bed, but Uma would not let him near me. He struck her and she fell, and her head hit the doorframe, and her blood leaked onto the floor. Her mind fell into the hands of The Mother and she was gone. In my angry grief, I nearly ended them both that night.

So far, I have kept my vow to Uma and have not avenged her, but the thought is never far from my mind. I told Talan I wanted to return home to my land, and she surprised me by saying that once the witch from who she hides Courtney was with the spirits, she would send me home. Now, watching her rage at Mr Cochrane only increased my belief that her promise to me was smoke in the air: Something that was unpleasant smelling and would evaporate later.

*

[Talan] – I had slept like the dead; a full 12 hours. Stiff from such a luxury, I showered and had my personal masseur attend me. He spent an hour removing the aches from my body, and another removing the ache of my libido. I dallied another hour being pampered with a mani-pedi, then showered again before strolling into the operations centre to catch up on events. On waking, I could sense Courtney to the west and Ethan a long way to the east; I was disappointed but not shocked that they still lived. I was surprised, therefore, when Cochrane described Ethan's fiery crash into Lake Superior in great detail.

Cochrane had been diligent in ensuring a thorough search and rescue operation was underway, which of course hadn't found a shred of evidence of an actual crash, but that didn't quiet my rage, which I let vent to the full. I was secretly annoyed with my momentary loss of self control – my self indulgence over the last few hours had allowed Ethan to escape our net –. but venting on Cochrane was cathartic.

The rest of the operations centre staff sat in silence as I lambasted Cochrane for his incompetence. Understandably, no one wanted to update me on anything when I had eventually calmed down enough to ask for updates on other matters. To let them settle, I stroked their minds and told them I expected a report from everyone when I returned from taking some air in the garden. Ten minutes later, I was receiving constructive reports as if my tantrum hadn't happened.

My priority was Courtney, who was in the wind. I could feel she was still in the central USA – most likely in Chicago – but neither the Mafia nor Cochrane's contacts could locate her. I considered flying closer so I could assist in the hunt, but now that I had earned my spot in the driver's seat in world events, I decided to be patient.

THE NUD<u>EST</u> DETECTIVE

The remaining Le Perjure members were proving equally elusive, and I guessed Courtney had found a way to contact them and convince them to make it hard for me to locate them. Again, it was a simple matter of keeping the pressure on, as time was on my side, but perhaps going after them to pick them off one at a time was a good use of my time. I would give that idea some thought.

A long-awaited invitation to meet President Millar had arrived. I didn't need to worm my way right to the top to be at my most effective, but I did want a little direct influence over the Commander-in-Chief of the world's most powerful army. The Joint Chiefs could get the job done, and I already had my tentacles around two of them, while making sure they had no problems from their boss. In three days, the POTUS was giving a television interview and there was a reception afterwards; I would be there. Most importantly, so would his Chief of Staff and Press Secretary, so I could kill, or at least ensnare, several birds with one stone.

Cochrane had little news about Booker, having thought him dead, and I hadn't thought to ask Antoni. His area of focus was typically North America unless he reached out through peer gangsters as he had with Japan's Le Perjure assassination. But he raised a finger – like a shy schoolboy – indicating he had something to contribute.

"I hesitate to mention this, Talan," he began slowly, perhaps still mindful of my earlier tirade. "Booker's name came up in something quite unrelated. I don't know if there is any mileage in it but will let you make that decision." I noted the cop-out, but I stayed silent, letting him take the risk. "We are closing out the work on the Chicago, er...recruitment of people to extort. You might recall a very attractive ex-Olympian, an Asian woman with a very muscular ex-Canadian Forces man. They run the charity that hosted the event. They have no value for you personally but were natural guests to invite under the circumstances. When we looked into them further, my organization became interested in their cash and access to hundreds, if not thousands, of sex workers around the world." He paused, as if afraid to take the next step.

"Go on," I prompted, projecting confidence into his mind.

"Well, the granola-munching do-gooders are trying to negotiate. They'll part with the cash but are refusing to give up their contact list."

"Why should I care? Are you wasting my time? Get to the Booker part!"

"Instead," he continued quickly, "they volunteered access to their next event in Vancouver taking place in a few weeks' time, and perhaps to subsequent events. We would get more cash on an ongoing basis. I was about to push back, as the list is worth more in the long run than the cash but had a look at the provisional guest list. Your Mr Booker and partner are on there as having accepted the invitation. It seems Booker was a schoolboy acquaintance of Max Stone, the man we are extorting, and Max is the brother of Marcy Stone, Booker's girlfriend."

Now this was interesting. Could it be a trap? As far as I knew, Booker didn't even know I existed and was blindly investigating who attacked him and his business interests. Could this Max be making a move against the mafia? Ex-forces operative against thugs? He might fancy his chances.

"Antoni, let's play it out. Have your men accept the terms, for now. Plan it out in the same way we have for all of the other events."

"Yes, Talan," he replied.

"Cochrane, a chance to redeem yourself. I want security at the event to be significantly upgraded. Who can you bring to the table to ensure we control the event completely?"

"The Secret Service are the best, but I don't have authority to detach them from the Presidential detail to put at your disposal. The next best would be private security contractors, many of whom are ex-Secret Service."

"I see President Millar in three days, so let me see how generous I can convince him to be. But in the meantime, prepare a plan to use your mercenaries in case I am unsuccessful."

19: A HINT OF BLUE

[Ethan] – Jeff shuttled us up to Glasgow, Scotland, dropping us off there. Then he headed off via Greenland, then Ottawa, Winnipeg, and eventually to Vancouver. We swapped over to a Dassault Falcon 7x, which had the range to reach Vancouver in one hop, even heading farther north than strictly required to give US airspace a wide berth. Talan appeared to have tapped into some serious US military capability, which made us particularly nervous. We would beat Jeff home by nearly 24 hours, but we wanted the Phenom's semi-stealth capability nearby. In fact, Darcy was working with her defence contacts on the feasibility of adding anti-missile defences similar to those used by Airforce One.

We were nearing Iceland when we connected via satellite into our update conference. The gang was all over the place, with Gia, Max, and Jim in Chicago; Courtney and Moy Lei soon to touch down in Nevada; and everyone else at home base in Vancouver. Marcy and I shared our update, then handed the floor over to the others.

"The hit in Japan was Yakuza," said Moy Lei, who was providing the next update. "Three separate assassins, each unaware of the other, all signalled simultaneously according to my mother's contacts. It was carried out to settle a debt to a Toronto triad boss, who was acting on behalf of the Polish mafia." This information was coming from Mochizuki Chiyome, Moy Lei's mother and head of probably the scariest and most secretive clan of assassins in North America. Many months ago, Chiyome had hired the Booker and Stone Detective Agency to locate Moy Lei, which is how we met.

"From what Kelsie and I have been able to gather from our surviving clan members, as well as various contacts," put in Courtney, "all of the assassinations were carried out by either US intelligence or organized crime resources. It would appear Talan has forged an alliance between the two groups. She also appears to have effectively severed my connection to US and

Canadian leaders, whom I have had influence over for some time and who would have been in a position to help me."

"This has obviously been a well-thought-through plan to remove Le Perjure," I added. "Do we know her motivation?"

"I suspect it is as obvious as it appears, Ethan. She is a power-hungry woman, determined to break free of her duty to the clan, and without the morals to go about it in a non-destructive way. She may have additional longer-term plans, but her freedom and being the most powerful person on the planet would be an end-goal in itself for Talan. I imagine she will graduate to starting her own dynasty, focussed on solidifying control and her power base."

"Your typical Bond villain, then," chuckled Max, then adding, "I have a question for the Nimbus on the call, I suppose. You haven't seen the video of her attack on us, but something was troubling me, which recently came into focus. Talan can be seen in the shots, and presumably she is immune to her own sexual broadcasting. But there were several others unaffected, such as the camera crew and security guards. I didn't think your power worked in such a targeted fashion. Can someone explain?" The silence that followed was telling in itself. Eventually Courtney stepped in.

"You are quite right, Max. I could drive a room to such behaviour, but it would be all non-Nimbus that would be affected; we Adepts can generally fend off each others' compulsions unless faced by a more significantly more powerful Nimbus. It's a broadcast, not a targeted effect. Talan appears to have another new trick in addition to being able to hide her mind. Jim, your technique relies on the consumption of a shared chemical to amplify the effect. Are there chemicals that block your power, or – in a room where some had, and some hadn't ingested the chemical – allow such a pronounced difference?"

"Aside from what Naomi is working on, I've never heard of a blocker. I don't think I could finesse a room as she appears to have done, but perhaps someone with more skill than me could.

But Talan has never had to rely on chemicals, so it is a stretch to think she is already better at it in a short time than I am, having practised for over fifty years. I would bet there is something else going on. I'll think on it."

We heard a phone chime over the link. Then Max and Gia whispered to each other before Max shared that they had just heard from Jakub that their proposal was accepted. They were to head to Vancouver to set up the event, and a contact would be in touch to ensure the arrangements were as the mafia required.

"They've taken the bait," finished Max.

"Perhaps," answered Marcy. "But that doesn't mean Talan will appear. If she is suspicious, she might settle for an assassination attempt instead. Pay a third party."

"We must develop a water-tight plan," I said. "There will be a lot of potential collateral damage if they decide to put a missile through the window. Max, can you spearhead a plan for us? As usual, whatever you need, you'll get. What else? Anyone?"

"SkyLoX and I believe we have located the data and back-ups of the blackmail material," put in Kelsie. "We can delete the primary copy remotely, but for the back-ups, which are housed on write-protected media in a laboratory in Venice, we need to get a resource into the facility to get physical access. We did look at options of remotely manipulating the electrical systems in the building to start a fire and turn off their fire suppression, but there are too many fail-safes to be certain of destroying the video files completely."

"And is that the only back-up?" I asked.

"We believe so, according to logs and the way the system is configured, but we are still doing our due diligence."

"So, we could destroy the material today, but risk missing a back-up, and then we lose the chance to kill the threat entirely. On the other hand, if we wait, additional copies could be made. And again, we lose the chance to destroy them. Correct?" asked Marcy.

"That is the balance, yes. And there is always the chance there were offline, memory-stick copies made from the camera before uploading to the cloud, of course. That wasn't how they were operating in Chicago, but we don't know if that holds true across the board."

"Would a reasonable approach be to wait until we are ready to strike at the Silent Souls Vancouver event? Take everything down in one coordinated set of strikes?" asked Gwen.

"With respect, Gwen," I answered, seeing a path of action emerging, "I don't think that is the right way to look at this. Each day this continues, criminals are exercising their leverage over the authorities. Many people are suffering terribly at their hands. Imagine if they had been successful at getting their hands on the Silent Souls' victims list, for example. While your suggestion might be best for our agenda, I think we need to move faster for the great good. And I see an additional advantage in moving much earlier..."

"You want to make it even more personal for Talan," cut in Marcy, reading my mind. "You want to cripple her organization and make it obvious it was us so she can't resist coming in person to Vancouver to get you."

"That's risky," gasped Jim. "That's brilliant," said Max, at the same time.

"If you do it right, I think she will certainly react," put in Courtney. "She is driven by rage and vindictiveness more than anything."

"How are we doing with identifying the list of blackmail victims, Kelsie?" asked Marcy.

"I think we have most of them. Once you see the pattern, it's not difficult, really."

"Here is what I think we need," I said, feeling ready to put a strawman of a plan on the table for the team to pick at and flesh out. "Max will focus on the Vancouver event; that has to be airtight. Gia and Kelsie will work up a plan to contact all of the victims. Do a trial run with the Police Commissioner who visited you. What was his full name?"

"Commissioner Gordon. Yep, truly. Don't say anything, we even had a laugh with him about it. He said with that as a family name and being with the police, where else would he end up but commissioner," chuckled Max.

"OK, sound out the good commissioner on what he would do if we convinced him he was free from the leverage. I hope we can convince all victims who would be able to strike back at the mafia to do so, in a coordinated fashion. If Gordon is game, we can move on down the list across the country. We should plan a coordinated take-down of the mafia, timed for the moment we destroy the back-ups and delete the main copies. That's your job Gia, if you will lead it?"

"What if there are still some memory-stick copies, Ethan?" asked Naomi.

"Ensure people are aware, but stress that we think it's unlikely. And stress, too, that even if a few people are still at risk, if we take the gangs down hard enough, there will be no one to use the material."

"What about the facility in Venice?" asked Kelsie.

"Marcy and I will pick up what we need in Vancouver and carry on straight to Italy. We will take Jim with us, and I would like to give these delta-blockers a try if our plan calls for them. We have some intelligence gathering to do and need to work up a detailed plan. Max, I'd like you to look over it once we have it worked out."

"What about us?" asked Courtney.

"We need to keep you moving and out of Talan's sights. Once you've finished at Creech Airforce Base, do you think you could get to Europe or Russia? You will be safer there, I imagine."

"I could, I guess, but I am not planning to let you and your team fight my battles and take all of the risks. Talan has a base somewhere, and I aim to find it. I'll keep moving, but I'll follow the Creech thread towards her as far as I can." There was silence on the call. My team were not used to dissent, I suppose.

"I respect that, Courtney, as that's exactly what I would do, too. We all would. My only request is that you consider my resources at your disposal. If you need something, Kelsie will arrange it: You only need to ask."

"That's more than generous, Ethan. Thank you."

"Hey, we *are* family, right? Literally." Everyone laughed. "I figure we could be in position in Venice in 48 hours. So, let's tentatively aim for 4 am Venice time, two days from now, as our action date. We can adjust from there. Anything else?"

"We have a couple of things from the lab," put in Naomi. "Firstly, Darcy debugged the blockers, and got an additional 20% size reduction, yet added almost 45 minutes to the battery. They run for almost an hour now. It might get better, but use that as a planning assumption for the Silent Souls event, Max.

"Secondly – you might recall – the day this adventure kicked off, I mentioned we had been experimenting with replicating Gia's fast speed. I think Max said he was first in line to try to take on Gia with the potential enhancement." A rare nod to humour from buttoned-up Naomi. She continued. "We are ready for someone to test it, and I don't think I can put it through the normal FDA channels."

"Are there any side effects, that you know of at least? How does it work?" asked Gwen. I suspect she knew the answer but proudly wanted her girl to show off a little.

"Most people think," began Naomi, "that the brain consumes the output of the optic nerves at a constant rate. In other words, if your eyes are open, there is a steady stream of information that the brain is processing. Recent studies using brain imaging have proven it is more like a series of snapshots, almost like frames on old movie reels. Think of two scenarios: As people get older, they often feel time moves faster and faster. This is because the rate of these snapshots decreases as we age, partly due to the neurology around aging, but also partly due to experience. We can solve visual problems with less data. The other scenario could be of times of acute crisis, say, an accident. Time seems to slow down. This is because the adrenaline and other reactions cause our brain to order faster snapshots. We need more information. Time seems to slow, and we perceive much more detail. Gia's fast speed is like the latter, increased by a significant factor."

"You mean she is consciously controlling this otherwise autonomic reaction?" asked Darcy.

"Precisely, yes."

"How can we replicate that?" asked Marcy.

"I think with time and training, most of us can do it to some degree. Many athletes across several sports are similar examples. If you practise hard enough, for long enough, it develops naturally. Although, as with most things, some people have a physiological advantage. In Gia's case, her Asian heritage is a factor."

"How so?" asked Max.

"In addition to learning how to do it, it helps if the optic nerve and surrounding eye tissue has more blood flow and, genetically, Asians have that already. We've created a drug from two fairly common, existing, prescription sources. Both are sold today, often in conjunction with each other, so we already know what the side effects are. In our case, the ratio is critical, and no one should ever emulate this without a doctor's supervision, of course. But we think we can prep the body to be ready to switch to fast speed. However, training is still required to make the brain consciously call for the increased bandwidth available."

"What are the drugs?" asked Darcy, more interested than the rest of us, of course. But we indulged her.

"One is a non-addictive amphetamine. The other is Sildenafil, in a significantly higher dose than your typical prescription."

A hearty, deep voice boomed laughter down the line. It took a moment to realize it was Jim. We asked him what was so funny, but he had lost control to the point he couldn't talk, and any attempt was like laughing in church: You just can't stop.

"Does anyone know why Jim's lost his shit?" asked Max, a little impatiently. Gwen and Darcy had joined Jim and were no use, so Naomi tried to bring us back together, with her sternest voice, which – in hindsight – didn't help once we were all *in-the-know*.

"I think what *some* of us find so amusing, is that Sildenafil has a few properties and side effects. We are leveraging an enzyme, PDE6, which is an inhibitor that works on chemicals in the blood vessels in our eyes, which control how dilated the arteries are, thus controlling blood flow. When PDE6 is introduced, it inhibits the process of contracting the arteries. So, the blood vessels dilate, more blood flows, and sets the condition for fast speed to be successful."

"I still don't get it," said Marcy.

"When the vessels relax, some people experience temporary cyanopia; they see a blue or cyan tinge to things. Gia gets that often." Naomi was getting uncomfortable, so I prompted her to continue.

"And...?"

"Well, that's PDE6. The drug is better known for its other enzyme, PDE5, which does the same for a quite different part of the anatomy. Well, for men at least. Sildenafil is typically sold under the brand Viagra." There was a short silence before we all joined Jim and the others.

"So, I will have much faster reactions, but have to fight with a huge erection?" put in Max. The conversation digressed from there for a while. Eventually, even Naomi lost her professional demeanour, but eventually pulled us back together.

"*ANYWAY*, as I was saying, we are ready to start testing, and I think Max wanted to get Gia on the mat first..." Laughing erupted again, and the call ended with very little additional productivity.

*

We had another seven hours to kill on the flight, and so Marcy and I got down to work with the plans Kelsie had transferred to our laptops for the Venice location. The site was a commercial data centre owned by Condatado, a private company that was part of a succession of shell companies. SkyLoX had provided enough information to convince us the site was an Italian organized crime facility, which hides in plain sight offering legitimate services covering the many servers that host their dark web and criminal data.

Although SkyLoX couldn't delete the blackmail video remotely, she had hacked the security video system and we could see staff and guards going about their work; we determined that every angle was being observed. The windows were covered with heavy steel shutters and the entrances, including the loading bay, had doors that would resist a sizable explosion. This place was built to keep the Guardia di Finanza, Italy's military police, at bay while incriminating data was deleted in the event of a raid. Even their electricity supply came from three separate, redundant feeds, backed by redundant roof-top generators.

We considered unleashing Jim's Adept power on them at a shift change when staff were coming and going through the door, or when the loading bay was open for a delivery. But we worked out that each potential access point had two sets of doors, which could not both be open at the same time, and the mantrap was monitored by a remote, off-site team who controlled the doors.

We were at a loss and I called Max, who suggested we check out where the data centre gets its cooling from. Modern servers create so much heat, there would be large vents somewhere that might be weak points.

As we neared Vancouver, we made a little progress. There were two sets of vents. A bank of air vents on the north side of the four-story building tucked just below the roof line. As far as we could tell it was covered with thin metal bars. An unlikely option. We were beginning to think we would have to dynamite the building.

Then we spotted the second vents designed to draw cooling water from Venice's canal system. Located five feet below the surface the ducts bring in water which then passes through a series of heat exchangers before being expelled through another set of ducts on the far side of the building. On the exit side, there were inspection hatches with padlocks that looked more like something we could defeat. Six hours later, we had a plan and we had picked up Jim, a protection team, some equipment, and fresh clothes, and were back in the air, Italy bound.

20: A SPRITZ OF PERFUME

[Gia] – I packed Max off to Vancouver with mixed feelings. He was understandably protective of me – I would normally kick his ass for showing it – but what had happened to us over the last few days had shaken me more than I could imagine. I had long since come to terms with the trauma of my youth, keeping the toxic residue locked in a tidy mental box, which had been torn open and tipped out into my lap. Having fought hard for my independence from the trade – seizing my life back – I had both softened and hardened; I now discovered that my confidence was brittle and my hard-as-nails shell, thinner than I knew. I hung onto Max for a good minute before chasing him out of the hotel-room.

Half an hour later, I was outside of Chicago police headquarters. The building is a blocky four stories of muted browns, greys, and glass behind four tall flagpoles carrying US, State, City, and military force flags. I didn't have an appointment, but I had an attitude. I marched up to the building's reception desk and was directed to the top floor. I negotiated my way through the metal detectors – I left my metal weapons in the car with Roxy but had a ceramic stiletto in my boot – and it was remarkably easy to find my way into the outer office of Commissioner Gordon. Getting past Ms Sales on reception was a good deal tougher. Two officers stood either side of the door to the inner sanctum, but they were not as menacing as Gordon's gate keeper, who had a glare that would shrivel a dragon.

"I don't have an appointment, but it is urgent I see the commissioner," I said, with authority.

"Everything he touches is urgent, young lady. What is it about?" We gazed at each other, and I swear she hadn't blinked since I stepped out of the elevator. I glanced at the guard to her left, and he looked embarrassed and deferential.

"It's confidential. Please tell the commissioner it relates to his meeting at The Folly with Gia Braekhus and Max Stone."

Something in my best shit-kicking tone must have annoyed her, because she just glared back at me, with an *is-that-all-you-got* expression. She waited me out. I played a hunch.

"I have a message from Jakub." I hoped the mafia had set things up so that they had ready access to the head of the police and that Gordon was told to ensure his staff would not be an impediment.

"Hold on," she said, instantly switching to friendly professional mode so fast my head spun. This woman was crazy. I liked her more and more with each second. She didn't use the intercom; instead she rose and walked through to Gordon's office. Twenty seconds later, three men emerged looking harried, with Ms Sales hot on their heels ensuring they didn't dally. "Go right on inside Ms Braekhus," she smiled. "Let me know if you need coffee."

I stepped between the guards and into a short corridor that opened into a wider anteroom where two men and two women sat, attending to the commissioner's needs. Gordon was at his office door, looking angry and not the least welcoming. But he held out his hand in a stony-faced greeting. I met his hard grip, and we stepped into his office. He closed the door behind us.

Gordon was at least six foot four and towered over me menacingly. He didn't appear to be trying to intimidate me; he was just angry, and I guessed that with each day, his predicament was eating away at him. His long face was topped with a shaved dome. His narrow jaw and chin made his head appear oddly triangular. It echoed his torso, which was a muscular, broad chest atop a narrow, fat-free waist. I couldn't see a six-pack through his plush, cotton shirt but I didn't doubt he was ripped. His tailored grey suit was sharp, and subtly set off his black skin. Technically, people of colour at the darkest end of the spectrum are not black, but a very dark brown, but I think Gordon might be the only truly black-skinned person I had ever met. His bright eyes were locked on me, his lips pursed together, his patience stretched, waiting for me to get to the point of my visit.

"Commissioner," I said in a soft, conciliatory tone, "before you shoot me, you should understand I am here as your friend, not your enemy. I have information I think you will want to hear. Can we sit?" He stared at me for a while, understandably skeptical.

"Denise – Ms Sales – said you had a message from Jakub," he prompted pointedly, not ready to let his guard down.

"I don't, but I needed something to get me past your gate keeper. Is she as fierce as she seems?" He laughed suddenly, his face lightening up several shades and relief transforming his features from steel to perhaps a soft iron.

"Sometimes I'm scared to leave my office," he chuckled, ushering me to the sofa off to the side of his desk. He took the matching chair to its side. "Look, I'm sorry. I guess you are in as much trouble as I am. I'm betraying my duty only because of the threat to my family, but it's tearing me apart. How are you and... Max was it?... doing?"

"The same. There is an evil and wrongness to this ugly situation that sickens me. And in the spirit of the trust I hope we can form, I will share that in my early life I was forced into prostitution, so I don't use words like evil and ugly lightly." I hadn't realized I had paused, lost in self-loathing for a moment, until he spoke.

"I'm sorry. That's hard. That explains your involvement in Silent Souls, which I greatly admire. I had a sister we lost to drugs ten years ago who was on the streets for a while... How can I help you, Ms Braekhus?"

"Gia, please."

"Then it's Wil. Short for Wilbur."

"Here's the thing, Wil. I'm looking for some help and your take on my proposal as to how everyone being victimized can escape the trap that we find ourselves in," I paused.

"That will be a neat trick. My *wife* doesn't even believe me. She thinks I have had an affair, am a closet swinger, and got my hand caught in the nookie jar. Me!"

"I've come to you Wil' because I've done my homework on you. Career, personal life...you name it. And you have a spotless record of clean living and integrity. I think you will give me a straight answer. If I presented you with a plan to take down the mafia, would you feel compelled to tell them? My plan includes protection for your family and the loved ones of anyone who joins us."

"Honestly? I would like to say I would keep your secret, but my decision would be based on exactly what you said: My family's safety."

"Good. We thought so. Then I'll take the chance and tell you." I had a sudden idea, switched direction, and asked, "But first, how are things at home? Your wife is angry, yes, but what is she doing about it? I know it's personal, but let's trust each other a bit," I pressed.

"We've done nothing but argue, and when I left this morning, she was packing her bags with no intentions of coming back." He looked lost and dejected, an expression he probably had never had on his face before, I felt certain.

I asked Wil to bear with me, and I messaged Courtney, who was at the airport. I was relieved when she advised she hadn't taken off yet. We swapped a couple of messages and she agreed with my idea.

"Wil, all of the victims acted the way they did because they received a dose of a new date-rape drug." This was the story we had agreed on, to protect the Adepts. "It's released in an aerosol form. Where ruffies make the victim compliant, passive, and almost knocks them out, this does the opposite. It's an uber-aphrodisiac."

"That would explain a lot. I had no way to account for my behaviour. But if my wife told me the same story, I would still be highly skeptical too, wouldn't you?"

"I would, true. But what if I told you I have a small sample, and she could experience it, under safe, controlled conditions. If I were her, my opinion of you would switch from slimeball to rape victim. My idea would be to offer any victim the option to have their family try a tiny sample and/or get as much counselling as they need to make things as right as they can get. All at no cost. And that is in addition to moving them all to a safe location for the duration."

"If there is a drug out there that can do what you say, society is screwed. Just carrying it could be considered attempted rape. I also know a lot of women who always wanted the female Viagra, too. The possibilities..."

"Hold on. The mafia doesn't know it yet, but we are almost positioned to take their supply off the market. It is our intention to destroy it all. Call your wife now, before she leaves, and explain. Tell her we will pick her up shortly and let her experience this for herself. Let's see if we can save your marriage. This will indicate if we are on the right path to convince others to help."

Wil nodded, so I stepped out into the anteroom. Ten minutes later, a wet eyed Wil strode out of his office – buttoning his suit jacket – with a renewed purpose.

"Have my car brought to the front," he said to Ms Sales, as he rushed by. Her eyes met mine, and I could see she deduced from his upbeat attitude that I had somehow helped her boss, and how much she had realized he was being tortured with something. She smiled and looked just a little less scary.

When we were in the car, with the privacy screen in place between us and his driver, I took out a state-of-the-art scanner and checked for bugs. Since SkyLoX had checked into the Wil's office's records I knew his office was swept daily, but the car was only scanned weekly. I didn't share that tidbit. Instead, I started to explain the rest of the plan.

"In less than 48 hours, we plan to delete all copies of the blackmail videos." I let that sink in.

"How could you do that?"

"Full disclosure: Some cards I am going to keep to myself, to save you from a conflict of interest. For example, hypothetically, if I had hacked into the criminal network, you would have to consider that a crime as it would require a warrant from a judge to be legal, correct?"

"That's right, but I don't see me arresting you for it."

"I hope not but forgive me if there are some gaps in my story. Silent Souls has some interesting connections, and Jakub picked on the wrong people. He just doesn't know it, yet. Max and his sister Marcy are ex-forces who have spent a great deal of their lives fighting abuse and sex trafficking. Marcy and her partner, Ethan, are silent partners in Silent Souls. Ethan, aside from being a multi-billionaire of a very altruistic nature, also has several business interests in the military-intelligence space. You won't believe the funding and capabilities he is ready to bring to bear to take these guys down."

"That's incredible, but he can't accomplish what law enforcement won't even take on. I wish he could, but I don't see it."

"Law enforcement is hamstrung by rules he isn't, and his funding doesn't have to compete with other departmental priorities. And he is not afraid to act, as he is well protected. You as individuals can't say the same, sorry." I felt genuinely sorry for him, recalling how I was blackmailed into doing things to protect my friend Jing when I was a street hooker in Alicante.

"No, and don't be. That is true. I'm scared for my family."

"What we are trying to set up is that the moment we destroy the leverage against you, we simultaneously offer everyone protection. We will do this regardless, but what we hope in return is that people like you, the victims in a position to take down the mafia quickly, will act instantly and aggressively."

"If I'm following, you are saying I will have my relationship heading back onto the right track, and for as long as Ethan will fund it, my family will be safe. And the leverage will be destroyed. Those circumstances would certainly free me to act without fear, but what evidence will I act on? I have to prove blackmail, and that would be hard without the drug. And even then, there is no proof we were slipped the drug. Or by whom. I would be ready to act but am powerless to. And we won't want to submit these videos as evidence, either."

"We agree and were thinking along a different line. Each jurisdiction will receive a package detailing a large amount of information about the mafia's other business interests, and nothing about their extortion using the drug. We know some people may have already been forced to commit additional crimes, which further compounds matters, and we would do our best to help in those matters, if the mafia tries to leverage that, too."

"That's great, but reading between the lines, these packages of information were obtained through illegal, if laudable, means. No judge will serve warrants for us to move on the mafia using that approach. And without warrants, it would take months to take any meaningful action."

"Ah...unless each jurisdiction had several members of the bench who were also blackmail victims. The blackmailer's playbook included such people at all of the events across the US and Canada. And we have their names, as well as those of most – if not all – of the other victims. We can use that against the mafia. Still illegal, but I'm sure many a blind eye will be turned. Admittedly, when this gets to court later on, things might get messy, but by then the underworld power vacuum will have been filled by others, and the mafia might prefer to be safe in jail than return to the streets."

"If you can do all of this, I would go for it. For sure."

We pulled up at Wil's house in the suburbs and his wife was standing on the sidewalk waiting for us. Her arms were wrapped tightly across her body, and her eyes were streaming tears. Her expression said she didn't believe a word of Wil's explanation. When I hopped out and offered to sit in the front so she could sit with Wil, she refused, and it was clear she was suspicious that I was one of the women he had cheated with. And maybe I was, although not on the video snippet we had been shown.

She climbed up into the front seat of the black Escalade SUV, and we drove in silence out to the airport. On arrival, we parked in a 'No Waiting' zone, but the driver briefly flashed his police lights to let security know we were on police business. We stayed in the car, and Wil asked his driver to get out and step away from the vehicle. A few minutes later, Courtney stepped out of the private terminal entrance glancing around nervously – worried about assassins, I was sure – and walked over to the car. I introduced her as one of Ethan's chemists, as per our quickly texted plan.

Courtney climbed into the driver's seat, shut the door, and pulled out a small vaporizer from her pocket. From our hurried texts to put this ruse together, I knew it was actually Moy Lei's perfume. Following a short explanation of the procedure, Courtney held a cloth over her nose and mouth with one hand, then sprayed a tiny amount of the substance within the vaporizer – the date-rape-drug – into the interior of the car.

After a few seconds, I felt an intense sexual urge. Even though I knew it was coming, and was revolted by it, I couldn't resist it. I wanted Courtney, Wil, his wife...hell, I was thinking of calling the driver back over. Anyone. And as quickly as it arose, the urge abated.

Wil's wife's eyes were wide with lust, then disbelief, and then guilt. She pushed open the car door and vomited. By the time we had pulled ourselves together, Courtney had rejoined Moi Ley in the terminal and now both were in the air heading for Nevada. The Gordons were tearfully hugging each other, while I sat up front with a very confused and uncomfortable driver. Who, if nothing else, was wondering how he would explain the strong smell of Issey Miyake perfume in which he found his chair, and now himself, smothered.

"Gia, I think you have us on board, but how on earth do you think you will convince all of the others to join us by tomorrow night?" asked Wil'.

"Well actually, I was hoping you would do that for us. By tomorrow we want every victim in Chicago on board, and we approached you because you are known locally as the poster boy for integrity. To retain the element of surprise and not cause the mafia to make additional copies of the videos, we won't inform the rest of the victims in other regions until the operation is under way and the videos are destroyed. We can't risk tipping off the bad guys. But we want to make a video to explain things to the victims, which will go out to them once the plan is in motion. We hope once they see this video, starring you and the Chicago chapter of this revolt, they will get on board quickly."

21: VENICE

[Marcy] – The debilitating pain from having our skulls poked open to insert the delta-blocker's slow-release capsule began once the anaesthetic wore off – about an hour after the insertion procedure – until the swelling reduced. We planned to penetrate the data centre at 4 am, and so we initiated the skull-cracking procedure – as we called it, for dramatic effect - at 11 pm. The capsule would release the chemicals slowly, protecting our minds from Jim's attack on the gangsters from 3 am until about 6 am. The dosage regulation units with their wires reaching from our packs to the sticky pads on our skulls would last an hour on batteries, but we should be in and out in about 45 minutes.

We had arrived in Venice in the early hours of the previous morning on a private jet into Marco Polo airport. Our team heaved our large pile of luggage and equipment onto trollies, and we cleared customs without incident, thankfully, considering some of the contents hidden in secret compartments were unusual, to say the least.

We pushed our gear through the labyrinth of corridors to the boat dock where our water transport awaited. The journey was awkward because we were transporting a twelve-foot long, heavy, steel pole, which was integral to our plan. It took a little back-and-forth to get it into our private launch, but we were soon on our way across the open water to Venice City proper. Although we appeared to be in a very wide bay, there were many shallows and so we followed the dredged paths marked by the frequent wooden posts.

We tracked up the north-eastern side of the tightly clustered group of 120 small islands that comprise Venice – each island joined to its neighbours only by small, humped bridges – and turned into the small channel next to the large train station. This brought us to the Grand Canal, the city's largest waterway that essentially bisects Venice and is its main thoroughfare. We bobbed our way through the charming 1200-

year-old architecture – which was eerily quiet at 3 am, as over 50% of tourists stay outside of Venice and only travel in during the day – and by 4 am turned off the Grand Canal into Rio di San Luca, along which our apartment awaited. We had chosen this apartment specifically because it was within two blocks of our target.

While Jim and most of the team ascended the stairs to the apartment, Ethan, Sara, Nell, and I transferred the steel pole straight into a gondola – which we had hired for the duration of our stay – and lay it along the deck, hidden from prying eyes. Our Gondolier, Alberto, helped us and asked no questions. Max's European contacts put us in touch with Alberto, who had carried out several small missions on behalf of Interpol and was deemed to be a confidential and reliable resource, unconnected with the Italian crime syndicates.

Sara was part of our protection team and had a very interesting past, which she had shared with me one night six months ago over a beer after she had joined me on a training run up the Grouse Grind in Vancouver. The Grind is a dirt and stone trail up Grouse Mountain, on Vancouver's North Shore, which climbs 2,800 feet over 1.8 miles. There is a bar at the top and the views are stunning whenever the weather is clear, but particularly good at sunset over a sweat-quenching beer.

Sara was born in the UK and grew up in a diving community. Her ambition was to join the British Special Boat Service. The SBS is the sister arm of SAS, the infamous army unit. Sara joined the navel cadets as a teen when the UK military were discussing opening the ranks of their special forces to women. This was twenty years ago, but it transpired that after she had joined that the modernization took much longer; the SBS only started accepting female candidates in 2018, and still have yet to see a female pass through into active SBS service. Sara had joined the navy but as these delays dragged on, she became disenfranchised and left the forces as a Lieutenant.

THE NUDEST DETECTIVE

Sara fought her way into the male-dominated work of deep-saturation diving for the oil industry – she is a glutton for punishment – and made good money for a decade. Then, as she says in her own words, she wised up: Why fight for the respect of idiots with dicks, diving in freezing water filling her lungs with poison and spending days of her life in saturation chambers when the Mediterranean Private Yacht industry was crying out for crew with her training. For six years Sara worked on private yachts in security roles, protecting the rich and sometimes the famous, and when required, could double as a diver for maintenance, or to train rich kids how to SCUBA safely.

It was when Sara was on one of Ethan's yachts that he discovered her – yes, he was one of the rich who wanted to learn some advanced SCUBA deep-level techniques – and he plucked her away to work on his Vancouver security detail, which she has been doing ever since. She was ideal for the mission we had to nail over the next 24 hours.

Alberto didn't know our plan but had agreed to work with us due to the rather large fee we were paying. He punted us slowly through several dark, narrow canals and under several bridges. Almost as if we were sightseeing, as opposed to embarking on a deadly mission, Alberto pulled out a flashlight and shone it onto a wall revealing some graffiti of a child in a life jacket holding a neon pink flare. In his broken English he told us he had helped the artist who painted it – who had stood on his gondola to work, as there was no pathway where the wall disappeared into the murky water – but he later found out Banksy had claimed the artwork. The debate still rages as to if Banksy was protesting the damage cruise ships are doing to Venice, or if it was a protest about the deaths of thousands of migrants escaping across the Mediterranean from the Middle East. Alberto thoroughly enjoyed refusing to describe the artist, which gave us the confidence that he could be trusted to be discreet.

We turned a final corner into the gap between two properties that loomed above us into the darkness. It was almost too narrow for our gondola and it was blocked ahead. We would eventually need to reverse back out the way we came. Alberto kept us in position while Ethan, Sara, and I manoeuvred our pole to the edge of the boat. The pole was wrapped many times in canvas, like toilet paper surrounds the cardboard tube. It had a cable at each end, and a third in the centre, the latter preventing the canvas from unrolling off the pole. The cables were three feet long, and had a fixing plate secured at the end. Ethan pulled the cable at his end and placed the plate against the wall of the building on our left; then, using a nail gun powered by a compressed air cylinder we had brought with us, he drove two thick bolts through the plate and into the building, securing the plate in place. He passed Sara the nail gun, and she repeated the process at the other end of the pole, making sure it was located at the same height above the water as Ethan's.

The three of us then slowly lifted the pole over the side and let it slip into the water, where it hung parallel with, and just under, the surface. I then used the same nail gun to fix a small device to the wall at the midpoint of the pole, again just above the surface into which the third cable that prevented the canvas unravelling fitted. We inspected our work, and decided it was unlikely to be noticed, as only the three fixing plates and the tips of the cable were above the water line.

We instructed Alberto to take us back to the apartment.

As previously agreed, Alberto disembarked with us and went to one of the rooms, where he would stay until we left without a device to contact anyone. We didn't want to take the risk that Interpol was wrong about him, so this precaution ensured there was no way he could warn anyone of our interest in the building we had just visited.

Ethan and I climbed to the roof to see how the other phase of our preparations were progressing. Jim had overseen the unloading and set-up of several microdrones and two larger

178

communications drones. As we arrived, they were just being launched, and we watched with interest as Kelsie's best drone operative – James, who had travelled with us on the plane – controlled them beside Kelsie from her console, which had been set up on the rooftop bar.

The console boasted a small forest of joysticks and other controls, several keyboards, and four screens. We stood behind and watch the operation unfold. First, a large communication drone wound up, then leaped up into the sky and was soon lost in the dark, with the sound dying almost instantly. On the screen we saw the view from the drone, which quickly travelled the few blocks to hover 600 feet above the data centre. It was set to auto-hover, and its purpose was to relay signals to other drones to ensure they were free of the interference of the brick buildings that composed the Venice skyline. The second communications drone would zip up to replace it if the mission took longer than expected and battery life became a concern.

Next, a micro-drone followed its big sister up and we watched as it found its way to the data centre's roof. Once there, James dropped the drone slowly over the roof at the west side and swivelled the camera so we could see the wall of the building. Per the plans we had studied, we could see two six-foot by six-foot ventilation shafts. Each shaft was capped off with chicken wire, to keep the ubiquitous pigeons from nesting inside. James piloted the drone to hover within two inches of the vent, then pressed a small button on his control. We heard a muffled 'bang' echo over the rooftops, and the screen went black. We didn't know if the small, shaped charge of C4 explosives embedded in the drone had done the job, but we had several similar drones to throw at it if necessary. We knew the noise would be noticed but didn't think anyone would be able to link it to any nefarious activity on our part, as the remains of the drone would have dropped into the canal.

Fifty seconds later, a second drone was hovering in front of the vent, and we were relieved to see a gaping hole in the wire. James pressed another button, and a six-foot-long wire dropped from the bottom of the drone; then he drove the little copter in through the hole, into the shaft. He landed just inside the grate, leaving the wire trailing outside. This would be the antenna that would assist in the relay of signals within the vent, which was essentially a metal Faraday cage, impervious to radio signals.

Two slightly larger drones followed their family over the roof tops and, one at a time, they entered the vent. James navigated them as close as he dared to the large, slowly revolving blades of the intake fan. He spun down their rotors, and at a command, the first drone opened a small hatch on the cargo container it carried, and tiny particles of vegetation were drawn into the building's airflow. These flora particles had been grown in Vancouver, and Jim had also consumed a good quantity of them earlier. We knew that the power of Adepts like Jim was greatly magnified when his targets consumed the same plant matter as Jim, providing a quantum connection and leveraging entanglement physics. This technique was proven to provide an efficient conduit for him to influence the people in the building when the time came. We still didn't know why female Adepts didn't need this assistance.

Now that we had the concept working, the six-remaining particle-carrying drones took off and hid themselves in the shaft with their sisters until we needed them. With nothing else to do, we recovered the communications drone and went to get some shut eye.

Our bedroom was small but well appointed, with white plaster walls and thick timber beams across the ceiling. Ethan looked at me with an expression that said *little Ethan is interested in playing, but the rest of me is knackered*. I agreed with big Ethan and left the kinky games alone for once. But we did manage a slow, cuddly sexual 'night cap' and slept until noon.

After we awoke, we ate fruit and yogurt and then risked playing tourist for an hour, to reconnoitre both the data centre doors and the surrounding area. Next, we walked with Eric, another member of our protection team, over to a building on the far side of Venice near the Arsenale della Biennale, where the building with the door's video surveillance and control was located. Our recce had confirmed that our remotely researched intelligence was sound, and we returned to the apartment to wait. That was twelve hours ago. Following several conference calls with the team in North America, we had confirmed the operations would proceed at 4 am Venice time, which was late evening at home. An hour from now our attack would begin.

The delta-blocker regulation units were six-by-eight-by-eight inches and were tucked neatly into a small backpack. A pair of wires ran up to two little pads, which were stuck with medical adhesive to the point where our necks met our heads; Ethan and I had both had our hairlines shaved to accommodate.

As the drug was released and took effect, we both felt out of sorts; flat and moody. When we turned on the regulator, that odd feeling died away and we were back to our hopped-up-on-adrenalin selves instantly. Next, we experimented with Jim sending emotions at us, gently at first, then turning the volume up in steps. If he hadn't told us he was doing it, and if Sara and Eric hadn't briefly succumbed to the effect next to us, we would never have known. Darcy and Naomi were wonderful. We turned off the units and recharged the little juice we had used, then sent the 'go' order to all of the people involved in the mission.

Up on the roof, James hit a button that caused the device holding the pole's middle cable to be released. The weight of the pole unwound the canvas, like a carpet being spread across the floor, in this case rolling it vertically down into the murk, hanging from the cables above. As it descended, it covered the underwater intakes for the data centre's water-cooling system. Pretty quickly alarms would be sounding as the temperature began to rise.

Sara was already in the water in SCUBA gear, having swum from our apartment's dock to within a few yards of the cooling water's exit point from the data centre. As the current reduced and then stopped, due to the canvas on the other side of the building blocking the inlet, she would be able to slip into the shaft and cut the padlocks securing the maintenance grate with bolt cutters. Five minutes later, she was heading back out of the shaft leaving two small explosive charges behind her, one on each of the impellers that moved the water through the system. When she was clear, she detonated both. This damage would not be fixed quickly.

Courtesy of SkyLoX's hijacked video-feed, we could see that things were heating up in more ways than one inside the data centre. The nightshift workers had become animated as they attempted to deal with the excess heat from the server farm. They switched the rooftop air-cooling into high gear to compensate. When we saw that, James dutifully opened the particle containers, flooding the data centre with plant life mentally linked to Jim.

While all of this was happening, Ethan, Jim, and I walked around to the data centre's main door, and signaled Eric. Eric and two of his colleagues forced their way into the building from where the doors were monitored and controlled and, ten minutes later, called to say that the occupants had been tranquillized: He had control of the doors and had taken all of the security cameras offline. As if to confirm his success, the heavy door in front of us swung opened with a hiss of hydraulics. We turned on our delta-blockers, pulled on gloves, pulled balaclavas down over our heads to hide our identities, and walked in.

Ethan and I had tranquillizer guns drawn and had silenced Glocks in specially extended, shoulder holsters for back-up. But we needed neither. Jim walked through the data centre as if he owned the place, filling the building with mental projections of fear so strong, it triggered the freeze instinct in the lizard brain of each person not wearing a blocker. Everyone we encountered either stood silently, lost in some trance or, in a few cases, had collapsed onto the floor. It was terribly eerie, and I noted Ethan and I were keeping closer together than would be optimal for such an armed breach.

Like most data centres, servers and other equipment was stacked onto row after row of computer racks, with a snake's wedding of cables connecting them all and their lights blinking furiously. We wove our way through this maze to a set of three rows near the west wall, which SkyLoX and Kelsie had determined were where the mafia kept its data. It was caged off from the rest by a sturdy wire fence. I borrowed a swipe card from a technician standing nearby, frozen in his tracks, and we let ourselves in.

SkyLoX had sent us a selection of mini-USB memory sticks and ethernet plugs, along with instructions as to where to plug them into. Once we had done so, we located the servers housing the back-ups of the videos and waited. Ten long minutes later, Jim was starting to show signs of strain from exerting his power with such force.

"How are you doing, Jim?" asked Ethan.

"It's better than in Chicago. We didn't seed the environment there with plant particles like we have here. But I don't think I can keep this up much more than another ten to fifteen minutes."

As if SkyLoX had heard him, Ethan's phone chirped with a message confirming she had deleted both the primary copy of the videos in the cloud and the back-ups here, and we could begin to remove the disk drives from the servers. We looked at the rack, and where – before – all of the disk drives had green lights blinking, the twenty-four of them of interest to us were now blinking red. Ethan holstered his tranquillizer gun, popped out the drives, and put them into the bag he brought along for this purpose. He was about halfway through when a message came through on my phone. I checked and it was instructions from SkyLoX to move two of the memory sticks to a new location. These sticks contained malware that enabled her to bypass the mafia's firewalls, which otherwise kept her out of certain systems. They had to be uploaded strategically and we had apparently placed two where they didn't do what was required. I went and moved her hacking tools as directed, then walked back to see Ethan pop the last drive into the bag. We started to move back towards the exit, taking our time in case SkyLoX needed anything else adjusted. But as we reached the exit doors, she messaged to say she now owned the data centre completely.

We left the building, crossed the piazza outside, weaving quickly down several of Venice's narrow streets emerging at Rio del Palazzo, a relatively broad canal that runs north to south. Sara and most of the protection team met us there in our launch, having cleared everything out of the apartment and releasing Alberto to his business. Once we were aboard, we sped quietly south, past Basilica di San Marco and under the Bridge of Sighs, which connects the interrogation chambers within the Doge's Palace to the New prison where the inmates were house, and out into the main waterway beyond. We turned sharply left and stopped at the first water-taxi pier to pick up Eric and the remaining team members, who were already waiting for us.

Once everyone was aboard, the boat's driver opened up the throttle, lifting the bow high as we picked up speed and headed south. Five minutes later we slowed, and the boat nosed through an archway and into a small dock at the north end of the island of Lido di Venezia. We disembarked and walked the short distance to the Nicelli Airport, which has a very small grass strip adjacent to a concrete ramp where helicopters can land.

We walked quickly over to a Quest Kodiak, a ten-seat plane designed to land and take off on short, unimproved runways. The pilot already had the engine running and warmed up. We threw our gear into the cargo area, scrambled in, and were already rolling down the runway while Ethan was still latching the rear door. We wanted to be out of the country before the police – or worse, the mafia – were aware that anything had occurred.

An hour later, we wound through several steep sided valleys suffused in a pink dawn glow to land at Innsbruck in Austria. The mission left us feeling tired but very pleased with ourselves. Our smugness evaporated when SkyLoX messaged to say she had analysed the data centre logs and had discovered that one additional copy had been made of the backed-up videos. It had been uploaded across the internet, and she was attempting to find out more about where this copy had been saved. All she knew at this point was that it was taken by somebody using very different protocols than Jakub's gang employed, and she suspected it was a government agency.

*

As we flew home, we tracked the progress of what we had come to call the "victim's-rebellion" as it unfolded. Firstly, an email and text message went out to each of the 237 blackmail victims advising them the blackmail material was deleted and offering a mix of counselling and relocation options to protected locations, which Gia had discussed with Commissioner Gordon. Almost everyone responded, and three quarters of them asked for protection for their families. Kelsie had worked hard to put solutions in place for everyone, from villas on private islands to suites on some of the super yachts we could access. We also promised to work on allowing sceptical partners to sample the drug in cases where people thought it would help mend relationship fences.

A few of the victims banded together to form a North American taskforce and invited all of the other victims to join. As we landed in Vancouver eleven hours later, Commissioner Gordon had already organised raids in Chicago. Other jurisdictions were already moving rapidly to gain arrest warrants based on the detailed information we fed them on gangland activities in each city's respective jurisdictions.

Gordon had let Gia tag along when his SWAT team went into the warehouse to arrest Jakub and his cronies. They met resistance and there was a short firefight, but when the dust settled and arrests were made, there was no sign of that gang chapter's leaders Jakub or Clay.

We spent the next 24 hours either sleeping or watching the take down of the Polish Mafia operation across North America. There were many loose ends, but within 36 hours from our drones entering the data centre in Venice, the back of the criminal organization was broken, and Talan had lost a large percentage of her unholy army.

22: MOMENTUM

[Talan] – Antoni had broken the news that his organization was under attack and had since been heads down on the phone, calling everyone he could to form a clear picture of the chaos. He was so immersed in this task that he didn't notice I had additional armed guards brought into the operations room. I had Nikki call Cochrane in from his home, and when he arrived – looking terrified at first – he relaxed when he realized it was the mafia that was in trouble and not him. By the end, he became smug and almost gleeful. That didn't help the rage that I had so far kept at a moderate simmer remain under control, and I glared at him, sending a jolt of fear into the room.

"Give us the room, please! All but Antoni, Cochrane, and Lindi leave. Guards – you wait outside the door, and the rest of you get a meal and return in 30 minutes," I commanded. When the door closed behind the last person, I demanded an update from Antoni, while holding both of their minds tightly to ensure I could detect any deceit.

"Starting in Chicago, I am hearing about extensive search and seizure operations on our places of business, both where we conduct drug, prostitution, illegal gaming, and other activities, as well as on legitimate interests through which we launder money. Even some of our businesses that are wholly legitimate have been visited. Most of the inner circle of leaders in each city have been arrested or, where they were stupid enough to resist the SWAT assisted raids, dead.

"In most cases, we have not been able to get lawyers in to see our people. But for the few that did, we are learning that the police appear to have very detailed information about our operations." He paused and scowled meaningfully at Cochrane and said, "It would appear we have been thoroughly infiltrated and very damaging information has been fed to the authorities."

"I swear it wasn't the US Intelligence Services," blurted Cochrane, looking quickly between Antoni and me. "Do the arrest warrants concern the extortion of high-ranking officials?

187

And why are our blackmail victims not providing cover?" That was a good question.

"No, they don't," replied Antoni, adding with a hollow laugh, "In fact, that piece is conspicuous by its absence. And it appears that many of those we were extorting are leading the charge to attack our operations right across North America. When I call them, they attempt to trace my calls." Then he hesitated again, clearly with more bad news he was reluctant to share, so I injected his mind with some confidence.

"Despite assurances our online resources were bullet proof, it appears that the cloud copy of our blackmail material was deleted at about the time this rebellion began. I have also heard from our cousins in Italy that they believe the data centre where the backups are kept has been compromised. The backups are gone, too."

I lost control of myself and leapt from my chair and into his face, yelling at him, a fleck of spit flying from my mouth onto his brow, "THIS IS COMPLETELY FUCKING UNACCEPTABLE! How can you miserable cretins have fucked this up so entirely, and so quickly?" I knew he had no answer, but I needed to vent.

"I do still have a copy. I downloaded it two days ago to my computer here," he weaseled, desperately seeking some cover from my anger. But it was too late. Part of my detached, objective self watched my lizard-brain self snap and flood both their minds with such emotion that they stood rooted to the spot, unable to physically react to defend themselves. I pulled the ornate cap off the ring on my right-hand middle finger, exposing a short needle dosed with a neurotoxin that would guarantee a slow, painful death, and jammed it into Antoni's neck. As he slipped first to his knees, and then to his stomach as his legs collapsed, I followed him down, yelling about his incompetence and the vengeance I would have. His mouth frothed and his eyes gradually clouded, but I would not free his mind to allow him to make noise. Only as his life force left his body did I release the two men.

"Have someone clean that up," I instructed Cochrane, who had witnessed the whole episode and was near panic himself. "Have the other Poles here killed, and don't make it too fast; they need to suffer. If people fail me, there are consequences. Get more of your resources in to fill their seats. I want a full report and some analysis as soon as possible. We will meet again in three hours, and you better have answers if you don't want to join Antoni."

I turned to storm out, but my eyes settled on Lindi. I had forgotten she was there, keeping my mind safe. Her brown cheeks were streaked with tears and based on her horrified expression, they were tears of anger for my actions, not sadness for Antoni. The judgemental bitch spiked my rage anew, and I slapped her hard enough that she fell onto her ass. She glared up at me. I leaned over her and warned her that if she ever wanted to see her homeland again, she needed to adjust her attitude. I doubt she could understand my words, but my actions were clear, I was sure. I stormed out of the room back to the residence, pausing only to ensure that Lindi had picked herself up and was following me. Until Courtney was dead, I needed this doe-eyed cretin, but I looked forward to ending her life, too.

*

Cochrane didn't have much news three hours later, but he convinced me he was getting organized quickly. There was no meaningful update on Courtney, who I sensed was in the western US somewhere, nor Booker, who I had perceived to be travelling somewhere to the north of Courtney. His home in Vancouver would be about right, I intuited.

In fact, it wasn't until our third meeting that useful information began to come through the US Intelligence Community. Cochrane had come through to the residence for this meeting, and I allowed him to eat with me on the terrace, looking out into the rose garden. I wished the thick screen of trees was not necessary, as it blocked the view out over the Potomac and reminded me of my need to hide, which I was getting very frustrated by. It would be over soon, I reminded myself.

"At last, I have news on several fronts, Talan," he began, looking relieved. "Booker and Stone just landed in Vancouver and made their way through the VIP customs channel declaring they arrived from Dublin. Per your instructions, we are tailing them at a discrete distance, and my last update had them almost back to their home in Yaletown."

"Let's hope he stays put and that you can keep tabs on him this time," I said with some menace, not wanting him to get too comfortable. I savoured him blanching as a result but let him continue."

"Next, we have a sighting of Mademoiselle du Caron." He handed me a photograph. It was a shot of Courtney walking out of an office. She had changed her hair colour and the way she dressed, but I recognized her instantly. "This was taken this morning at Creech Airforce Base, where we controlled the Istanbul strike from. There is no record of her visit, and this picture was discovered by computer facial recognition from Creech's weather-reporting system, as du Caron doesn't appear on the base's security cameras, either. She obviously didn't know about this camera system, so we were lucky we caught her with this angled shot."

"I can guess what she was up to," I said, "but what else have you found out?"

"As there is no physical trace or record of her, aside from this one shot, we have to speculate based on some related information. The drone pilot, Ed Bains, has no memory of meeting her. He logged three hours of his time that morning completing online training, but the training system logs do not show matching activity. There are various security camera malfunctions we can align to the route du Caron likely took. And although she doesn't appear on the security system, a rental car appears in the carpark and vanishes again, without being seen at the security gates or on camera. We did get its plate, however."

"Well, that's something. Go on," I encouraged.

"We've tracked the car back to the airport rental office, where we have video of her getting out and into a black Lincoln Navigator, which is also a rental. No faces are visible, but we can see her and three other individuals who we believe are a protection team."

"Any idea where they are now?"

"Again, using traffic-camera surveillance history, we tracked them to McLellan Palomar airport, where there is a drop-off record for the SUV. A private jet took off 45 minutes later, with a flight plan to Richmond, Virginia. The plane is registered to a company that has an arm's-length relationship with one of Booker's companies. It could be coincidence, but I believe du Caron is working with Booker, though how they are connected we don't know."

"She's following the thread from the assassins, hoping to find me. We will have to make sure she does. What else?"

"Max Stone and Gia Braekhus, Booker's friends who are setting up the event in Vancouver, have popped up again."

"How so?"

"Jakub Nowak was the leader of the Polish mafia chapter in Chicago, and their contact. He was driving to their warehouse just as the SWAT team moved in to take it down. Apparently, he was at a red light, one block away, as SWAT shut the street down right in front of him. He watched the attack unfold then withdrew, but had the light changed a few seconds earlier, he would have been shot or arrested."

"Tell me why I care," I said, hoping he would get to the point instead of talking up his stories to sound important.

"Our friend Braekhus was at the scene and went in alongside the commissioner, who was being extorted by us but was also helping execute the take down, rather than moving to protect us. But that isn't the interesting part. Once he was at his safe house, Nowak started to investigate events leading up to the arrests. He discovered one of his men had some secret video footage taken earlier in the week. It's of a group breaking into the warehouse. The hidden cameras were deployed to identify someone suspected of skimming but caught this instead. Here, watch," he said, passing me his computer tablet.

The 20-second scene showed Stone and Breakhus moving through the building, accompanied by an old African American. The most interesting part was the total lack of reaction from the mafia, who just stood there, trancelike. I knew immediately what I was seeing.

"We don't understand this," said Cochrane, watching my reaction to the video. "It's like the mafia are spellbound. We would guess some sort of mass hypnosis, or a neurotoxin or gas perhaps? The few survivors of the arrests Jakub could reach, who were at the facility when the breach occurred, have no memory of anything unusual."

My lover, Guance, used the same technique to move through crowds facelessly, and I had witnessed it often. I would have known if Stone or Braekhus were Nimbus when I caused them to join the orgy at the Silent Souls event, so the Nimbus must be the third person, the black man. What I didn't understand was why Stone and Braekhus were not trancelike, too. Could this man target his talents like Lindi? Normally only Nimbus are immune to such emotional broadcasts.

"I want close-ups of all three intruders, as detailed as you can get them, and quickly," I commanded. Cochrane relayed the instruction to Nikki via phone, then returned his attention to me.

"Incidentally," he said, almost as an aside, "that is the best video of the intruders, but there are a couple of segments that show them working on computers in the warehouse. We suspect they were hacking in. And it could be where the mafia intelligence was gathered, which led to this rebellion."

Then it hit me: Booker was working with Courtney, and whoever this new Nimbus was, in Chicago. My mind reeled. He was behind this whole effort. He must know about me through

Courtney. I felt him in Europe somewhere at the time the Venice data centre was breached. I was both angry and impressed. This also explained why we had not been able to locate the remaining Le Perjure members. They should have been easy to pick off, cut off from resources, but Booker had taken them under his well-funded wings.

How much did Booker and his gang know? He has already stripped me of my mafia army, and now Courtney is coming to Virginia. Do they know about my grip of US Intelligence? They must suspect.

I know I am not a patient person, and this last year of quietly building my resources had me at my wits' end. I reminded myself that, despite the disaster with the mafia, I was still in the driver's seat. Patience might be the smart move, but I knew I was a creature of momentum at heart. The moment felt like the nexus point, where I must emerge or fail. Sitting back and consolidating for a year is not in me, I know. Booker might be baiting a trap in Vancouver, but I knew I wouldn't avoid it. My personality only really allowed me one way forward, and that was to go and spring their trap. But I would go with overwhelming force and trickery. Anything to win. I wouldn't be stupid and get overly target-focused and miss a flanking attack – as I already had, I realized, with the mafia – so I spent a moment reviewing my base here and asking myself if I was safe. Or did I need to move?

"Antoni said he downloaded a copy of the videos, right?"

"Yes, we found them along with the emails from Jakub detailing what I just showed you on Antoni's laptop. They arrived after Antoni's death."

"Could someone trace the download back to here?"

"Unlikely. It would take a very well-organized hacker. In fact, probably a state actor."

"I want you to arrange a reception for Courtney. Nothing in person, though. She will know immediately if someone near her is watching her directly. Find her transport in advance and put a tracker on it. Get drones in the air and track her remotely. Use roadside camera's, hotel security systems or whatever you need, but stay away from her. And Cochrane, if you lose her, what happened to Antoni will seem pleasant compared to what I will do to you, understand?" He nodded quickly, the sweat that had been on his brow throughout seeming to glisten brighter.

"How are you coming along with the plan to control the Vancouver event?"

"It's booked at Grouse Mountain resort, which overlooks Vancouver, and I have an advanced team in place doing reconnaissance and watching for anything unusual. I've contacted several ex-Secret Service contractors and have begun the process of moving weapons and other assets across the border from Washington State into British Columbia. We have just over a week to put this together."

"Contact Jakub. We need him in place in Vancouver to continue to act as a contact point. We have to assume they know about us, and that this is bait. They will be suspicious of Jakub now that his organization has been destroyed but set him up with a believable cover that he is acting independently, trying to regroup. Don't reveal a link back to us but assume they will suspect there is one."

"If we think this is a trap, why go ahead with it?" asked Cochrane, puzzled.

"We might yet pull out, but let's see if we can find a way to reverse their trap on them. All of the players from Vancouver in one spot is hard to resist. In fact, after my meeting with POTUS tonight, Lindi and I will travel to Vancouver. I don't want to be too close to Courtney when she gets here."

"Do you want us to kill Courtney?"

"Maybe. But watch her for now. I want a plan for two scenarios; one to capture her, the other to kill her."

Nikki stepped out onto the terrace and passed me some large printouts of the three people who had breached the warehouse in Chicago; I studied them for some time. I was looking for anything of use, but especially anything that would explain how non-Nimbus could resist the effect that the African

American was causing on the mafia. I didn't see it until the very last picture. A thin wire ran from Stone's backpack up to his head, leading to what appeared to be a sticky pad, much like doctors use to tape heart monitor wires to patients. I thought about it: *Could someone develop an electrical shield of some sort?*

"Cochrane, you are aware I can control you with my mind. Even I don't know how I do it, but I think Booker might have collaborated with the du Caron bitch to develop some sort of electrical shield. Look here, in this picture. I need to know how to jam or disrupt that shield."

"I have some ideas already. Something we've tested to take down enemy operations centres. I'll research it more and get back to you. I don't have anything else to report. We should get back to the operations centre. There is much to do."

He stood up, and he and Nikki began to leave. I was feeling much better. It had come as a shock to realize how close Booker and du Caron had come to getting the better of me, but now I felt the tables were turning. In fact, I deserved a treat, and it wouldn't hurt to reward this better news.

"No, wait," I said, flooding them both with the sexual urge I myself felt. "Both of you go and use my shower while I finish thinking. I'll be through in ten minutes and expect to see you both naked in my bed by the time I get there." I dismissed them with a wave and went back to looking at the photographs, while I finished off the small bowl of strawberries and cream I had been slowly working on throughout the discussion.

23: A GIFT

[Ethan] — We had slept some on the flight back from Europe, so the first thing we did was collect Elvis and take him for some exercise. Wary of revenge attacks from the mafia, we went to Vancouver's Waterfront Helipad, and I flew us up into the mountains, believing we would be impossible to track. I put down at Wigeon Lake — less than 14 miles to the northeast, nestled behind Coquitlam Mountain — an area that is not easy to approach on foot. Marcy and I lounged on the bank to take stock, while Elvis dug around in the brush, paddled in the cold lake, and nosed up a deer trail to look for adventure.

To get some exercise, and to appease the dog, we hiked about two miles into the hills. We sat down on a large boulder and looked at the stunning scenery. It was amazingly peaceful taking in the valleys, peaks, and towering clouds, with Marcy tucked in under my shoulder. All too soon, it was time to wind our way back to the lake, fire up the helicopter, and return to the battle. We dropped Elvis back into The Crazy Bean and envied the fact he was already asleep in front of the fire before we had our lattes-to-go.

We walked into a group update call to learn that the most interesting news was that Jakub had reached out by email to Gia and Max. He asserted that he still had copies of the blackmail material from Chicago and would expose their activities if the Silent Souls commitment wasn't met. We all recognized it was a bit of a farce and assumed Talan was behind it, as opposed to it being a legitimate attempt by Jakub to extort Gia and Max. We played our part, Gia acting compliantly, and went along with his demands. We were not confident that Talan would show up in person, but we wanted to appear to be playing into her hands.

Next up after the call was a visit to Naomi, who gave us both a thorough medical check, including brain scans and blood work, to ensure there were no adverse reactions to the delta-blocker. We answered many questions that both she and Darcy asked; they also shared that they now had a version of the chemical that could pass through the blood-brain barrier, so the painful skull penetrations were no longer required.

We had a light meal and then returned to the lab, as it was time to test out the fast-speed drug. Max had already tried it and marvelled at the effects, although he was a long way from mastering the benefits the drug brought. There were three steps: get used to the sensation; train your brain to speed up capturing data; and practise fighting when equipped with the faster information flow. This latter step was particularly important, as the timing of our movements, strikes, and blocks were all impacted, and we had to relearn and adjust.

Marcy and I both took the drug, swigging it out of a test tube like teens trying our first shooter. Naomi had added a pineapple flavour which I'm sure would factor into whatever nickname we would eventually come up with for the concoction. It took about 45 minutes before we noticed the first subtle differences, such as the depth of the grain of the wood on the desk; or that the words Naomi was writing changed in width, depending on how much ink was released from the pressure she put on her pen as she wrote. Glancing out of the window, I could see floatplanes out over Bowen Island to the west with a clarity I never could before.

"Ethan, catch," said Gwen, as she tossed a small roll of medical tape to me. My hand shot out to catch it, but I closed my fingers too quickly, the tape bouncing off my now-closed fist. But I caught it with the other hand, without thinking, before it got halfway to the ground.

"You can start your recalibration exercises now," said Naomi, grinning at Gwen. "You too, Marcy." Darcy had created a computer system that was a combination of the electronic game Simon Says, a martial arts training mannequin, and a mad spider. We both stood before a vaguely human-looking contraption that was covered with lights, poles, and an assortment of things that flashed or moved. A light would come on randomly, and the idea was to react and touch it to turn it off. At the same time, an arm would move, and you had to touch a button on it to make it return to where it started from. There were ten lights and twenty things that moved in total, located from floor level to as high as we could reach, and a few feet either side of us.

The system began slowly at first and we worked quite hard to spot a light or movement, understand what was required, and react to touch the appropriate button. The buttons were small, and some precision was required to hit them as they moved.

As we mastered the slowest speed, the system automatically sped up, based on how fast the computer driving the program detected our improvements. And as we tired or lost concentration, it slowed.

We were both tiring after 30 minutes, but of course had made a competition out of it and neither of us wanted to lose. I think we were both relieved when Naomi stopped us and showed us the results.

"We ran some baseline tests with people who are normal non-athletes, like Gwen and I, and some hyper-fit people from the protection team, who are already trained in complex-fighting systems. The tests were done both with and without the drug, and some with a placebo. All improved with practise, but you can see from this graph that your reaction and accuracy using the drug is seeing a 15-20% improvement already. The regime requires you rotate using this trainer for 30 minutes, then go to the dojo and spar for 30 minutes, then rest for 30 minutes. We want you to do this three times per day for the next three days. On the fourth day, you will spar without the drug in your system in the morning, then with the drug in the afternoon. Then we will reassess.

We moved through to the dojo, where Marcy and I faced off on the mat. It felt good to be just the two of us.

"Buckle up, Booker. I'm going to hand you your ass," said Marcy, already launching into a series of rapid strikes. I noticed they were a bit rushed and wildly off target. I started to laugh, but the sound died on my lips when I realized my blocks were equally terrible. I saw Marcy's weight change to her back foot and instantly knew a head-kick was coming. I went to step back into a low defensive posture and tripped over my own feet. We both landed in a heap, with Marcy on top laughing.

"This is crazy," she said. "My brain feels as sharp and fast as it ever has, but my body feels drunk," she groaned. "A two-year-old could beat me."

"They won't have to," I countered, "because I aim to master this before you, and I will kick your butt." She suddenly reached between my pants and squeezed my cock, waking little Ethan from his slumber.

"Let's see you fight with an erection, smart ass," she said, leaping to her feet, only to stumble again. The rest of the afternoon was a shambles, but we felt we were improving by the time we went for dinner. That night we experimented with the side effects of the drug well into the night.

By the end of the third day, we were all making good progress. None of us could beat Gia, but she was certainly having to work harder to take us down. Day four was the most depressing, as we sparred without drugs.

We had discovered that 'Hard Colada,' as we had nicknamed Naomi's discovery – part piña colada, and part... well, the Viagra side effect – lasted for about five hours. We experienced minor bouts of depression when the effects wore off due to the lack of amphetamine in our system, and the drop in visual acuity. Day four, sparring had the depressing combination of feeling like seeing the world in a dark DVD quality, after living in a bright 4k world, coupled with once again being out of sync with our bodies.

After a couple of hours in the dojo, we felt we were back to our old selves, only to dose up on Hard Colada again in the afternoon. It was disorientating, but we agreed we were beginning to get a feel for the sudden gear changes. Little Ethan was very confused, but rarely grumpy about it.

Our twice daily calls rolled by with updates from Courtney and Moi Ley in the D.C. area, who were working their way about government circles but not locating any strong links to Talan's whereabouts. Gia's victim-rebellion was still going strong. Many arrests stuck, some didn't, but the damage done overall to the Polish mafia was long term. We had little doubt smaller clusters and gangs would re-emerge over time, where their competition hadn't already moved into their territory, but we wouldn't see any multicity, organized crime to the degree that they had grown too with Talan's orgy-generated assistance.

Max's plan to protect the Silent Souls event, which was now just four days away, would be revealed in detail tonight. He had had his head down planning, bringing in logistics and personnel, and visiting the venue. Gia and Max had met Jakub, who had introduced them to a new contact. Garrett Driskel was hard and competent, reported both Gia and Max, and clearly cut from a different cloth than Jakub and the mafia. Max was sure Garrett was special forces trained. No bluff or bluster, just a dangerous, quiet professionalism.

Garrett's team was slowly woven into Max's, and there were several headbutts as people fought for position. Garrett was quick to keep his team in line and deferred to Max often, making many very positive contributions to security. Max was exhausted, as he had to double plan everything; once with Garrett, then a second time to build additional contingencies about which Garrett couldn't know. We completely trusted Max was on top of things but were anxious to understand the details. With three days to go, the full briefing couldn't come soon enough.

Of Talan there was little sign, except for a brief flash of her mind on the day we arrived back in Vancouver. Courtney said it was like a blanket was dropped suddenly, and she could feel Talan out east. But then the blanket was replaced seconds later, and Talan vanished from her mental radar once more.

The last report today was from Naomi, confirming she was satisfied with the updated delta-blocking chemical, which was now a gel capsule we could swallow as opposed to a pinhole through our skulls. Darcy had also finalized the design of the blocker's electronic part. It was now in a hardened case, a little smaller, with a two-hour battery life. The connector to the pads that were stuck to our skulls was now translucent, and very hard to see, and the pads themselves were replaced with versions concealed in prosthetic skin, an idea lifted from the local film industry's special effects department. Marcy and I donned the black-tie outfits we would wear to the event and did a full dress-rehearsal. The delta-blockers were all but invisible, especially for Marcy, whose hair would almost cover them if worn down.

Our meeting broke up, and Marcy took off with Gia for a girls' lunch and catch-up. Jim and I had agreed to take some sandwiches and walk the seawall for some fresh air. We had 90 minutes of freedom before I had to be back in the dojo for another session of Hard Colada-empowered sparring, at which Gia would once again kick my ass, I was sure.

*

[Lindi] – The *nakele umthakathi* – Talan – was asleep, so despite her instructions to stay below decks, I climbed up, sat on the roof of our boat, and took in this amazing crush of people she called a city.

Talan had taken me through the skies in her flying machine and we had come straight to this boat, which was almost as large as some villages from my land. It could hold a hundred of us if we squeezed in, but Talan only allowed a fraction of that to climb on board. Most were for her security or her comfort. Cochrane had visited and left again.

We had left the boat a few times to look at the buildings she said the man called *Booker* lived in; he who was the focus of her rage and why we were here. We also met Jakub – whose mind felt as corrupt as Talan's – as well as a man called Garrett. It felt like he was a hunter, or a warrior from my tribe; a hard man, but not unkind. But he kept bad company, so I didn't warm to him.

I sat on the front of a boat and wondered at the city in front of me. I hadn't seen much more than the garden in the last house, but these giant buildings swarming with people was a sight I could tell people about when – or rather, *if* – I return to the village. The wall separating the city from the water was crowded with people running or riding on what I learned are called bikes; two wheeled but somehow well balanced, it seemed. I would love to try to ride one. But it was the buildings that dominated my attention: Each as tall as a large dune but, instead of sand, they were glass and metal, woven with white stone. So tall that people ride in cradles suspended from the roof to clean the glass, as there could never be a ladder tall enough. All of this filled with more minds than I could follow.

The sights and sounds were so captivating I almost missed the sorcerer sitting on the wall at the marina's entrance, eating bread, talking to another man. The sorcerer was one of the few here with skin the colour of mine, and he was clearly an elder. I climbed down off the boat's roof and, using my mind to hide myself from the two men on the deck of our boat, I slipped onto the walkway to which our boat was tied.

I slowly made my way closer. The sorcerer's aura – his glow – was clear and bright. His mind was clean to the touch. I determined he was a witch-sorcerer, like the man who took me from my land. But better natured. He suddenly stopped talking to his companion and looked around, his eyes settling on me. He had felt my light touch. He was old, but quite gifted. Most wouldn't have felt me. I let my aura shine brightly. I wanted him to see I was clean, too.

He stood and approached, his friend following. I suddenly wasn't sure. I could still feel Talan sleeping, and I deftly shadowed her mind so she would not wake up until I lifted my shade. I stepped out from the post, behind which I thought I was hidden, and waited for them to come to me.

"I see you, stranger," he said, in Talan's language.

I nodded, wishing I had the words to reply rather than just the understanding of his thoughts.

"My name is Jim," he said. He touched his chest as he said it.

"Lindi," I replied, reflecting his gesture.

"What brings you here?" he asked. Again, I didn't have the words to reply, so I used one of the few phrases Uma had taught me.

"I have only small words, Jim," I said hesitantly. "I understand much more than I can speak,"

"Do you think she is lost?" his companion said. I touched his mind for the first time and got a shock. He was clean and strong, like Jim, and he had the mind of a witch, not of a dull person like Cochrane or Uma. His magic was asleep, and it seemed it had never been used. This was new to me. Surely, he would prefer to wake it and let it grow.

"Do you need help?" asked Jim. I wanted to say yes, but then he would want to know more. He was almost as strong as Talan, but I sensed her strength would last longer than his. He would tire quickly if they fought, which I suspected they would if they met.

"Do you have family with you?" his companion asked. He seemed genuinely concerned for me. He was sweet. As much as I wanted to talk to these witches, I decided it would only lead to trouble. I reached into their minds and faded their memories of me. I nudged them back towards their bench and their food, and I turned to walk back to the boat. I was sad, as I rarely met witches with their strength and purity. I would have liked to know them better. Jim was nice, but I was particularly drawn to his companion. I realised I didn't ask his name. I reached back to his mind but couldn't easily determine what he called himself. I can't read thoughts that the owner is not thinking at the time. His mind was full of concerns and worries, but high among them were the thoughts for my safety. I determined that this man was special. I closed my eyes and concentrated on how his mind was laid out and how it worked. I left him a gift. I hoped he would find it one day.

*

[Ethan] – The face of the African girl we had met on the seawall stayed with me all afternoon. She looked about 12 or 13 years old, and like she had walked out of a movie. Her eyes were haunting. She had that overly thin look of an Adept, and Jim said she was a strange one. Her Nimbus was one of the brightest he has seen, yet he could barely feel her mind. What he could feel was calm and quiet. A teenage Nimbus is normally chaotic and uncontrolled, and their aura has yet to bloom. He suspected she looked much younger than her years, which is not uncommon in his experience. With hindsight we weren't sure why we didn't invite her back with us or attempt to connect with her folk. Strange, now that I think about it. Stranger still was that I didn't feel the urge to go back and find her; that area of town felt unwelcoming.

The sparring went well that afternoon, and we felt good as we showered. I tried to make a move on Marcy in the shower, but she playfully fended me off. She told me to save my energy for tonight, as she had been thinking of an idea to torture me. I was completely receptive to whatever she planned but couldn't see why it was an either/or situation. "More is better," I'd said. She just put one finger on my lips and said something about needing the pressure to build, then kissed me and stepped out of the shower. I was so distracted I didn't notice her flip the shower down to freezing as she stepped past the control, and as I jumped around to push it back, I heard – then felt – her towel whip through the misty air and sting my butt. *Cow!* I hurried after her, suddenly realizing we would have to move it to get to Max's briefing on time.

Max had the Oscar Peterson board room set up for the presentation, and he took us through the plan as if he were briefing a bunch of generals. He was sharp, on point, and concise. He outlined the tactical benefits of the venue he had selected for the Silent Souls event. Nestled atop the mountains overlooking Vancouver are several small ski resorts. In the summertime, they are used for hiking and climbing, and are world-renowned for downhill trail-biking. One resort has facilities to host corporate or other events. The terrain made it easy to strictly control access, and the locations was far enough from any built-up areas to limit collateral damage, should Talan try to employ missiles or explosives as she had in Turkey.

We had leveraged the new contacts we had with law enforcement and the military – courtesy of saving them from Jakub's extortion – and the resort we had chosen went live this morning with protection from a ring of high-frequency radar and missile defences, which are normally only used when Heads of State visit Canada. These resources were hidden, and Garrett's team was kept in the dark about their presence.

At the venue itself, a complex set of metal-, chemical-, and explosive-detecting electronics and sniffer dogs were in place. The woods were patrolled in a tight pattern even now, three days out, and the inside of the venue had already been thoroughly searched twice. As caterers and others involved in staging the charity event were hired, they unknowingly went through a ferocious background check – as did those on the guest list – and were searched diligently as they came and went.

On the night of the event, only six of Garrett's team and six of Max's would be armed; all other weapons would be kept outside. Guests would arrive by helicopters that we would provide exclusively. The one road into the event would be blocked off and, unknown to Garrett, monitored by Kelsie via microwave-linked cameras.

The airspace around the site had a high-density laser-scanning system – similar to but much more accurate than conventional radar – which would detect drones down to the size of a football. Sonic disrupters were deployed to take down anything non-military. These disruptors were similar to those used at major airports since the Gatwick Airport drone incident in 2018, which had cost the UK authorities over 65 million pounds. We didn't have time to develop a foolproof method of discerning friend from foe in the small drone space, so this meant we couldn't use drones either.

All of the air defences were controlled offsite by Kelsie, together with a team on loan from the Canadian Armed Forces. Everything onsite was controlled by an operations centre Max ran, which had one of Garrett's men in attendance to ensure close coordination. Both Max and Garrett would be seated with guests at the event, mingling with the crowd, looking for up-close threats.

Gia took us through the who's-who that composed the guest list. Most of Vancouver's powerful and wealthy had accepted, and some wanted to bring their own protection teams. Tactfully refusing them, yet keeping them from pulling out due to their egos, had become one of the biggest problems for Max.

We lost ten minutes when the briefing was hijacked by discussions around outfits, make-up, and shoes, but we eventually got to the final items: Our blockers and special cocktail.

"The current thinking is that Ethan, Marcy, Gia, and I – plus the leads of our two full time protection details – will wear blockers. That leaves one spare blocker on the shelf in case of technical problems," explained Max. "End-to-end, the event is four hours, so we will need to replace the batteries halfway through. If we stagger the timing of when the battery changes happen, we retain good coverage across the team. Naomi confirms we can take an additional dose of blocker chemical then, too."

We discussed various alternative options but couldn't improve on anything we had heard.

"What about the fast speed drug?" I asked, avoiding using the nickname at this more serious moment. "There are pros and cons to using it."

"Garrett's team are real professionals, Ethan," said Max. "They seem like really tough bastards. I'd bet Gia could take any of them, but the rest of us will be matched or better. Some of our protection team, those from the SAS or similar, may put up a decent fight if the fists fly. I think we will need the edge Hard Colada will give us."

"Do you think it will come down to a fist fight?" asked Marcy.

"I doubt that is their primary plan," answered Max. "I must assume they are planning for Talan taking control if she comes and, if she stays away, long range attacks using explosives or missiles. Or they might have found a clever way to smuggle explosives or additional guns into the venue. There are problems with those plans."

"Like what?" asked Gwen, her mother hen peaking out.

"The obvious one being that guns or missiles would create a high mortality rate for their team, too. They might win, but they would die."

"But would they care if Talan has brainwashed them?" said Kelsie.

"Maybe not, but then there is the risk of failure. We might get lucky fighting back, or the missiles might miss. Anyway, I think Talan will want to be up close and personal. Don't you Courtney?" said Max.

"I do. I feel strongly that she will put in an appearance. I think your blockers will be your biggest advantage. Are you sure I shouldn't come back to Vancouver?"

"No," I said firmly. She had suggested it several times, and I repeated our belief that if Talen sensed Courtney in attendance she would resort to a missile-type attack killing everyone at the venue.

"How is your investigation going?" Marcy asked Courtney.

"Actually, I think after a week of nothing, I might have a lead," replied the Adept. "I've discovered that the man on the ground at Creech who was directing the attack was a CIA operative working for a man named Cochrane. From contacts in

Langley, whom Moi Ley has been cultivating – she really has a gift for this work, by the way – we've found out that Cochrane has been on a special assignment for almost a year."

"Do we know what he has been doing?" asked Marcy.

"I met with his superior, who believes Cochrane is working in Pakistan on Taliban-related work. I highly suspect that is not the case. I could tell the man had had his mind worked over by Talan. I could feel her fingerprints on him. She isn't very subtle."

"I've been working with Courtney on this for the last few hours," cut in Kelsie. "SkyLoX and I have a theory: She eventually traced the download of the blackmail material from the Venice back-ups, through a forest of firewalls and proxies, to a small facility at Fort Belvoir, which lies just south of Washington DC. Cochrane's credit cards showed activity all around that area, too. We are wondering if we stumbled over one of Talan's hideouts. It matches the approximate bearing for Talan that we plotted in our analysis of the helicopters that tried to intercept you near Detroit, Ethan."

"So, if Talan doesn't come here, she might be there, working with Garrett remotely?" I asked. "Should we split our team and attack there at the same time?" I didn't like that idea. I would rather lose Talan than put the attendees at the fundraiser at more risk than they already were. Max and Marcy, who had better tactical planning brains than I, jumped in to say we should keep the Vancouver plan intact. With that agreed, we spent an hour planning how to reinforce Courtney going in to Fort Belvoir simultaneously with the Silent Souls event here.

I felt we were as prepared as we possibly could be three days out from the showdown, so we adjourned the meeting and enjoyed a light meal and some small talk together.

*

We took the elevator back up to the suites with Gwen, Naomi, and Elvis. Our respective suite doors face each other across an eight-foot corridor, where often there is a tug-of-war as to which apartment Elvis will sleep in for the night. Elvis will typically solve it by sauntering over to one door or the other, depending on his mood, and sitting down to wait to see what the adults do. Tonight, the decision seemed more straightforward than most occasions, as both Elvis and the adults seemed to think he should stay over with the women.

As soon as the door closed behind us, Marcy came at me with long, deep kisses, grinding herself into me, and slowly removing my shirt.

"Have I got plans for you, Slave Boy," she cooed. "I may have been shopping, again." *Crap!* Marcy isn't shy to pop into sex-toy stores, but has discovered an even wider range of options online, some of them that will tailor items to her specific design and whim. There were very few I didn't enjoy, often in a painful way, but I felt most nervous when I sensed Phoenix had been creative.

"Pour us each a glass of red wine and come through to the bedroom," she instructed, as she pulled my belt from my pants, slung it over her shoulder, and sauntered away as only a sassy woman can.

I opened a 2006 Cakebread Cabernet and trickled some into two wide-brimmed glasses to get the air into it quickly. Even the sound of the wine pouring, and the fruity aroma being released, built the erotic tension. I kicked off my shoes and socks – I hate it if I end up naked everywhere except for my socks – and gingerly followed Marcy through to the bedroom. The blinds were down – they aren't always when she teases me – and soft and sexy R&B tones filled the darkened space with a sensual mood. I noted a vanilla- and coconut-scented incense stick smouldering in the corner and hoped the smoke alarm didn't sound while I was tied up.

I saw that Marcy had been unpacking something; the wrapping was on the small table in the corner, but neither she nor the contents were in sight. I put both glasses down on the table and sat on the end of the bed with nervous anticipation.

"Why don't you take the painting down and put your cuffs on," she shouted from the bathroom, sounding busy with something. Our bedroom is 800 square feet, slightly oblong, with full-length windows on two sides, one of which led to a small balcony. On the third side of the room is our custom four-poster bed – what else – and the last side hosted two features: a ten by four-foot mirror and a piece of art the same size, spaced equally to divide up the wall behind them. Both the art and the mirror stand about three feet into the room, suspended a foot from the floor by cables from the ceiling. The walls behind the features are tastefully divided into bookcases, air conditioning outlets, a wet bar, and several other features that served both their obvious utility function, but also concealed a range of hidden areas: The safe, which is easy to find, contains our throw-down items that we're not afraid of being stolen; a much harder-to-find safe for weapons and other secret items; and a third hidden area, our cupboard of kinky toys.

I picked up a remote control from the bedside and tapped a code into it's keypad enabling the controller to access the rooms secret features. In addition to controlling the blinds, music, and environmental settings, it could now open the toy cupboard and activate hidden winches to lower the painting and mirror. The painting is an authentic 18th century masterpiece of a couple entwined in a moonlit forest-clearing, oblivious to the small audience of animals curiously, but not creepily, observing them. The lovers were lost in each other, and the animals were radiating a sense that nature approved of the union. I lowered the work to the floor and unhooked it from the cables. Then I rolled it on its wheels, which were subtly built into the frame, to a point behind the mirror and leaned it against the wall out of the way.

In a matter of moments, we could connect four separate cables to ceiling winches, which we could then organize for our use in whichever way our kinky minds could think to.

From the toy cupboard I selected and put on a black pair of two-inch, heavy, leather wrist cuffs, then sat back on the bed.

Marcy emerged with a tray covered by a cloth to conceal whatever mischief lay beneath. I stood and picked up our wine, handing a glass to Marcy. We clinked our glasses, sipped, and then kissed, fondled, and tasted each other for a good 15 minutes until we were both becoming quite excited.

Marcy broke away, caught her breath, led me over to the cables, and locked both of my wrist cuffs to one of them. Using the remote, she drew my hands up with the winch until they were a few inches above my head. With those out of the way, she undid and removed my pants, leaving me in my Saxx Vibe briefs. As was typical in these moments, I was quite erect and excited, but it was apparent to anyone familiar with little Ethan the addition of the Hard Colada had firmed even his posture up a notch further. Marcy took her time. She traced the outline of my engorged penis for several long moments while she stared into my eyes, kissed and tweaked my nipples sharply, and ran her fingers softly around any and all erogenous areas.

She gave my butt a playful slap and disappeared into the cupboard to return with a custom leg-spreader. It was a wooden three-foot pole that had been beautifully carved and varnished, with a broad leather cuff at each end. She knelt provocatively in front of me and attached a cuff to each of my ankles, forcing my legs wide apart and allowing me a glimpse down her tank top. Taking the remote once again, she raised the cables so that my arms were taught, and my feet barely touched the floor. I was stretched out like an upside-down letter Y, and vulnerable to whatever she wished.

She stalked back to the cupboard, her heels clicking on the hardwood, and returned with our safety shears. They could cut through thick leather and rope quickly in an emergency, and my Saxx briefs offered no resistance at all as she slowly sliced through them and peeled them away. Little Ethan sprang out in full glory, rejoicing at his freedom and clearly ready for action.

Next came a blindfold. Marcy stood behind me reached up and slipped it over my eyes. She kissed me and paid some attention to my favourite areas. Then she gave my butt cheeks ten hard slaps each, warming them up nicely, ordering me to count the strokes out loud and thank her: "One, thank you, Phoenix... two..."

Then she left me hanging alone for some time, wondering what she was up to. Suddenly, just under my left arm, a sharp prickling sensation made me jump, though in my predicament I couldn't move far. Marcy giggled with laughter, delighted with the results. Needles pricked in a lazy yet sharp line down my left side, across my butt, and back up my right flank. I couldn't stand still. It was both tickling and stinging me, all at once. For what seemed like a minute, the sensation shot unpredictably all over my legs and torso and had me flailing around in response, much to Marcy's apparent pleasure. The blindfold came off suddenly, revealing a medieval-looking implement I hadn't seen before, held up by Marcy's long, sexy, red-nailed fingers hovering in front her impish face. It was all metal, comprising a long handle – similar to a toothbrush but thinner – with a gleaming, spiked wheel at one end. The wheel was about an inch in diameter, ringed with two dozen or so very pointy needles. She spun the wheel with her finger, like a cowboy might twirl his spurs, and giggled with joy.

"This is a Wartenberg wheel. You like?"

I squirmed away as far as I could and answered, "I'm shocked I am so ticklish. I'm not normally in the least, and I *never* squirm in such an unmanly manner."

"Well, big man, I have something else, too. But little Ethan is way too full of himself to try it. I thought this little wheel might help shrink him, but it's had the opposite effect," she murmured, in a faux-Marilyn Munroe voice I didn't know she could do; she smiled innocently up at me. My mind shrank, imagining the sensation again, but that traitor between my legs had a mind of his own today and was clearly yelling, "Bring it, babe!"

Marcy lifted a chair over from her dresser, placed it in front of me, and put the tray-of-mystery on the bed where she could reach it. She sat, held up and spun the Wartenberg like a sadistic wheel-of-fortune, then began to run it very gently up and down my shaft. I didn't dare move a muscle, focussing entirely on the exquisite sensation. She added a little bit of pressure, and I flinched, so tempted to yell my safe word. If I said "amber," she would know I was at my limit and she should ease off a little; if I said "red," she would stop so we could regroup. Although I didn't say anything, I think she sensed I was at the edge, so she kissed little Ethan on his forehead once and threw the wheel onto the tray.

Next Marcy pulled out a tube of cream, which smelled of tangerine, and slathered some all over my manhood. Things were at full stretch down there, blood rushing in and veins standing out to form what she referred to as erotic ridges. I felt myself starting to rush towards climax and my testicles grow tight.

"Hold it, mister," Marcy said, in her strictest Phoenix voice. "I said I wanted him to shrink, not grow!" She gave him a light slap, then picked up the wheel again and slowly dragged it along his length. I was up on my toes. It stung. In a good way, though. Marcy reached back to the tray and retrieved a silk bag with what appeared to be marbles inside. She wrapped the bag around my balls – *yikes... cold.* The bag held small balls of ice.

"Marcy, there are nicer ways of making it shrink," I gasped.

"Yes, but I want to play, not finish you off, silly. I want to see how much control you have when you are eager, revved up, and full of Viagra," she chortled.

When she had me shrunken and soft, she pulled a chastity cage from the tray. We had played with cages a few times, but normally under my clothes when we went out to dinner. She liked to wear the key on a necklace or bracelet and tease me with it all night, threatening to leave me locked up or lose the key. She even had some cages that vibrated or gave small electric shocks as directed by her discrete remote control; surprising me with a zap as I ordered my meal from the server was a favourite. Of hers.

Satisfied I was small enough to fit, Marcy opened and slid the hinged metal ring part around and behind my balls. Then she carefully slid the cage over my shaft and locked it to the ring. Little Ethan was in jail until Marcy let him out using the key. Normally cages are very snug and tight fitting, even when its 'contents' are flaccid. I was just noticing that this was more roomy than normal when Marcy explained why.

"So, lover, this cage has teeth. On the inside are sharp points, facing inwards. Not a problem while you are soft, but if you get even half hard, they will bite you," she laughed. "And if you get very hard, which will be difficult under the circumstances, the pressure will activate an electric shock to keep you in line."

"Well, I don't think I am incented to get hard at all. You are scaring the crap out of me," I said wryly, just as that traitorous nutjob of a penis of mine began to throb and swell with mindless anticipation. I felt the cage stab me in several places almost immediately.

Marcy stood, removed the chair, and walked over to her wardrobe, stripping her clothes off slowly as she went. She looked amazing, and I was already struggling to keep things contained down below as she slowly slid her knickers down her thighs, bending over to slip them over her shoes, which she kept on. From her closet she pulled a hanger with some of her sexiest lingerie on it, which she knew was some of my favourite things she wore.

I was bitten several times as Marcy slid herself into the outfit, lingering over certain fun areas – spending time on herself – and warming up Little Marcy.

When she was in her racy outfit, she walked to the sex-toy cupboard and returned with a leather paddle and a batter powered, vibrating wand. When she turned on the latter and held it against the top of the cage, causing the whole contraption to tingle, I got my first electric shock. It was pretty sharp, and I jumped in place, unable to move.

"Yowee!" I growled. "That's mean!"

"You have a safe word, Slave Boy. I don't' mind if you want to stop, but no editorials, or I will gag you!" That idea brought on the second shock of the night.

"Oh look, you seem to like this Hard Colada, Ethan. You can't control yourself at all, can you?" She proceeded to paddle my butt and thighs for several minutes, and I was bitten and shocked repeatedly. I was getting lost in sub-space, not sure which part of my body to pay attention to as my breathing ran fast and shallow. She slipped the blindfold back over my eyes and continued the treatment, mixing it up with the Wartenberg wheel.

I was getting very worked up when she suddenly stopped. I felt the cage being released, and then I was in her hands and mouth. But not for long. I exploded in a very short, intense orgasm. I could see stars behind my tightly shut eyelids, and my muscles were clamped down tight on the sensations refusing to relax as if they were consciously trying to extend the amazing sensations. I hung for a moment and Marcy stood against me, her head on my shoulder, her hands on my neck.

"I'll let you down now, and you can pay me some attention. You've been neglecting me, Ethan. We can measure your recovery time to see if that is faster with Hard Colada, too."

24: THE BEAST RISES

[Gia] – When I get the chance, I take time for myself most mornings to maintain my mind and fighting skills through a regime I have perfected over the past decade. In the summer, when it is warmer and dryer, I like to get outside to my favourite spot at Spanish Banks.

The Spaniards Juan Carrasco and José María Narváez first mapped out the Vancouver coast in 1791, followed by Captain George Vancouver a year later with his own cartography voyage of the area. Neither the Spaniards' nor Vancouver's charts recorded the stretch of shore between what is now the University of BC and Locarno Beach. This omission was corrected by Captain Richards of HMS Plumper in his survey of the area in 1859. He bestowed the name Spanish Banks to recognize the efforts of the two Spaniards nearly 70 years earlier. An oddity in the name is that there is only one bank, so it should not be plural.

My regime starts with ten minutes of yoga to stretch my muscles and clear my mind of trivia such as the area's history; when I am ready, I begin with Tai Chi, which to me is like yoga to the music inside my head. The slow pace brings balance and, if done correctly, strength, too.

My Kung Fu routine – the name actually referring to any skill acquired through diligent learning and practise – begins with the flowing Shaolin style. My first teacher adapted by mixing the northern style, which emphasizes fast and powerful kicks, and the southern style of immovable stances and fast footwork. My kata routines then transform into karate styles, kickboxing, and end with some movements from the Brazilian martial art, Vale Tudo.

It is not unusual for my 30-minute routine among the trees that line the beach to draw a crowd, and I am used to blocking the onlookers out while I focus on perfecting my form and timing. I suddenly became aware that some men had breached the natural bubble of respect looky-loos typically adhere to;

they were clearly moving purposefully towards me. I pivoted out of the series of kicks I was in the middle of and settled into a defensive stance – my weight on my back leg, and my arms out loose at shoulder height – and surveyed the scene.

Five hard-looking men formed most of a circle around me, leaving a small gap that led through to the few cars that were parked nearby at 6 am. The door on a red sedan opened and a tall man stepped out, slowly unfolding himself into the six-foot-eight Clay from Chicago. From the car's other door emerged an angry looking Jakob. The two strode across the path and thin strip of grass, and together they completed the circle. I turned and reset my ready stance so that they were in front of me, and my back was to one of their goons, who I kept in my peripheral vision by tilting my head at 45 degrees.

"Something on your mind, boys?" I said, calculating options and angles, which didn't take long given I was out in the open. If there were no guns, I would just react to their attack but try to stay out of Clay's reach, due to his massive size; if there were guns drawn, the only defence would be to run and zigzag. Despite what you see on TV, a moving target or someone more than 20 feet away is really hard to hit with a pistol. Their formation didn't favour a machine gun unless they were suicidal.

"Revenge, you stupid bitch!" barked Jakob.

"Hey, we paid you 15 million bucks, and this is the thanks we get? What more do you want?"

"Our business is gone, and most of my family in jail. Clay's sons and my grandson are both dead. Killed by the SWAT-pigs. The only thing I want from you is to hear you scream for a long time before you die. In the car, now!"

"I've got to tell you, Jakob, your sales pitch needs some work. I didn't like the *give me the list* idea, and I certainly don't like this *come quietly and we torture you* idea, either. What else are you offering?"

They had obviously expected this because the goons started to close in rapidly from all sides at once in a well-choreographed motion. None of the goons drew weapons, but Clay reached into his voluminous jacket and pulled out a pistol. Jakob pulled another from his waistband. Before they had a chance to point them at me, I was off. I took three quick steps backwards to build up speed, turned, and dove into a cartwheel from which I vaulted up and over the head of the goon who had been rushing me from behind. He was quick enough to reach for me, but I swatted his hand away with one arm and poked him in the eye with a straight finger jab as I passed over him.

I landed and kept running at full speed, trusting that most of the goons now stood between me and the men with the guns. I was a good 30 feet away and jinking left, when I heard the bark of the first pistol. I immediately jinked left again as several shots followed me along the shoreline. I surged right suddenly, heading away from the soft sand, which would slow me down, towards the trees. I glanced back and saw one man down – clutching his eye – two more pursuing me on foot, and the rest running for their cars.

I slowed a little, drawing the pursuers closer and allowing the others to get into their vehicles, from where they couldn't shoot effectively. When I judged it right, I reversed direction and in 12 paces reached the spot of my choice to make a stand against the two men running full speed towards me. I stopped dead in my tracks in a stance. It would be foolish and unpredictable to clash with them on the run, but that obviously had not occurred to them; they kept barreling towards me.

I sidestepped to the left and tripped the first man as he passed; then reversed to the right, catching the other man by surprise with an elbow to the throat. I heard his trachea pop and knew he would never breathe through it again. He turned to fight me before his mind caught up to his new reality, as he soon realized he couldn't breathe; he grabbed his throat, tumbling to the ground with a gurgle. I ran around him and then headed straight at his partner, who had pulled himself up but was bleeding from a gash on his forehead from his fall. This time I ran straight at him, hitting him with a kick to the sternum. I combined my forward momentum with the energy I could generate using my whole body as a whip, planting one foot on the ground, and surging around an up, driving my other foot on target at full strength. Such a blow can stop hearts if placed just right, but I was about an inch and a half left of optimal. But I heard the satisfying sound of several ribs cracking as he went down hard.

I checked both men for guns. They were unarmed. I hoped the rest of the goons were, too, but I had to assume they would arm themselves from caches in their vehicles. I ran and entered the trees just as the first car drew up and hadn't put much wood between me and the bad guys before I heard the bullets thunking into tree trunks.

I turned so that I was at 45 degrees to the treeline, running back against the way the cars had come, so that they either had to turn around or reverse to follow me. Before the trees blocked my view, the last thing I saw was one car doing the latter and the other two standing empty as their occupants pursued me on foot.

I had jogged from home to Spanish Banks, with no car to run back to, so I decided to pick off my pursuers and work my way back to their cars, in hope that they had been stupid enough to leave me some keys. As I passed under the thick, tan-coloured branch of an Arbutus tree, I grabbed it and swung up. I stilled both my movement and breathing as I listened to the enemy approach. I heard two distinct sets of footsteps and panting, which sounded about right. There had been five goons plus Clay and Jakob. One was down with no eye, and two down by the edge of the trees. Two cars reversed, so my quick math added up to two men on foot in the woods. It was possible either Clay or Jakob had changed tack, or some yet-to-be-seen goons were nearby, so I had to be careful.

My other challenge was a beast in my head that had begun to roar at me when I saw Jakob step out of his car. The beast was two-headed: one had the ugly face of their involvement in Talan's rape-fest and connected through time to the other, the sexual abuses of my teen years and the death of my sister-friend Jing. All caused by animals like him. That beast in me was a rage I fought to contain, as it would make me fight poorly. It was urging me to throw myself at the men and rip their faces off with my hands. That might work with little Jakob, but it could be fatal with the much larger Clay. I pushed the beast down deep inside me but whispered to it: *Soon... soon!*

The two men slowed, deciding to do the smart thing and listen rather than run blindly into a trap. Unfortunately for them, one stopped right beneath me. They both had their weapons drawn and were signalling to each other. Dropping onto someone like they do in the movies takes them down but leads to a very unpredictable landing and is not recommended by professionals. I judged my jump to land on a sound footing on a bare patch of even ground, right next to the attacker below me. He was so shocked, I simply snatched the gun from his grip, turned, and shot his partner – who was moving away from me – in the back of the head. I deftly stepped back, pivoted, and shot the other man – whose gun I had just taken – between his stupid, surprised eyes. All known goons down, I turned my attention to their leaders.

I moved to the treeline and paralleled the road in the opposite direction to where I had last seen Jakob's car heading. I couldn't hear anything except the very distant sound of sirens. I popped my head out of the woods, looked down the road, and quickly pulled my head back in again before someone could shoot it. Both Clay and Jakob were stopped fifty yards away, standing with their car between themselves and me and the tree line. I could see why they were management. Much smarter than the goons.

I edged back 15 yards or so towards them to where one of the goons' cars sat. I couldn't hear its engine, but the exhaust pipe was vibrating and let out a hint of vapour. This answered my question about car keys. When the remaining mafia looked away, I slipped out of hiding and crept into the driver's seat.

Slowly at first, so as to delay Jakub and Clay detecting me for as long as possible, I reversed the car towards them. I lined Clay up. He was about the size of the car, it seemed. I was less than 20 yards away when Clay's head snapped my way, and I floored the accelerator, the SUV leaping backwards in response. Clay's shooting arm was most of the way around towards me when I was still ten yards away. Should I duck away from the shot and risk his body coming through the rear window and hitting me, or jump out and clear, and risk the car swerving and missing him. I ducked and prayed to the safety-glass gods.

I heard a double 'thunk,' then felt the wheels bounce over something. *Sounds promising*, I thought, and risked a look out of the door, keeping my head low. Right below me was Clay, his face bloody and eyes shut. A dazed Jakub was on his ass a dozen yards back having been shoved there by the impact. Clay's gun was on the ground near me. I rolled out, stood, and shot Clay through the head. Or I would have if it hadn't clicked empty. I had no idea how many bullets the pursuers had emptied into the woods. I walked over and retrieved Jakub's revolver, which worked much better. It was a 45 calibre, and a single shot splashed Clay's brains across the ground and the car.

Jakub looked stunned and was still pulling himself up. I took a moment to wipe my prints off both guns I had touched, then dumped them onto Clay's body. Then I turned to Jakob and let the beast loose. I barely remember closing the distance and digging my fingers into his face. Everything else was a blur after that.

I came back to myself in the woods covered in blood and scratches. There was a gouge in the flesh of my thigh that a lucky shot must have carved, which I was only noticing now that the adrenaline was fading. At my feet were my gym bag of clothes, a towel, and some water. I don't recall retrieving it, but I was glad I had. The bag also contained my phone. I thought about calling Max, but I knew he would abandon planning for the event and head down here. Instead, I called Kelsie. She had a team who monitored the police wavelengths and confirmed she already had drones overhead the scene and two cars approaching, just in case the "guns fired" dispatch call had anything to do with me.

I told Kelsie where I was hidden in the trees and we agreed on a rendezvous point away from the gathering police presence. While I waited to be picked up in my sports bra, having made a compress from my workout shirt, Kelsie and I agreed I would get cleaned up at the apartment, remove any gunpowder residue and blood, then head back to the scene. Enough people see me work out there several times a week to give the police a description. I needed to go back and convince the police I was caught in the middle of a gang shootout and had escaped into the woods to safety.

It took three and a half hours, a visit to the station and Aiden to convince the police they had nothing substantive to charge me with, or at least I hadn't been the instigator. A call to the National Gang Crimes unit confirmed the Polish gangs were in turmoil, thanks to the intervention of one of the extortion victims in Montreal who was assigned to that division of the RCMP.

By the time I got home, Max was up to speed and was torn between spanking me and hugging me – he smartly chose the latter – and we found 30 minutes to cuddle up and celebrate being alive, before joining Ethan and the team for a catch-up call. My experience was the sole topic of discussion. The summary was that we had to assume Talan now knew we were all connected, and she was being lured into a trap. Emotionally, we were all up for the risk, so we spent an hour trying to decide what the smart thing was to do. We elected to go ahead, limiting Talan's opportunity to attack us before we got to her.

Max stayed home and completed the preparations for the event. Jim was with him 24 hours a day; we felt another Adept's presence might be the biggest deterrent to Talan trying anything. Moy Lei and Courtney were in Washington, a force in themselves but guarded by Roxy and a beefed-up team. The rest of us, including Kelsie, Darcy, Naomi, and Gwen, left to fly unpredictably around the planet for a couple of days.

25: THE NUDEST DETECTIVE

[Marcy] – The big night arrived at last, and we were nervous and jumpy. I'd recently seen a meme that read, "Afraid of being alone in the dark? Don't worry. You are not!" We had no sense of who Talan might corrupt to come at us and it had us on edge.

We had to assume Garrett's team was working for her but, so far, their behaviour was impeccable; Max informed us that they had genuinely improved the security at the venue. Using facial-recognition technology, we had confirmed each member of his team's identity, regardless of the names that appeared on their official credentials. All were pretty reputable private contractors, made up of ex-special forces, law enforcement, or – like Garrett – ex-US Secret Service Protection Detail. But the critical question was, were they in possession of their own minds?

This morning, per our plan, Max quietly approached Garrett – one top security professional to another – and they had an off-the-record discussion. Max revealed that we suspected he had been hired by Clay, Jakob, or some member of their organization, which was now in tatters. He asked if they were still getting paid and offered to double their money to walk away. Garrett politely declined, advising his contract had been taken over by an old and confidential contact from Washington. They had worked for them on other occasions and would not renege, out of principle; it would kill any future business in his small professional community.

We considered flying Courtney back for a brief period to confirm if Garrett or his team's minds had been altered but decided against it; we didn't want to scare Talan away. Besides, tonight Courtney would infiltrate Cochrane's residence and confront him.

We returned to Vancouver in two separate jets, arriving via the Canadian Forces airport at Comox on Vancouver Island. This seemed less predictable than any of the mainland possibilities. Kelsie set up camp in offices provided by the base commander, who is one of Max's Canadian Forces buddies, and got to work ensuring she was plugged into her myriad electronic assets.

Ethan, Gia, and I changed into our black-tie outfits in a room at the back of the hangar and took a dose of Hard Colada that would last at least three hours. Then to confuse any potential attack timed for our arrival, we were ferried in a fleet of six helicopters – most were empty – directly to the venue.

When we were about a mile away from touch down, Ethan and I switched on our delta-blockers. Max was on the ground to meet us as we landed, looking handsome and all grown up in his tux – I'm one proud sister – and was also already wearing his blocker.

Max had one team member assigned to each one of Garrett's contractors, watching them closely. He also had a few floaters dressed as security, as well as some floating around incognito among the guests.

Everything in the venue had been screened for drugs, explosives, poisons – even radioactive isotopes – in case Talan took a lead from the Russian GRU playbook. But aside from some ecstasy, cocaine, and pot smuggled in by guests, the venue was clean. We had one last, quick meeting as the bulk of the guests were landing. We gave Courtney the go-ahead for her mission, which was deliberately timed to coincide with our event, then we put on our game faces and began to mingle with the crowd.

Those of us participating in the event drank mocktails – no alcohol for us – as we glad-handed and hob-knobbed through the reception. I stayed close to Ethan, and Gia was with Max.

As the dinner portion of the evening began, we had to split up, as it would have looked too odd if we didn't spread ourselves around the various tables to help host Vancouver's rich and famous, who were also typically sensitive to social snubs. But we had ensured the tables were arranged so that I was back-to-back with Ethan and Gia was adjacent to Max.

Ethan stepped away from his guests, pulling out his phone, and had a brief conversation with someone. As he returned to sit, he leaned close and whispered some troubling news: Courtney's team was off the air and not responding to Kelsie's calls. Kelsie had drones watching the residence they had entered, and there was no sign of unusual activity. Hopefully it was a communications glitch, which was not uncommon in DC when the government reacts to some incident and jams signals in case the incident is terror related. A back-up team would enter the property in ten minutes if nothing was heard from our DC team.

Max stepped out for a few minutes to check the perimeter, before reappearing and texting everyone a code which meant that all was quiet at our event here.

As dinner and drinks flowed, the guests chatted brightly and perused the prospectus of fund-raising opportunities. A door prize was awarded, and the owner of a Vancouver-based conglomerate now had two weeks on Ethan's yacht, which they would probably pass on to someone else to enjoy or enter it as a prize in some event of their own. That's how these things work, apparently.

All of our team got a text shortly afterward from the back-up team's leader in DC. It read: "Entered without challenge. Property empty. Assume our team compromised and abducted. We are looking for their egress route. Stand by." I looked at Ethan; his face was ashen with concern. I wondered if this meant Talan was in DC, which would mean that at least we wouldn't have to worry about her here. Just her bombs or poison gas.

I got up and caught Gia's eye, nodding towards the ladies' room. She made an excuse and followed me. We passed by the ladies' room and stepped through a door marked "Private" at the end of the corridor, where we could talk without fear of being overheard.

"How are you doing, Gia?" I asked. I was scared but thought she must be reliving her and Max's rape at the Silent

Souls event they attended in Chicago. She is really good at shutting off her emotions, but she blanched at my question and uncharacteristically and subconsciously placed her hand on my arm, drawing support.

"I won't lie and say this is fun. I'm jumpy as hell. A waitress stumbled over a chair leg just now in my direction, and I nearly kicked her in the face." I must have looked alarmed because she quickly added, "I didn't. Don't worry."

"Gia, sorry to ask about your previous encounter, but I wanted to check something. I think you said that at the event in Chicago, both you and Max felt unusually horny and overly casual during the build-up and the dinner. The sex acts at the end of the evening were the culmination of something that built up for over an hour beforehand."

"That's right. I was conscious of it at the time, but it didn't feel like anything I needed to worry about. In hindsight, it was a glaring problem. Why?" she replied.

"I don't know about you, but I feel the least horny I've ever felt and the opposite of casual; I'm on full alert."

"Me, too. Tonight feels very different from last time. Either Talan is not nearby, or she isn't using her Adept powers on us. Or these blockers are negating the sensations," she said thoughtfully.

"That's what I was thinking, too. I want to turn mine off, and I want you nearby so you can take me down if I do anything of concern," I proposed.

"I should turn mine off," she objected. "I am more likely to recognize the feeling!"

"That's true," I countered, "but there is no way I could take you down if you reacted strangely. I'd just get a butt-kicking."

I reached under my skirt, through a deftly cut seam, and retrieved a small dart gun, which I held loosely at the ready. Gia stepped back and reached into where her voluminous dress wrapped around her cleavage, which was where the battery for her blocker was strapped with adhesive tape and flipped off the power. We stood and looked at each other for a minute. She flipped it back on and said she felt no change whatsoever. I texted this information to everyone, visited the ladies' room for real, took a moment to double check my blocker was working, and then returned to my table.

Throughout the auction, several messages came in from Kelsie, who was monitoring events from Comox. Our microwave cameras and the drones situated outside of the missile defence ring didn't detect any threat. There were no unexpected radio or other airborne communications in the vicinity. Our people in the venue's control room reported that nothing unusual was occurring.

As we reached the culmination of the event, pledges had reached 15 million dollars, with the last item that remained to be sold for at least another million. Ethan had donated a small Rembrandt from this private collection, worth twice that much, with a million-dollar minimum reserve.

The auctioneer was at his podium, his gavel poised; the Premier of British Columbia and his twenty-something-year-old niece were already on the stage, ready to formally present the masterpiece to the winning bidder. Ethan and Gia made their way to the podium, Ethan to give some background on his donation, and Gia to be ready with closing comments after the award. The stage was tastefully decorated, with the previously won prizes arranged as a backdrop to this final item's sale, and audio-visual team had the lighting focussed in to raise the atmosphere – all tricks borrowed from high-roller auctions to help the donations flow to their maximum.

The Premier's niece had stepped away momentarily, drawn to one of the prizes behind her, the latest gaming platform; she was disappointed she wouldn't be taking it home. This new, high-tech model had just been released two days ago and it was all but impossible to get one's hands on them. The Premier had almost outbid all comers, raising half joking questions about who was paying for it, as his bid was $50,000. In the end he was outbid by a big-name athletic clothing retailer who wanted it for his son.

The Premiere's niece lifted a flap on the top of the unit when suddenly, as the music stopped to make way for the speeches and the crowd settled, a high-pitched whine became audible above the hubbub in the room. All of the security personnel went on full alert, their heads swivelling wildly to detect the source of the noise.

There was a modest flash. We were plunged into darkness, with only the moonlight streaming through the venue's glass, domed roof and the various skylights leaving the room silhouetted in silver. It was eerily quiet for a second before nervous voices and calls for lights replaced the silence. The music and the air conditioning had ceased; even the ceiling fans were spinning down. The dim light revealed the security team had pulled their weapons from their holsters, but no targets had presented themselves. I realized that without conscious thought, I'd pulled my Glock, too.

With my other hand, I reached into my purse and pulled out my phone to see what the control room or Kelsie could tell us. My phone was completely dead, despite my pressing buttons on it, uselessly trying to revive it. I could see others had the same problem with their devices.

I was suddenly filled with warmth and desire. The urgent concerns of a moment ago faded, becoming trivial and distant, replaced by a pressing need spreading out from my crotch, up through my belly to my breasts. A part of me knew this was Talan's doing, but why would I care about that now? I wanted sex; the urge was building rapidly. I looked at Ethan, who was looking at me as well as taking in the room. I looked around and people had started to move closer to each other. Was this going to happen? I had never had an orgy fantasy in my life, but suddenly it seemed like the best idea.

The Premier's niece stepped to the centre of the stage and was joined by a small Black teenager I had noticed sitting with them earlier. The niece dipped her head to remove her wig. Then she carefully pealed off a thick layer of prosthetics from her nose, cheekbones, brow, and ears. Plucking a cloth napkin from the nearest table and wiping away makeup from her face, Talan emerged from her disguise.

I felt rage begin to rise within me, and I hoped it would trump this unholy lust. I felt a desperate need to get to Ethan, who Talan was now looking at like the predator she was. I fought the compulsion for sex as hard as I could. Though I was losing that battle, I at least had some sense of what I was seeing: Like me, Max and Gia appeared to be struggling; but not Ethan. He appeared totally consumed and in Talan's thrall. He stood stupidly holding his erection through his pants, like many of the other men in the room were. Garrett was also fighting Talan's spell; he appeared confused, but he obviously sensed Talan was behind it and kept trying to raise his gun in Talan's direction.

Aside from Talan and the mystery teen, only two people in the room looked fully in control of themselves. Both were guests who owned legitimate property businesses that had unsubstantiated links to money laundering. Each walked over to the nearest person with a gun drawn, disarmed them without any objection, stepped up next to Talan, and trained the acquired weapons on the crowd.

A wave of abject and crippling fear rolled through the room, pushing away the sexual pressure. It heralded Jim, who then burst through the kitchen door and locked his eyes on Talan and her three companions; they were the only people unaffected by his unleashing his full Adept power. The rest of us cowered and stared around seeking a sabre tooth tiger or some other monster. Four people fainted and collapsed, another grabbed his chest and I feared he was having a heart attack.

One of Talan's gunmen took aim at Jim and, for a moment, my fear for Jim overrode the fear he was pumping into me. With a crude bang from the gun, Jim went down hard, a spray of blood painting the women behind him crimson. The fear he projected on us dissipated quickly, and sexual desire reasserted itself. The teenage girl looked on in horror and, for no reason, the man who had shot Jim collapsed in a heap. Before I could determine who had had their wits about them to shoot Jim's murderer, the desire for sex and compliance swept me up and I felt my body getting impatient and hot. I realized I had dropped my gun to free my hands so they could claw at my outfit; a most inappropriate move, but I didn't care.

"Quiet! Everyone, quiet!" shouted Talan, and although a small part of me wanted to scream back, most of me was eager to listen. After all, her voice dripped with honey and might tell us we could have sex soon. I wanted to hear that. I needed her permission. The room was silent within seconds. The only sounds were of us breathing lustily.

"Ladies and gentlemen. Premier, Mayor, and our late Nimbus," Talan said, looking at Jim's body with what appeared to be some genuine sadness. There was one less of her race, although she had singlehandedly done the most damage to her own species.

"You came here for a show, and I won't disappoint. I will let you quench your desires shortly, but to set the scene, I think we need a sacrifice. Blood rites always add to these gatherings, I find. Mr Booker, step forward." As he complied, docile, I tried to tap into the panic I was feeling for him; the small part of my brain that was fighting back, hoping that emotion might overcome Talan's grip. I looked at Gia, who had tears streaming down her face but was helpless, too.

"If any of you are concerned for Mr Booker," Talan continued, "you need not be. Booker is a filthy murderer, you see. He killed my lover in cold blood, and today I will have my revenge. I will also kill Ms Braekhus and Mr Stone before I leave, for meddling in my business interests. But not before I force them to debase themselves again and relive the pain." She turned to me.

"And Ms Stone. Alas, you too. Aside from the company you keep, I don't think I have a score to settle with you, but you are way too dangerous to leave alive after I kill your partner. I don't want you doing to me what I am about to do to Ethan, after all." She laughed at her own joke. "But you can help me make Ethan suffer just a little more before I end him. You will fuck Garrett here, in front of Ethan. And I will make sure Ethan enjoys watching you do it, too."

Garrett turned his head my way and our eyes locked. He was fighting her, too, I could tell. But I also sensed it would do neither of us much good.

"Booker, strip off! I want everyone to see you debased and humbled. And I want them to see you erect at the sight of your woman being taken by another. You might as well enjoy it, too, as it will be the last thing you will ever see – except for my face."

As if he hadn't a care in the world, Ethan stripped. Her control over him was complete, and I saw no sign of a struggle on his face. In fact, it was blank and emotionless. And when directed, I moved over to Garrett, despite fighting every step.

When Ethan was naked, he dropped his clothes, without thought, alongside his delta-blocker, which presumably had been neutralized by whatever killed the power. His gun was still holstered and sat atop the mess.

"Friends. The powerful and rich of Vancouver, I present to you Mr Ethan Booker, the world's nudest private detective in all of his glory. I admit he is a fine specimen who could entertain me for hours, except that I despise him," yelled Talan, her voice becoming manic. "Here, boy," she ordered. Ethan walked slowly over and stood an arm's length to her right. Awaiting his fate. Even as my hands started to undress Garrett, and his worked on the remains of my dress, I tried to hold out hope. I had to find a way to overcome Talan's grip. I locked eyes with Ethan, and he looked back at me. There was a hint of recognition and, slowly, a single tear formed and rolled down his left cheek.

Talan pulled at the handle of her purse and it came apart, revealing an eight-inch-long ceramic blade, which looked wickedly sharp.

I felt the sex-compulsion ratchet up another notch.

"Ethan, I'm really disappointed not to see an erection. I rarely find anyone who can resist my charms. Perhaps it's broken? You won't be needing it, so perhaps I should cut it off.

What do you think?" threatened Talan. Ethan just nodded slowly and helplessly.

At times like this, humans do amazing things. They find wells of untapped emotion to beat the greatest adversity. Their bodies release so much adrenalin that some have been granted the strength of ten people and lifted cars to free trapped children. That small part of me that still fought realized that that effect was a possibility and our only chance. My mind sought something of enough consequence to harness to fight back. Images of abuse at my father's hand flooded my mind. I returned for a moment to when I was told Max had been killed in the Middle East. The death of my first husband. The bullies at my high school. I opened up all of the mental boxes I had these terrors buried in and let the pain and horror rise up. These memories stoked a deep, deep rage within me, and I rode it hard, encouraging it.

Garrett had my dress undone and was working it over my shoulders. I looked him in the eye and saw only sorrow. He was still fighting, too. I willed him success. I put my hands on his chest and pushed him back a step. It was an incredibly hard thing to do.

"Oh Marcy, you are a fighter," laughed Talan. Her compulsion increased enormously, and the room went into motion, with people pawing at whoever was nearest. I dropped to my knees, the desire to free Garrett from his pants unstoppable. I instantly knew I was beat, and my hands rose as if they had their own mind and settled on his belt.

I looked at Ethan, who was staring back. I managed to mouth a "sorry." I saw his eyes soften. A look of forgiveness.

Talan stepped closer to Ethan, placing the blade of her knife on his cheek. A tiny prick of red spawned at its point. She was whispering to him, her face a mask of hate. Talan stepped around him, dropping the knife to his throat. She wanted to stare into his eyes and watch his life drain away. Then, with a percussive crack, Ethan head butted the bridge of her nose, driving his brow deep into her face.

The room suddenly spun violently, and I vomited – as did several people around me. Some people collapsed as Talan's heavy spell blanked out completely in her shock. I was enveloped by an intense feeling of isolation, closely followed by a wave of agony and rage as Talan's uncontrolled mind pumped out what she felt as her consciousness caught up with Ethan's attack.

Ethan hit her again, but instead of hitting her with a throat strike, which seemed to be his intent, his knuckles glanced off her shoulder. He instantly reversed into an elbow strike, whipping his torso around to build power and speed, but he mistimed it and it glanced off the top of Talan's head instead of connecting with her temple. Talan stumbled, but recovered enough to thrust her blade into Ethan. He keeled over and hit the deck hard, lying still.

My brain was screaming *no, no, no* so loudly my legs were deaf to another part of my minds demand they carry me to Ethan's side. This can't be happening. I tried to shake myself to motion. I let the urgency bloom and I gulped for breath. *Move, move, move...*

Talan stood over him, knife poised to finish things, when a gun fired. She reeled around grabbing for her shoulder; Max was on his knees near Jim and lining up another shot. He fired, and the second of Talan's gun men went down. My wonderful brother's skillfully trained arm swung back to aim at Talan. I looked for my gun but had left it ten feet away. Garrett was wrestling in his discarded jacket for his holster, but it was tangled.

People were recovering all around and standing up, blocking Max's shot. Talan stumbled back, grabbing her teenaged companion as she ran for the exit at the back of the stage. A wave of fear hit us; a weaker version of Jim's, but it was still enough to stop us in our tracks. A few moments later it faded, and I could stand again.

I ran to Ethan, nearly colliding with Gia and Max as they went after Talan. I gently rolled him over and examined his wound. Talan had aimed at his heart, no doubt, but the knife had glanced off a rib and gouged his shoulder. There was a lot of blood, but it didn't look fatal. Garrett appeared at my side with a first aid kit, ripped a compress from a packet, placed it over the wound, and applied pressure.

My thoughts went to Jim, who already had two medically trained people working on him: the Head of Surgery from Vancouver General who was a guest, and a medic who was a member of Max's team. They sat back suddenly, and I heard the whine of a defibrillator. Then I saw Jim's body jerk and the team restarted CPR.

26: AN UNEXPECTED TURN

Jim died twice in the next hour while we waited for transport to get him to a hospital. The field training of the doctor and the medic's combined at the party was enough to bring him back both times, but his blood loss was becoming an issue. His visible wounds were quickly staunched but he was bleeding internally.

Nothing electrical worked within half a mile. No phones, no radios, and no transport. We knew Kelsie would have organized some sort of rescue, so we just had to hang on. The first to arrive was an RCMP helicopter, which just beat the team Kelsie had arranged to the single helipad. The RCMP assumed ground command but were not interested in saving lives. They herded everyone into the ballroom and refused to listen to our pleas to medivac Jim and Ethan.

Kelsie's helicopter circled and was about to put down on the ski slope above the facility when the RCMP ordered them to leave the area. Ten minutes later, two large American army Blackhawk helicopters descended from the sky. The RCMP aircraft lifted off to make way for one – and assumed an overwatch role hovering above us – and the other Blackhawk settled onto the ski hill where Kelsie's helicopter had tried to put down. Roughly 30 soldiers and specialists spread out through the venue and surrounding area, either searching for threats or setting up hazmat tents.

Only once the military had determined that the area was safe did they allow a medivac unit they had called to land and take on Jim and Ethan. Four soldiers accompanied them; the rest of us were detained, questioned for two hours, and then forced to provide a blood sample. We were kept on site another three hours while these samples were tested, before guests and staff were allowed to depart on a fleet of helicopters Kelsie had lined up for us. Throughout all of this, we were kept in the dark by the RCMP, despite vociferous protests from the Province's most influential people, including the Premier.

Gia and I sat together as Max shared with us his deduction that the military response was due to Talan having killed all of the electronic devices and power supply. He guessed, correctly as we confirmed later, that she had hidden a miniature EMP device in the game console that was in the auction. An Electro Magnetic Pulse – EMP for short – was first discovered to be released during the detonation of a nuclear weapon. The effect is to disrupt and shut down anything operating on electricity within a wide radius. The military has long since found ways to create the pulse without the nuclear radiation and devastation of property, and more recently has found ways to create mini versions, which just take down a city block. It appeared Talan had her hands on an even smaller, more tactical version.

The US and NATO have satellites constantly circling the earth monitoring for nuclear and EMP events, and Canada has an arrangement with the USA where the latter will cross the border immediately to help determine the source if such emissions are detected on the west coast of Canada. The RCMP and the men from the Blackhawks had practised this scenario annually for the past 20 years and were not about to let anything disrupt the script they had developed. This nuclear alarm apparently lay behind the delay in Jim being medevacked to hospital. Nothing could leave until the authorities were sure there was not a second device hidden at the venue.

Once the investigators had determined there was no radiation or damage but that an EMP had been deployed, the mountain and surrounding area had been locked down and the questioning had begun. The embarrassing reports of rampant emotions caused investigators to quickly conclude an exotic drug of some sort must have been released into the air, hence the blood tests. When nothing was found in our blood other than alcohol or – in some cases – recreational street drugs, they let us go.

Gia, Max, and I boarded the helicopter Kelsie had sent and the pilot – the first person who could give us any news of the outside world – gave me her phone; Kelsie was already on the line.

"Ethan's fine," she said, without my having to ask. "Just stitches and a pint of blood. Jim's critical and in surgery. They are both at Vancouver General and the pilot will have you there in about ten minutes. What happened? We had lost all contact with the entire mountain." As we lifted off the slope and descended rapidly down the mountainside towards the hospital just on the far side of the city, I filled Kelsie in on what we knew and suspected. She advised there was still no word from Courtney and Moy Lei, but that a tunnel had been discovered through which they must have been taken.

Vancouver General has a helipad on the roof, but it was occupied by the medivac aircraft that brought in Jim. I assured our pilot we would intercede with Transport Canada should the need arise but having flown often with Ethan she needed no encouragement to complete several highly illegal manoeuvres to deposit us on the playground of the children's wing.

Ethan was with Gwen and Naomi, who were all pacing in the waiting room. Kelsie had them flown back when they had lost contact with the mountain, in case Naomi's specialized knowledge of some of our group's physiology would be needed. I flung myself at Ethan, who was wearing a borrowed T-shirt and pants; he had a strapped-up shoulder and still had some flecks of blood on the side of his head. He flinched away slightly due to the pain my uncontrolled embrace caused, and I stared deeply into his eyes, somehow trying to double check his many reassurances that he was fine.

Also present in the small waiting room were two soldiers – two others waited outside – and two of our protection team. As I examined Ethan for scratches, I noticed he was wearing a delta-blocker, presumably brought over by Naomi. We couldn't discuss events in front of the security teams, so all we could do was settle in and hope Talan wasn't homing in to finish the job while we waited for news of Jim.

Jim was still under the knife when the lead investigator from the mountain event, who refused to identify which branch of government he worked for, arrived to question Ethan and Jim. He would have a long time to wait to talk to Jim, but he took Ethan away for an hour. I had no idea how Ethan would explain standing naked in front of the room and the ensuing attack on Talan, which had presumably been described by many who were at the event. We were told we could go home but not leave the city until further notice, so we sat and waited for news of Jim, Courtney, and Moy Lei. The soldiers that had guarded us wished us luck and left with the investigator.

*

Jim was released to intensive care four hours later, but the problems did not stop there; people treating him were falling sick, as were other people in the ICU. Naomi had already declared she had been acting as Jim's GP and so had been able to work closely with the medical staff. She surmised that in his troubled and drugged state, his Adept brain was leaking emotions that were the cause of the sickness, which she had experienced herself while in his recovery room. Citing various allergies Jim didn't actually have, she tricked the attending doctors to substitute a different sedative, one that Naomi knew would calm Jim's unconscious outpourings.

Max arrived, exhausted. He had left Garrett to clean up things at the mountain, flown down to the heliport at the harbour front, and taken an Uber to the hospital. It was now nearly 3 pm and we needed a plan, believing Talan would have had time to regroup, increasing the risk of an imminent attack. Max had already thought of this and had a proposal.

"Ethan, Marcy, Gia, and I are Talan's primary targets," he began. "Jim is a threat, too, of course, and he isn't going anywhere soon. We need to protect him, but we need to be on the move to stay out of Talan's sights. And we need to find Courtney and Moy Lei."

"I'm not leaving Jim's side until we know he can protect himself," cut in Ethan, bristling, and stepping into Max's space.

"Respectfully, Bro, that's tactically unsound and stupid. If Talan determines we are all in one spot, she could put a shoulder-launched missile through the hospital window. You are putting innocents at risk for little defensive gain. You know Jim wouldn't see that as acceptable, and neither would you if that were you in that bed." The two men stared at each other. Eventually, Ethan backed down, reluctantly accepting the wisdom.

"Our standard protection teams are aware there is some weird shit going on. They've made comments and tried to understand it for months, but we kept them in the dark. The team members we had in the event room experienced it first-hand and talked about it - even more than they talked about their boss dropping his kit in front of the crowd," laughed Max, trying to ease the tension.

"Jeez, I'd forgotten about that," Ethan winced.

"I've already ordered new business cards, Ethan. *The Nude Detective,*" I said, piling on.

"I want permission to bring our regular security team who have experience with Talan into the fold. Not to tell them all of the details but tell them enough so they could wear the delta-blockers and stay and protect Jim. The rest of us need to get moving, get some rest, and go find Moy Lei and Courtney – if they are still alive. Let's stay hard on this bitch's tail. Let's not let up and give her time to get too organized to come at us again."

There was no arguing with my brother's logic so, with our blessing, he went off to talk to the protection team. An hour later, we left them to it. Two were resting in cars in the hospital parking lot, while the other two guarded Jim, Naomi, and Gwen, who was glued to Naomi's side. In addition to these four who would wear blockers 24/7, were six others who were not in the know. It was the best we could do until Jim was fit enough to move. The rest of us went home, changed, collected whatever we thought we could use, briefed Aiden that we were busting the 'don't leave town' directive, and headed to the airport. An hour later, we were asleep in our seats as our plane climbed north, around but not over the Silent Souls venue – which was now a temporary no-fly zone – on a looping track that would keep us well out of US airspace. We wanted to stay out of the reach of the CIA but get to the east coast, where we assumed our missing team members were being held captive.

Umiujaq Airport – also known as Cold Lake Airport – is nearly 800 miles north of Montreal as the crow flies and was our refueling stop. Normally below freezing here, today it was a balmy 4 degrees Celsius, so we sat on the ramp beneath the plane to eat while the pilot set up for the next leg. Ethan was ravenous and ate two meals, his body presumably needing energy to repair his wounds. We had slept most of the way across northern Canada and there hadn't been time for a group debrief, so when we finished eating, we set up a call with those left behind in Vancouver and caught up.

Jim was improving rapidly, his unusual body consuming massive amounts of sustenance as quickly as Naomi could convince his doctors to supply it. She hoped that by tomorrow, he would be ready to move to the Booker Building, where she could support Jim better than the hospital could. She was preparing her lab for any eventuality, as well as scheming with Aiden to break Jim out of hospital when the time came.

What we all wanted to know was how Ethan had managed to overcome Talan's grip at the last moment and save us all. His blocker was dead, yet somehow, he had found the strength of will when the rest of us could not.

"It wasn't like that, actually," he began, looking a little sheepish. "When the lights went out, I felt the compulsion, as you clearly all did. But after a few moments, I realized I could push it away fairly easily. Don't ask me how. I felt the effort draining me, it was hard work, but not impossible."

"Why didn't you smack Talan earlier?" I asked, as surprised as everyone else looked. I began to feel anger and shame stir within that Ethan had let me go so far with Garrett before he acted.

"By the time I realized it, and trusted it, she had two guys on the stage covering us all with guns. I was trying to plan something when Jim ran out and got himself shot. Of course, at that point I wished I had just acted first and thought later, but it wasn't how it played out. Poor Jim." Ethan paused in thought, then continued.

"Another thing I found troubling was what I saw as I watched the guy who shot Jim very closely. He was only four or five feet away from me; it was like the light in his eyes just went out, and he crumpled to the floor. I imagine Talan did something to his mind and killed him for shooting Jim, and I didn't know if I could withstand that, and didn't want her to do whatever it was to the whole room. I waited her out until I was in striking distance, from where I felt certain I could do the most damage."

"That took guts, Ethan," put in Max. "And I'm sure you will get invited to a lot of parties now that most of Vancouver knows you intimately now." I hit Max on one shoulder, just as Gia clipped him around the ear.

"Yes, that was interesting. Please forget everything you saw. When I got close and she came for me with that knife, I knew I had her. I struck, but I think the Hard Colada threw me off. I know we practised it, but it was like the first time we tried it. I missed every punch by a mile. Then I collapsed with exhaustion."

"I think the rest of us collapsed because Talan sent out some sort of shock wave," Gia said. "Perhaps it was that?"

"Maybe. I felt the wave and saw you all go down. But I had been struggling with the strain of pushing off Talan for a few minutes and felt my energy was just being sapped. I had nothing in reserve. I didn't say anything, but I was feeling very depleted all day. I had wondered earlier in the day if I had a flu coming. At the hospital I talked to Naomi about it, and she took some blood. She has a theory, and when we stopped off at home, she took me down to her lab and did a quick MRI. Did you conclude anything, Naomi?"

"I did, as a matter of fact, but I wanted to talk to you alone. I don't share patient information without consent."

"Go ahead," laughed Ethan. "This group is family and they just saw me naked, so I have very little left to hide." He winked subtly at me.

"You had told me before Marcy and the others arrived that you were less effected than the others at the event. That got my mind whirring. The blood sample you gave me suggested I was not barking mad, and finally the MRI confirmed my suspicions."

"Go on," said a suddenly more serious Ethan.

"Adepts' blood has an enzyme unique to their physiology. I theorized that it is required to convert their food more efficiently, given their brains require more energy. It relates to why Adepts are so lean – even gaunt. Your blood was rich in that enzyme. It has never shown up in any of your previous blood tests. The MRI confirmed my hypothesis: Your fourth neuron, which was dormant in all previous tests, has switched on and is lit up like Moy Lei and Jim's."

We were all stunned. Ethan was staring at me with what looked like his *will-you-still-love-me-now-I'm-an-alien* look that he wore when he first discovered he had a delta neuron. I wanted to reassure him by jumping his bones but, with everyone there, I settled for pulling him into a hug and warning him that jokes about him having a bigger brain than me would not go down well.

We all had replacement phones, since ours were destroyed by the EMP, and Ethan's rang now.

"It's Roxy," he said, pushing the buttons so that her call joined our group conference and everyone could hear.

"Roxy, where the hell are you? Is everyone OK?" he asked.

"No, Ethan. I'm sorry," she croaked, her voice hoarse. I took her apology to mean she had let someone get hurt on her watch. "I have Talan and Cochrane next to me. Moy Lei and

Courtney are in the room, too, but are heavily sedated. Out cold. Talan just killed the three other members of my team in front of me... they've been like a family to me..." her voice broke into sobs. She had known all three for several years and they were like family to her. There was a long moment of quiet, though which we could hear Roxy crying softly.

"God. I'm so sorry, Roxy," said Ethan. "This is on us, not you." The noise of the phone being pulled from Roxy's ear heralded Talan's angry voice coming onto the line.

"You are a very hard man to kill, Ethan."

"Back at you, bitch!" retorted Ethan. His face didn't reflect the emotion he put into his voice, and I knew he was more in control of himself than he appeared. He wanted Talan to think she had his measure.

"What do you want?" he asked, after a moment of sounding like he was getting himself together.

"An exchange. You for your remaining bodyguard and Moy Lei. I would ask for Marcy, Gia, and Max, too, but you would never trade them, of course. I'll settle for you for now."

"I'd want Courtney, too," Ethan's tone brooked no debate.

"Let me be clear," cut in Talan. "Du Caron's dead, whatever happens. She is too much of a threat to me to leave alive. But I want her to see you die and know that the remainder of Le Perjure are dead, too, before she follows her clan. You will bring me one of those clever devices that block Nimbus powers in return for a quick and painless death, and your two friends will go free and unharmed. With your device, I can wake up Courtney and let her watch me slit her throat." Everyone in the room was silently signalling Ethan not to make the deal, but he waved us away.

"I thought you Nimbus were immune to each other's powers. Is Courtney so much stronger than you that you are scared of her?" Ethan was baiting her. He didn't want to appear too compliant.

"She's strong enough to spoil my enjoyment of slitting her throat, let's put it that way. And if you are insolent again, it will cost Storm here her eyes." Talan sounded like she was trying to appear relaxed, but the hatred and malevolence came through, nonetheless.

"Tell me where you are, and you have a deal," he said, letting resignation creep into his voice.

"I'll get back to you with instructions." The line clicked, and Kelsie confirmed the call from Roxy's phone had dropped off.

"You are not going to her, whatever the cost," said all of us in various ways, simultaneously. "She'll just kill you all, anyway." Max finished the thought we were all thinking.

"I hope it doesn't come to that," replied Ethan, emphatically. "But if I have to, I will. In that case, I'll need every trick I can use. Naomi," he barked, in a harsh tone, "what went wrong with my Hard Colada at the venue?" I knew he was under stress but taking it out on Naomi was offside and he felt me giving him the side-eye and closed his eyes to recompose himself. But before he could apologize Gwen jumped in.

"Hey, back up there! We all knew it was an experimental drug and discussed the risks."

"It's OK, Gwen," said Naomi. "If I had to speculate, I think Ethan's metabolism has sped up, driven by his delta neuron switching on. Perhaps he has to recalibrate his fast-speed training and get used to different reflexes." Her voice sounded tight, and her tone suggested she was hiding behind her professional persona. It seems that Ethan had hit a nerve.

"Naomi, Gwen's right. That wasn't fair. No excuses, but there is a lot to take in. Sorry," he offered.

"Err...guys," cut in Kelsie. "There is another caller in the virtual waiting room. It's Jim's line. I'm allowing him into the call now."

A few clicks later, an unmistakable baritone came through the line, rough and whispery, but very much Jim. "Hello. Are you there?" before dissolving into a painful coughing fit. Everyone on the call was cheering and peppering him with questions. Looking around the group here, there wasn't a dry eye to be seen.

"Guys, stop, stop!" coughed Jim, and we made an effort to suppress our relief and delight so we could hear him. "I can barely keep my eyes open, and this idiot here," he seemed to be referring to one of the guards in his room, "he wouldn't give me my phone until I threatened to climb out of bed and hit him."

"That's because you nearly died and need to rest, Jim," said Ethan sternly but kindly. "Doctor's orders."

"Sshhh! You don't understand. Talan. I can sense her. Whatever was blocking her from me has stopped. If I could move, I could find her."

"You won't be moving for a while, Jim," put in Naomi. Jim ignored her and continued after more coughing.

"Ethan, did you see her?" whispered Jim.

"Who? Talan?" answered Ethan.

"No," coughed Jim. "At the event, just before I got shot. The Black girl from the seawall. She was standing behind Talan."

"I saw a young girl with Talan," I replied.

"We met her on the seawall in Vancouver? When?" puzzled Ethan. "Are you sure, Jim? Now you say it I almost *can* see her. But it's like she's standing in a mist."

"Absolutely. Her aura is unmistakable. Quite different from any Nimbus I've ever met. Her energy was in the room, too. Each time I focused my mind on Talan, trying to break her grip on you, my energy just disappeared into the girl's aura. Like she was sucking up my power. Never seen anything like it. I'd bet Talan hasn't developed the ability to hide herself. I think her young friend was masking Talan's mind from us. But now she's stopped."

27: THE SNIPER TRAP

[Talan] – Booker's helicopter landed at Davison Army Airbase under the special clearance Cochrane had arranged. I sent him his instructions 48 hours ago and he was following them to the letter. The operations room was monitoring him closely and reported that he was the Eurocopter's sole occupant and flying the aircraft himself. They reported he had been searched and that, as instructed, he was unarmed and not wearing the device that blocks my mind. The reception committee made him change into clothes we supplied to foil any potential smuggling attempt, and he had compliantly climbed into the SUV I sent to fetch him, without incident.

Cochrane's team had agents deployed all over the fort, as well as on the far side of the river. He had arranged for both lasers and radar to scour the nearby airspace for any aircraft, including drones. Anything larger than a football would be detected and shot down by the fort's defences. The only drone in the area was the one we were controlling; it circled overhead, feeding high-definition pictures of my compound and a half mile radius around us to our team. It was an unarmed, military Predator from the Washington defences. DC is monitored 24/7 by drones that carry visual-surveillance cameras as well as sensor pods that detect radioactive and chemical activity, which might pose a terrorist threat.

"What is the status of our sniper team?" I asked.

"All eight report their status as green, with the target zone in sight. Our observers watching our sniper nests report nothing untoward, and the observers searching for counter-snipers also report no threats."

The mansion's rear garden was open to the north and south on the sides, but the house blocked the view from the west, and the row of thick trees at the fence line blocked the view from the east. On the two open sides, between 600 and 850 yards out, eight 40-foot towers had been erected on poles or in truck-mounted cranes – similar to those that repair traffic lights – with a sniper nest mounted in each.

Each sniper nest was a thick steel box with a four-by-six-inch hole through which the sniper could aim and fire down into the garden. The ground around each nest was protected by army personnel. I had spent time with each sniper to ensure they had no qualms about following my orders. It took time, which is why my directive to Booker had been to arrive here today, 48 hours from when I first told him I had his people hostage.

Two overlapping sniper detection systems, which fire lasers in all directions and detect any light rebounding from a surface with the signature of a telescopic sight, scanned the perimeter constantly but could only detect our eight shooters.

"And our guests in the yard?"

"Courtney du Caron, Moy Lei, and Storm are staked out in the sniper kill-zone, and the doctor reports the two Nimbus are in a medically induced coma, as ordered."

"Then let's go and meet Mr Booker."

Cochrane, Lindi, and I walked across the patio and over the lawn to where three bodies were propped up in chairs. Their arms and legs were tightly fixed to the seats with medical-grade immobilization cuffs – the types used at asylums. Both Nimbus were asleep, with a drip inserted into their arms that supplied the drugs that kept them that way; Storm was awake and glaring at me with hatred.

Ten feet in front of their chairs was a three-sided shelter with a flat roof. The shelter was steel and would stop even a 50-calibre bullet from a Barratt rifle. Lindi and I stood in the shelter, while Cochrane went to stand between the chairs occupied by the two sleeping Nimbus. He dismissed the doctor monitoring the prisoners.

As Booker was marched into the garden, I took the pistol from the table in the shelter and held it by my side, just in case. Cochrane reached into his jacket and pulled another from his holster and pointed it at Moy Lei's head. The two guards escorting Booker brought him to a mark we had painted on the floor of our little stage, and one of the guards handed me a large, padded envelope. Inside was a small box with electrodes on wires, presumably the device to block Nimbus energy.

"How does it work, cousin?" I asked Booker.

"Attach the electrodes here, and here," he said, pointing to spots high on the back of his neck, "and flip the switch. Green light means it is on. Battery is good for three hours. I was thinking of selling them online."

"Hilarious. You try it first. I don't want to get tasered, thank you." As I spoke, I flooded the yard with my mind. Booker, and everyone awake except Lindi, flinched. Good. I was a little worried after Booker fought off my power on the mountain top but, seeing him now, I decided I had correctly concluded it was a final rush of adrenaline from his impending death. This time I would be smarter, and he wouldn't get within eight feet of me.

One of the guards put the electrodes on Booker and turned on the device. Aside from a short bleep and the green light flashing then staying on, nothing happened. Satisfied, I had the guard fasten it to my neck; I took the unit and held it in my free hand, then sent both guards back to the house.

"I've kept my end," said Booker. "Let Roxy and Moy Lei go. Then you can do what you want with me." *How naïve*, I thought.

"Actually, no. None of you will leave here alive. And I don't think Marcy, Gia, or Max will see the month out." Then I nodded at Cochrane to wake Courtney up.

"You are a lying bitch," Ethan said, pointing his finger at me aggressively.

Cochrane pushed a button on the side of the valve on du Caron's drip, cutting off the sedative. Then he took a syringe from the table next to her chair and emptied its contents into the plastic pipe leading into her arm, to speed up her awakening. After a few seconds, she began to come around.

"Hello, Auntie," I said. It took but a moment for her to understand her predicament. The intense pressure from her mind smashing into mine brought stars dancing before my eyes and made my knees faulter. Cochrane went down like a rag doll. Booker took a step towards me as I stumbled, seizing the moment he had obviously hoped for, but I steadied myself and kept my gun trained on him. It would only be a matter of time before du Caron's mind brought me down, but we had a prearranged contingency: When the operations centre staff monitoring remotely by video saw Cochrane fall, they quickly reopened the valve electronically to sedate du Caron again. I felt the pressure in my mind begin to subside and smiled. Cochrane pulled himself to his knee's, massaging his temples trying to clear his mind.

"Good try, Booker. But it will take more than..."

And then Cochrane's head exploded, filling the air with a red mist and a lot of brain.

*

[Ethan] – Napoleon – and several other famous people – have been credited with the phrase similar to, "Your battle plans are great until the first shot is fired," but I prefer the version attributed to the boxer, Mike Tyson: "Everyone has a plan until they get punched in the mouth."

We had done a lot to prepare for this moment, but there were too many variables for a sound plan. I knew that there was a good chance we would end up winging it. And it didn't take long, as the boxer had warned.

I reflected on how we got here. Naomi and Aiden had sprung Jim from hospital against the doctors' wishes, but Jim had been adamant and persuasive. He allowed them half a day to fit out a private jet as a mini hospital, and he, Gwen, and Naomi flew down to Florida. To reduce the risk of Talan sensing him, Naomi kept him sedated; however, during the flight she woke him every 30 minutes so he could take a mental bearing on Talan, mark it on a map, then let himself be put back to sleep. It wasn't very accurate, but it did correctly suggest Talan was close to where we found her today.

This position matched the location SkyLoX had traced the extra copy of the extortion material to, which increased our confidence significantly. SkyLoX had breached Talan's operations centre several days earlier by following the thread of the download, and we had been able to overhear much of the planning for the mansion's defences over a microphone she had compromised.

Max's contacts had supplied information about the defences of the fort, and the drone protection and security systems. Last night, Darcy piloted a special drone she had developed – ironically, for the CIA – into the base where Washington's defensive drones are housed. SkyLoX had accessed the base's computers and determined the drones' schedule. Darcy's drone flew under the Predator assigned to today's mission and rose to affix itself with a special adhesive to its belly. It reconfigured its rotors and some panels, so it looked like another sensing pod, and piggybacked a ride. It had been circling above Talan's property for the past 15 hours, feeding us intelligence. We watched the Adept eating breakfast with Cochrane and our friends being placed on the lawn.

Kelsie's contribution was to take out the sniper nests; knowing that a drone bigger than a football would be detected didn't deter her. She and her team sent 16 of the tiny units with the shaped charges that we had deployed in Venice to attack the snipers. Each sniper nest now had two charges attached to the poles that held them aloft. Kelsie detonated them all simultaneously once she saw our pre-agreed signal of my pointing at Talan, which she observed via the piggybacked camera feed.

Max was on a 52-foot wonder called the Sally-Jane. She was a converted car ferry – with its original flat bottom and bow-ramp – that had been upgraded to be a tender for one of my yachts. It was posh enough to fit the styling of a mega-yacht, yet still able to deliver ATVs and other toys directly onto a beach with its capacity to ground its bow and drop the ramp. It was an ideal playboy landing craft, too.

Having been flown in from the British Virgin Islands on a borrowed C5 Galaxy cargo plane – courtesy of the major who had been forced to hunt us in Detroit – the Sally-Jane was slowly working its way upriver past Talan's property. Hidden below decks was an eight-person assault team and their breaching equipment. Mounted on the mast, shrouded in a fake satellite dome, were two hydraulically controlled sniper rifles. The gimble and gyroscopic design automatically stabilized the rolling motion of the boat in a similar way to how warships' canons maintain their accuracy as the vessels pound through the waves.

Max stood at the targeting station, aiming the Barratt M82 rifles by computer and joystick. Instead of a lens, which an anti-sniper system would detect, a complex series of mirrors were used, none of which ever were perpendicular to the laser sensors which foiled the anti-sniper defence. The array of mirrors each caught different fractions of the target area from several offset directions and were reconstituted to an accurate targeting image on his screen by a custom computer system.

In the final go / no go meeting before I flew in, we knew that – despite all of this preparation – it would come down to several risky moments: Talan testing the blocker on me, rather than making a guard wear it and seeing if they could resist her power; the device was in perfect working order, but no one present had taken the drug, so it was useless. We had never even tested it on an Adept. Naomi doubted it would be effective, anyway. The next unknown was whether Talan would wake Courtney and Moy Lei and, if so, could they overcome Talan. We didn't know how many guards would be present in the yard. And we didn't know the purpose of the structure that was protecting Talan now.

The majority of the team advised not to risk the rescue, but I insisted – and Marcy surprised me by agreeing with me.

Under the skin of the wound Talan's knife had made, I had a subcutaneous radio receiver; buried deep in my ear was an earbud. I could hear Max talking me through his firing angles as things unfolded. He could see Cochrane but not Talan nor Lindi – Jim had recalled her name -- and wanted to use an option where I ran, hopefully drawing Talan out of cover for him to shoot. Through a series of clandestine signals that we had practised, I vetoed that idea in the moment, believing Talan would just shoot the hostages and then me.

My pointing at Talan had triggered Kelsie to detonate the explosives attached to the sniper towers, and my earpiece confirmed she had toppled them all. Max killed Cochrane, and the Sally-Jane was heading to shore at her top speed, which unfortunately wasn't particularly fast. We planned on four minutes from the 'go' signal to the boat beaching and the assault team blowing their way through the fence to the garden. Talan was holding the only gun here and, while she was alert enough to stay out of sight of Max's rifle, I knew that we didn't have that long. None of this factored in the response time from the others in the mansion; playing for time was the only card I had left, so I set about it.

"I saw you in Vancouver," I said to Lindi, who stood looking between Talan and me. She nodded slowly.

"She's been hiding you from us. How?" I asked Talan.

"I don't know how she does it, but it doesn't matter now. Once I kill you and Courtney, I won't need to hide my mind anymore." She clearly was unaware her mind had been visible for nearly 48 hours. Was that deliberate on behalf of this enigmatic teenager?

"You'll kill the girl then?" I asked. I wanted to create a division between them if I could. It would help delay things if I could start an argument. The girl certainly looked shocked at the suggestion. "How do you control her? When I met her with Jim she seemed honest enough."

"I have leverage over her family in Namibia, but I think she just wants to go home. She isn't educated enough to get there on her own, and I'm her only link."

"I can take you home, Lindi. Or Jim could."

"How do you know her name? And when did you meet in Vancouver? Oh, forget it. You are just playing for time. You have something else in that bag of tricks, don't you?" Talan looked around, trying to detect a threat. Then she turned the gun towards Roxy. "Let's get this done, Booker. You are all as good as dead, but I'll let you pick who goes first."

"Jim?" asked Lindi.

"He's in critical condition, I'm afraid. He is kind. He risked himself even further to help us locate Talan." I answered, ignoring Talan's order to pick her first victim.

"Why Talan hurt you? She hurt Uma," the girl said, in terrible English.

"ENOUGH!" yelled Talan, raising her gun and sighting on Moy Lei. I ducked and ran, zigzagging as I moved. I hadn't risked another dose of Hard Colada, but in that moment, I could have used it. I was too slow, and Talan swung the gun and fired. My right leg collapsed, and pain shot through my thigh. I tried to move towards Talan, but there was no way. I nearly blacked out. Talan had the gun pointed at my head and was grinning maniacally. I looked at Lindi.

"She hates me because I killed her man to protect someone I love. I tried to stop Talan from hurting good people like Jim, Roxy and Uma. Hide your eyes little one..." I whispered with regret.

I filled my mind with thoughts of Marcy, and how she must be feeling watching this play out via the drone. I looked up to the sky, hoping she would see me saying goodbye. Out of the corner of my eye, I saw Talan's aim shift towards my head.

"NO!" yelled Lindi. I looked just in time to see Talan's eyes freeze and the light go out of them. Just like the man who shot Jim's had. Talan folded slowly to the floor, twitching for a moment as her brain no longer instructed her muscles. Then she lay still. As I passed out, I heard a muffled explosion that I hoped was Max and the cavalry breaching the fence.

EPILOGUE

I poured a top-up round of prosecco into the flutes of our friends, who were gathered in our suite admiring our latest piece of art. Marcy, Gia, Max, Gwen, Naomi, Kelsie – and of course Elvis – were here for the 'morning after' breakfast.

Last night, as the sunset turned the private beach on Gambier Island golden – the beach opposite where I was nearly caught naked, which kicked off this whole series of events – Gia and Max slipped rings onto each others fingers and said the important words: "I will," "I do," and, in Max's case, "Hell, I caught myself a honey-mama." Not only were they married, but they were also parents-in-waiting. After breakfast they were bound for Montreal.

The honeymoon was deferred until the baby came, as they felt compelled to get Silent Souls back on track and had an additional gift-cum-headache to bring to life. As we took out the Mafia, SkyLoX had very thoughtfully recovered the millions we had transferred from Silent Souls. Recalling my extreme discomfort sitting across from detectives Webb and Bell and our discussion about money laundering, I had asked her to take it back and find a good use for it with some other good cause. I had intended to replace it with a donation. But the nine mayors who had become entangled in Talan's extortion scheme each donated two million, on the proviso that fifty percent of the money went to setting up Silent Souls offices in their cities, to serve their respective state or province.

Max had been so impressed with Garrett, who was not involved in Talan's scheme, that he talked me into hiring him and some of his crew to replace the people we had lost. Garrett and Roxy got on well, and we speculated on whether time would bring them together.

The artwork we were admiring was a photo Marcy had taken in Namibia, which we had blown up to be eight feet high by four feet wide and now hung in our living room by two discrete winches set in the ceiling. I know, things are getting out of control in the winch department.

The photo, which was mounted on stretched canvas and artfully daubed with glue to add texture where needed, was taken while we were in Namibia for the grand opening of Lindi and Jim's lodge.

We quickly learned how Lindi had been abducted and felt compelled to help. Marcy cried with Lindi as the tale of Uma's death was retold. Meeting Jim and me, and finally deciding that the people in this land, as she calls it, were basically good, she concluded that in rare cases, killing to protect is the better – if regrettable – option. This had given her the confidence to break her forced allegiance to Talan.

Marcy and I still hadn't connected the dots that it was Lindi who had killed Talan and the man who had shot Jim; that revelation came later. We fled DC within the hour of the assault team's rescue and were in Florida at Jim's bedside within four hours. I had x-rays and tests done, my field dressing changed, and was given on a course of painkillers and antibiotics.

It was touch-and-go with Jim. The strain of the trip to triangulate Talan's location was a tipping point and for several seemingly endless days we prepared for the worst. From the moment Lindi saw Jim in hospital, she refused to leave his side. Anyone who tried to remove her soon changed their minds or – as we found out later – had them changed by Lindi.

Jim eventually pulled through, proving again what a tough old bird, he is. As he improved, he practically adopted Lindi, and eventually determined she came from the Namib – a coastal desert in Namibia. It was Jim that Lindi took into her confidence, and in her language of witches and sorcerers explained how she had sent Talan and Jim's shooters' minds to the spirits. Slowly Jim gained from her an understanding of an unheard-of range of talents. He came to believe she was working on a whole new level, way ahead of any Adept he had ever met.

The most shocking revelation came when I was talking to Lindi about the day Jim was shot, on the mountain above Vancouver.

"Talan told me I must hide her mind, and the minds of the two men with guns," explained Lindi. "I kept waiting for you to stop Talan, and grew more and more angry with you when you did nothing. I could feel that you had accepted my gift, and Talan had little power over you, yet you pretended that she did. When Jim was shot, I blamed you for it because you didn't act against Talan until it was too late for Jim. Only to save yourself at the end. But later, I realized I was wrong."

"I don't understand," I replied. "What gift did you give me?"

"Your witchcraft," she replied. "You let it sleep, so I woke it for you." I realized it was Lindi who had somehow activated my delta neuron – the fourth neuron.

Lindi permitted Naomi to scan her using one of the MRI machines at the hospital in Florida and we were surprised by the results. We expected a fourth, or maybe even a fifth neuron. Something to explain Lindi's elevated powers. The surprise was Lindi's brain was the same as Marcy's or Gwen's. A standard human brain. We had no explanation for her abilities, so Lindi's answer was the best we could accept so far: She is a witch.

Gwen had the idea first, to set up a lodge to help the Nimbus. The idea got legs and morphed into a lodge in Namibia, close to Lindi's home village. Its primary focus was to help Namibian's with dementia; secondarily, anyone from Le Perjure or elsewhere in the Nimbus world was welcome to come and work with Lindi on their abilities.

Moy Lei formally joined Courtney in Le Perjure. Even so, the clan was still short of numbers to continue to influence the world as they once had. But her clan had many members, both men and women, who had a dormant fourth neuron, similar to me. With Lindi's help, many agreed to have Lindi activate it for them, and with time and training, Le Perjure would regain its strength. The year 2020 – and maybe a few after that – would show us what humanity would do when left to its own devices.

Marcy and I had flown out for the lodge's opening and had an amazing time. Phoenix had come out to play and we enacted one of my long-time nudity fantasies, that of being staked out naked in the open.

The dark red dunes surrounding Sossusvlei, a spectacular clay pan inhabited by 1000-year-old, seemingly petrified trees, are relatively new. The sand, which is the most amazing fiery red at sunrise, has had an interesting journey. It starts far from Namibia's west coast, where the dunes are located, instead originating on the other side of the continent in the Drakensburg Mountains. The Drakensburg erodes and deposits sand, iron, and other ores into the Orange River, giving its name. The river flows over 1400 miles across the country to the Atlantic Ocean. For much of the journey the river is below the surface of the land. Ownership of diamonds carried from the mountains and deposited along the route have resulted in several historic battles.

A hundred miles off the Namibian coast, the weather system plucks the orange sand up with seawater in the cycle of cloud and rain formation, and the landward airflow dumps the sand at the southern end of the Namib desert to create the Dunes.

"What a magical place for my Slave Boy to enjoy his fantasy of being staked out." said Pheonix.

The Dunes are in the Naukluft National Park and are best seen at before 9am each morning. Tourists queue up at the Sesriem gate to enter the park at 6.45am, make the 37-mile drive to the dunes, and try to be atop these massive hills of slippery sand for when they look their best. Of course, Phoenix had me fly us in early in a rented Robinson R44 helicopter.

The dunes are numbered and Dune 45 – which is 45km from the gate – stands at 557 feet high. It is one of the most visited attractions. The dune next to it rarely has visitors as there is a small lake in the valley separating the two, which although mostly a dry lakebed, makes the dune unattractive to visit. It is, however, wonderful for climbers of Dune 45 to photograph from the viewing point. On one particular day two weeks ago, anyone with a very long lens and eye for detail would have seen a naked man staked out in an X-shape, sweating, and looking back at them with playful chagrin.

I don't know how many tourist photos I am hidden in from that day, but I do know that if you know where to look – and you have to get up close – I appear as a blob in the gallery wrapped photo we were all admiring this morning. Phoenix had left me there for an hour while she hiked over and took this picture.

That night, I confessed to Marcy something that had been on my mind since the Silent Souls event where things went so wrong. The thrill of being caught naked had waned. Part of the enjoyment was the taboo, the feeling of *what if I get caught and am seen naked?* And now that so many people had, and continued to joke mercilessly about it, I felt perhaps that that kink's time had come to an end.

Last night, I took Marcy aside on the beach on Gambier where it had all started and recounted my boyhood adventures, but being there didn't rekindle that lovely, thrilling dread.

My interest in continuing to explore our kinky side hasn't diminished in general, and Marcy and I have a growing list of ideas to pursue. But as we stood there last night and laughed about our journey, Marcy had another surprise.

"If there is anything you want that Phoenix would find overly stressful, it may have to wait seven and a half months, honey," she whispered, dropping her head onto my shoulder. It took me a moment, but when the penny dropped, I hooted and swept her up and hugged her with joy. Apparently Hard Colada and birth control pills don't mix, but we were both delighted.

We didn't want to steal any of the thunder from Gia and Max, so no one but Marcy, me, and Elvis – who was there for moral support when Marcy took the home pregnancy test – are aware.

Standing beside the picture now, I grinned like an idiot and looked into Marcy's eyes, and she knew I was thinking about both our desert adventure and the child we were thrilled about who could grow up alongside Max and Gia's.

I am still wrestling with what to do with my new-found Adept status. Lindi confirmed I can work at developing powers or, if I wished, she could take her gift back. The latter has some appeal, as I don't really want to live twice as long as Marcy; however, Marcy thinks our kids having a dad around twice as long is cool. For now, I've decided to leave things as they are until my children are born. If any have an extra neuron, it might help me decide.

END.

ACKNOWLEDGEMENTS

My fantastic partner and fun collaborator, who believed in my writing ability — perhaps before I did – and who helped me maintain my drive and discipline (no pun intended). The only personal fan club I could ever need.

Anita Kuehnel, whose unrivalled editing skills (and matching tact), combined with some invaluable story suggestions, helped me make a better book.

Zenia Platten, a published author of fantasy fiction. I highly recommend her young adult book, Tethered. It was an honour to have an established author edit my book. She is so insightful and taught me a great deal.

The women, men, and recently acknowledged variations — in our new non-binary world — who have battled for equity and recognition for their gender, race, age, orientation, and/or kink.

The many brave people who have researched – often at significant professional and personal risk – the psychology, physiology, culture, history, and evolution of BDSM and similar topics. Fascinating stuff. Thanks to their efforts, and freely shared findings, I was able to reach a more educated viewpoint than would have been possible in previous decades.

I encourage anyone with an interest in BDSM to do their own research and form their own opinion. Whether you end up with a conservative or liberal viewpoint at the end of that journey, at least it will be based on the new data, which didn't exist before this century, instead of the dogma from the 1900s and before.

The inventors of the internet. A fascinating part of my journey was realizing how the internet allows us to amass data to combat stigma, and provides the ability to connect and find out that we are not alone. A dramatic acceleration to social change. If we are ever to reach fairness and equity in our lifetime, the internet is invaluable to our quest.

ABOUT THE AUTHOR

If you read the Acknowledgements, you will find that the author was inspired by the courage of many people, over many generations, who risked the backlash of stigma associated with some of the topics contained in this book. But, this author is not that brave. Well, I'm not! Melissa Jane, or MJ as I've become to know her, is my beloved pen-name. That admission dispensed with, I affirm that the following is all me.

At school, I was a lover of math, the sciences, geography, and sports, with little use for the likes of foreign languages, history, and written English. The latter is now, of course, a handicap (see Acknowledgements – thanks Anita).

In my pre- and early teens, I read encyclopedias galore; quiz books, locations of countries, their cities, populations, and their flags. At the time I felt incredibly knowledgeable, compared with my peers, but looking back, I'm sure I was more of a Cliff Clavin. If you feel that some of my novels have a few too many sex or technology factoids, this is why. Let me know what you think about any aspect of my work via my website: www.melissajaneparker.com

Some of my early literary influences were: — E.E. Doc Smith's Lensman series, anything by Asimov, Piers Anthony's Xanth and Adept worlds, James Clavell's Shogun, and Eric Van Lustbader's Linnear series. Later in life, Rothfuss, Rowling, and Mr. Martin's Game of Thrones (if he would just finish the damn series) fuelled my love for Sci-Fan, while Ken Follet, Dan Brown and P.T. Deutermann built on my interest in historical fiction. Lee Child, Chandler, Grafton, Baldacci, Larsson, and James (P.D.) are some 'go to' authors for detective novels; and in case you are wondering, I prefer Joey Hill, Tiffany Reisz, and Jacqueline Carey to E.L. James. The best book I have read in a long time is Esi Edugyan's Washington Black, for which she justifiably earned another Giller Prize. Ms. Edugyan has strong affiliations with Victoria, BC – Vancouver's near neighbour. There is something about this part of the world which is good for authors, and I hope some will rub off on me. A close second to Esi, in my admittedly biased opinion, is my daughter's latest effort.

Lightning Source UK Ltd.
Milton Keynes UK
UKHW022121240222
399201UK00005B/155